THE PRODIGAL OF LENINGRAD

DANIEL TAYLOR

THE PRODIGAL OF LENINGRAD

A NOVEL

PARACLETE PRESS
BREWSTER, MASSACHUSETTS

2026 First Printing

The Prodigal of Leningrad: A Novel

ISBN 979-8-89348-022-1

Library of Congress Cataloging-in-Publication Data
Names: Taylor, Daniel, 1948- author
Title: The Prodigal of Leningrad : a novel / Daniel Taylor.
Description: Brewster : Paraclete Press, 2026. | Summary: "Based on real historical events, including the extraordinary wartime tours of the Hermitage's empty galleries, this book is an unforgettable story of human resilience, and a profound meditation on art, faith, forgiveness and healing"-- Provided by publisher.
Identifiers: LCCN 2025034326 (print) | LCCN 2025034327 (ebook) | ISBN 9798893480221 trade paperback | ISBN 9798893480238 epub
Subjects: LCSH: Gosudarstvennyĭ Ėrmitazh (Russia)--Fiction | World War, 1939-1945--Soviet Union--Fiction | Saint Petersburg (Russia)--History--Siege, 1941-1944--Fiction | BISAC: FICTION / Historical / 20th Century / World War II | FICTION / Christian / Historical | LCGFT: War fiction | Christian fiction | Novels | Fiction
Classification: LCC PS3620.A935865 D63 2026 (print) | LCC PS3620.A935865 (ebook)
LC record available at https://lccn.loc.gov/2025034326
LC ebook record available at https://lccn.loc.gov/2025034327
10 9 8 7 6 5 4 3 2 1

Published by Paraclete Press
Brewster, Massachusetts
www.paracletepress.com

Printed in United States of America

Dwell on the past and you'll lose an eye. Forget the past and you'll lose both eyes.

—Russian proverb

So let their children die of starvation. Let them be cut down by the sword. Let their wives lose their husbands and children. Let the older men die of disease and the younger men die by the sword in battle.

—Jeremiah 18:21

In the terrible years of the Yezhov terror, I spent seventeen months in the prison lines of Leningrad. Once, someone "recognized" me. Then a woman with bluish lips standing behind me, who, of course, had never heard me called by name before, woke up from the stupor to which everyone had succumbed and whispered in my ear (everyone spoke in whispers there):

"Can you describe this?"

And I answered, "Yes, I can."

Then something that looked like a smile passed over what had once been her face.

—Anna Akhmatova, "Instead of a Preface" in *Requiem*.

Rembrandt van Rijn, *The Return of the Prodigal Son.*

CHAPTER 1

June 1941

STARVATION WAS THE MOST NATURAL OF ALL THE MANY WAYS TO die in Leningrad in the winters of 1941 and '42. Withhold nutrition from any living organism and it dies—no further cause required. But starvation was the furthest thing from Daniil's mind when he heard the announcement that Hitler had developed an appetite for dining on the Soviet Union and that Leningrad was a main course. Instead he thought first of his paintings.

Of course they were not *his* paintings. They were Michelangelo's paintings, and Raphael's paintings, and Caravaggio's paintings. And, most precious of all to him, they were Rembrandt's paintings.

Technically, of course, they all belonged to the Hermitage, the greatest art museum in the world as every Russian claimed, meaning they belonged to the State, which is to say to the great Soviet people. They were encouraged to refer to "my Hermitage," and they did.

The great collection had gotten its name because its original collector, Catherine the Great, had in the eighteenth century reserved its viewing mainly for herself. "Only the mice and I admire all this," she said smugly. The rooms of art were her private, anchorite-like "hermitage," hence the name. Fortunately for everyone, Lenin had put an end to private ownership of most everything, even one's body, and over time many additional masterpieces made their way to the great public museum in the city now named after him.

If the Nazis take Leningrad, they will take its treasures, as conquerors have always done—and always will do, thought Daniil. And there were no greater treasures in the world for the docent than its works of art. For Daniil was not just a citizen of Leningrad and a lover of art, he was a docent at the Hermitage—a guide, an interpreter, a priest of the Imagination. Well, perhaps more an unordained monk than a priest, for he was not an artist himself, and not even a paid employee. He guided for love, eventually the only love left him in what was a difficult life.

If there was any ultimate meaning to human life, and he was not sure there was, it was to be found in the spirit, and the highest expression of the human spirit was its art. He knew that things of the spirit were under threat in a materialistic age, especially when materialism was the official policy of the state, which made protecting those past creations of the spirit from a rapacious present all the more critical.

The invasion started in the dark hours of morning on a Sunday. Few if any of Leningrad's more than three million inhabitants knew of it when dawn broke, though approximately half of them would soon die because of it—just as the passengers of the Titanic had no knowledge when the ship left Southampton of the iceberg that patiently awaited them many miles away.

It being a Sunday, the docent was scheduled to guide. Up to this time, he volunteered mostly on weekends, the rest of the week spent at his office job—a job that paid his bills but starved his heart. Sundays were busy at the Hermitage, especially in the summer, the most popular galleries packed with citizens and, usually, with soldiers and seamen. They didn't hear Molotov's radio announcement of the invasion late that morning. But word spread quickly, and the vast museum, composed of multiple buildings, miles of corridors, dozens of staircases, thousands of windows, and endless works of the spirit was almost empty by noon—a kind of prophetic emptiness.

Hitler called his invasion Operation Barbarossa; Stalin called it a treacherous stab in the back; the docent of Leningrad called it impending sacrilege. The masterworks in the Hermitage must be protected. Which meant they must be sent away—deeper into Russia, into the mountains, into secret places. And it was his job—his calling—to help.

Fortunately, perhaps, this was not the first time that Hermitage art had to be hidden to be saved. The first time was when Napoleon underestimated the Russians. The second time was when it looked like Kaiser Wilhelm might come knocking. There were already thousands of crates in storage from the World War I exodus, and there was already a plan.

The mastermind of the plan, quite literally, was Joseph Orbeli, the head of the museum. Not only were the crates ready, there was a long list of which works of art would go in which crates, many of them already labelled. Orbeli, an Armenian by birth, was in his mid-fifties but already looked like an old man—thinning hair, shuffling walk, long beard. An academic with a prominent forehead, he could have easily passed as an Orthodox monk, but his was an orthodoxy of the mind and imagination.

The invasion began early Sunday morning, and the evacuation began that afternoon when some of the most famous paintings were moved to the Special Vault—a series of rooms with reinforced doors and without windows. The Hermitage employees placed on air-raid watch were told to spend the night at the museum and to remain round the clock thereafter. Finland was known to be eager to get back the land they had lost in the short 1939 "Winter War" with the Soviet Union, and air raids were feared. The packing up of the art began in earnest the next day.

Because he knew the German habit of gobbling its neighbors, Orbeli had stockpiled huge amounts of packing material since the beginning of the war in Europe in 1939—tons of packing paper, cotton wool, crumbled cork, and wood shavings, and miles of oilcloth. Government officials were known not to be happy about this. They thought such preparations might offend their new treaty friends, the Germans.

Everyone helped pack and crate—guides, guards, researchers, restorers, administrators, cleaners, curators, secretaries, and, yes, docents. They were joined by artists and art students from the city, military personnel, and by many others.

It wasn't enough.

The timeline called for everything to be trucked and trained away in six days. The museum had not only thousands of paintings, but also endless statuary, some of it—like the multi-ton statue of the smirking Voltaire—huge. Some pieces, such as the gigantic, solid jasper, nineteen-ton Kolyvan Vase—eight feet tall and its bowl fifteen feet across—were too big to move.

In addition, there were hundreds of thousands of coins, ten thousand pieces of jewelry, and countless fragile objets d'art. Experts came from the famous Lomonosov Porcelain Factory to pack porcelain and chinaware. Most of the exhibition rooms and hallways had no electric lights, but work could go on almost round the clock because the sun shone near constantly in the White Nights of early summer.

To save time and space, the paintings were removed from their frames, which were left hanging in place on the walls. Twenty to sixty small- to medium-sized paintings could be laid flat in one crate. The large paintings were carefully removed from their gilded frames and wound onto large rollers, ten to fifteen canvases per roller, with tissue paper layered between them, then wrapped in oilcloth and placed in long pine boxes—a kind of coffin of the Imagination. In this way, the artists of the ages—and all their subjects—mingled with each other in unimagined ways, rolled together and boxed in a desperate attempt to survive the war beast. Thus Ruben's *Bacchus,* Titian's *Danae,* Murillo's *Boy with a Dog*, Watteau's *Capricious Girl*, and Van Dyke's *Self-Portrait* could potentially all meet, wrapped together in a precious and priceless roll in a pine box.

All the paintings, that is, except one. One painting alone was deemed too important, too beloved, too *sui generis* to be treated like the others. The only painting to get its own crate was Rembrandt's huge *The Return of the Prodigal Son.* Even in the God-mocking, priest-murdering, church-razing center of scientific materialism, this transcendent rendering of a story from the Bible was deemed too important to share space with any other masterpiece.

A young man in rags, kneeling at the feet of his father, whose hands are placed tenderly on the son's shoulders, with a surrounding audience of a judgmental older brother, a family friend and possible counselor, a servant girl, and, barely visible in the dark shadows, perhaps an emotion-filled mother. A painting of Rembrandt's old age, maybe even his last, maybe even unfinished, painted by a man who knew what needing forgiveness was all about.

The docent stood and watched as the experts removed the *Prodigal* from its frame. He felt himself near weeping. The painting was as much a part of his life as his heartbeat. He made sure to see it every time he came to the museum, even if only to pick up his schedule. It was possible he would never see it again. Nothing was dependable in wartime. The painting might be destroyed. As might he.

He thought back to the first time he had seen the *Prodigal*. It hung as a framed print in his grandfather's office when Daniil was a small child. His grandfather was then a historian and valued knowledge of the past the way a miser values money. His grandfather explained the painting to him, saying that the boy would understand it better when he was the grandfather's age. At the time Daniil could not imagine the possibility that he could ever be that old. And now he was a grandfather too.

It pleased the docent that the painting he both loved and feared was so honored and protected. He had stood beside it and spoken countless times to groups ranging from schoolchildren to pensioners to politicians. His aim was to help them better understand the greatness of what they were seeing with their eyes. Soon he would be creating the painting with words for those left with nothing to see.

The docent did not pack the painting himself—it was a job for experts—but he spoke to the painting as it was removed from its frame.

"Return to me, prodigal, just as you returned to your father."

Crating and packing went on around the clock all week. Many of the crates containing the most valuable paintings were temporarily stored in the great Hall of Twenty Columns. All through the night of July 1, soldiers loaded the crates on an endless stream of trucks heading for the train station.

The train itself was a mobile fortress, a battleship as much as a train. Stretching five hundred yards long, it was pulled by two engines (with a third going ahead to scout the way), had an armored car, a flatcar in the middle with an antiaircraft battery and another at the end, four Pullmans for especially valuable works, two passenger cars carrying soldiers and Hermitage staff (and, of course, some members of the secret police to keep an eye both on the art and on the people rescuing it).

As a further precaution, even the train's engineers were not told their final destination. As the American war posters said, "loose lips" and all that. Ironically, some of these treasures would find their way to the basement of the Ipatiev mansion in the distant Ural mountains, the very place where the royal Romanov family, the one-time putative owners of many of these treasures, were once kept before their secret execution twenty-three years prior. People were dispensable, paintings were not.

Orbeli accompanied his precious charges to their sendoff. He stood far down the platform along the length of the train, next to a lamppost. He held his hat to his breast, tears wetting his face, a final salute to his departing children, unsure of their return.

CHAPTER 2

July 1941

THE INABILITY OF HUMAN BEINGS TO FULLY REALIZE THEIR circumstances is a constant in the human experience. When the Nazis launched their invasion of the Soviet Union in the early hours on Sunday 22 June in 1941, the Leningraders, like all Russians, were both shocked and angry. Molotov announced the assault with a faltering voice on the radio in the late morning. (Stalin was in such a state of shock that he was unable to function for days.)

How perfidious were the Germans, everyone agreed, to betray an ally and violate a treaty signed less than two years prior! How slanderous to use as an excuse the supposed threats of Soviet troops stationed near the German border! (While explaining their own staging of troops as practicing for an invasion of Britain, out of range of British bombers.) But most of all, how foolish to take on the great Red Army! Did they not know history? Had they never heard of the delusional Napoleon?

Yes, shocked and angry, but also entirely too optimistic.

Within a week of the invasion, the local authorities ordered the civilian population to turn out to dig trenches and tank traps south of the city. Over a million citizens—The People's Militia—answered the call, including schoolchildren. Patriotic enthusiasm reigned. Stalinist oppression, especially apparent in Leningrad since the assassination of their beloved mayor Kirov in the purges of the 1930s, was forgotten. The Motherland was under threat! She must be defended!

It was chaos.

Women showed up in sundresses and sandals. There was little equipment, less organization, and no training at all. There were more parasols than shovels. The few rifles were in the hands of people who had never fired one. They couldn't even march, much less fight. Meanwhile the Panzers were sweeping through the Baltic states toward them.

But they were still far away. Food was plentiful in the stores. Plays and concerts continued unabated. The restaurants were full. Citizens sang patriotic songs on the streets and in the squares. A billboard declared, "Leningrad is not afraid of death—death is afraid of Leningrad." It was the season of the famous White Nights of Leningrad, and people were out late, as was the sun.

On 3 July, Stalin, now recovered, gave a speech on the radio. He spoke of "the heroic resistance of the Red Army" and claimed that "the enemy's finest divisions and finest air force units have already been smashed and have met their doom on the field of battle." He pointed out that Napoleon had been defeated and Kaiser Wilhelm had been frightened off, and he promised that Hitler's army would be crushed. He ridiculed the idea that the government had made a mistake in signing a nonaggression pact with Hitler, saying it was only because the Soviet Union was a "peace-loving state."

At the same time, Stalin acknowledged the looming fascist threat and mixed a warning with his exhortation: "There must be no room in our ranks for whimperers and cowards, for panic-mongers and deserters; our people must know no fear in the fight and must selflessly join our patriotic war of liberation against the fascist enslavers."

He closed with a flourish—"Forward to victory!"

The docent happened to be in his neighbor's apartment at the time. They listened and were not impressed. The neighbor, Aleksandr, was especially contemptuous.

"What is it about us that we swallow this stuff? Why are we so passive—first with the czars, now with the Bolsheviks? We have a congenital appetite for lies. We've had twenty-five years of lies piled on top of lies—a tall wedding cake of lies. The Man of Steel they call him. I call him the Man of Confection—sweet lies with bitter consequences. He murdered the priests and turned the monasteries into brothels and museums of atheism. He starved the kulaks for resisting the theft of their farms. He had Kirov assassinated, the best mayor our city has ever had. He hates us because of our tradition of free-thinking artists and intellectuals and our associations with Trotsky. He has no love for us, and we return the favor."

The docent knew Aleksandr could only talk this way because he felt safe with Daniil. Those few sentences in the presence of an informer—commonly called a "whisperer" and as familiar as fleas—would earn him the attention of a firing squad or a long vacation in the labor camps. The thought of the camps sent a spasm of guilt through the docent, as it always did.

"Be careful of your words, Aleksandr; your children are nearby."

By the middle of July the mood in Leningrad had changed. A kind of pragmatic pessimism set in. The People's Militia was being wiped out (though losses were kept secret). Patriotic slogans gave way to threats to those who did not join the impromptu citizens army. "Do you not want to defend the Motherland?" A bullet to the head, administered without trial, awaited those accused of injuring themselves to avoid participation. (Soon enough it would be much easier—as it was in the thirties—to get a bullet in the head than a loaf of bread.)

Other precautions began to be taken, including sandbags and wooden ramparts around Falconet's huge equestrian statue of Peter the Great in Senate Square. The local myth, which people now fervently wished to believe, was that as long as the statue stood, Leningrad would not fall. Other statuary was buried in the Summer Garden for protection from bombs and shells.

Brilliant military strategists that they were, the authorities counseled women, should the Germans enter the city, to throw rocks and douse the enemy with boiling water. Once the Panzers made it north of the Luga River, a hundred miles to the south and west, the amateur citizen-soldiers died by the thousands. Slogans proved ineffective against artillery shells.

Despite Stalin's admonition against them, rumors became the common currency. Rumors replaced propaganda just as propaganda had long since replaced news. The fear of spies was omnipresent. Stalin's famous paranoia became the people's paranoia. The first German reconnaissance flights took place over the city. Food rationing was announced on July 17. Soon the first bombs and shells would violate the city.

Optimism gave way to dark humor. When wooden tanks were placed throughout the city to fool the Germans, Aleksandr said to Daniil, "O yes, wooden tanks to defend us. Perhaps the Nazis will cooperate and drop wooden bombs." Told repeatedly that the Red Army was winning, he responded, "More winning like this and Fritz will be knocking on our door, asking, 'What's for supper?'"

The day after food rationing was announced, both rhetorical bravado and flippant cynicism gave way to genuine horror. The authorities had ordered that all children under fourteen be evacuated, creating panic and resistance. Children were loaded onto trucks and driven away, chased by wailing mothers. They were sent to train stations, sometimes waiting for days to leave because there were so many. Some of the youngest lacked any papers and had only their names written on their hands, which soon were smeared and unreadable.

Consistent with the universal absence of accurate information and the incompetence of leaders, trainloads of children were actually sent towards the advancing Germans, headed for youth campgrounds in the south. One such train arrived at the Lychkovo station, packed with children and their guardians. A child looking out the window in the distance said, "Look at all the balloons in the sky." It was German paratroopers.

The train sat in the station waiting as more children from the region arrived, perhaps three thousand on the platforms and in the train altogether. Then appeared the Nazi fighter planes from over the horizon, flying low. Mere chaos turned to carnage.

A collective shout went up from the platforms, spiking the fears of those inside the train. The bombs sniffed out their targets with tragic accuracy, blowing up whole rail cars. As many as could fled the train and platforms in all directions into adjacent fields, some clutching dolls. Fighter planes made repeated passes, strafing the children. People on the ground could see the faces of the pilots. Exploding bombs left body parts hanging in trees.

Accurate numbers are often casualties in war, but some estimate two thousand children were massacred. The Germans later said they didn't know they were children. The Soviet authorities said it never happened. "Hostile and provocative rumors" said the officials in Leningrad.

The bodies, uncounted, can still be found in their mass grave in Lychkovo.

The mothers of Leningrad rioted. The police kept them from coming to the train station to search returning trains for their little ones. Families vowed never to part from their children again. "Better that we die here together." The authorities called off the evacuations.

After the beginning of rationing, hoarding became commonplace. Stalin's call for "self-sacrifice" gave way to the oldest and deepest of all human motivations—self-preservation. Food started to become scarce. The initial ration of food, not much less than what was consumed normally, was soon cut, the first of many such reductions to come. The shelves in stores were increasingly bare. Leningrad became the City of Long Lines.

To make matters worse, hundreds of thousands of refugees flooded into the city, fleeing the German advance from places like Pskov and Novgorod. The docent found it painfully ironic and said so to Aleksandr.

"Imagine. The Nazis are surrounding us from the south, and the Finns, trying to get their lost land back, have blocked us in the north; to our east is a massive lake and to the west is the Baltic Sea. And these people think they have fled to safety? They have fled Purgatory for Hell."

CHAPTER 3

Winter 1928

The grandfather had already enjoyed years in the Soviet internment system before he graduated to the Special camps. At first jail. Then prison. Then one of the regular camps that spread throughout Russia like bubonic sores. Now a Special labor camp. The only place to graduate to from here was the grave, a graduation long wished for by many of its inhabitants. It was your last act of loyal citizenship in the Worker's Paradise. You were not sent here for reform, or even for punishment (because the crimes were largely a fabrication), but simply to eliminate you—after extracting a bit of labor. Death was their ultimate goal, and the authorities tried hard to make it your goal as well.

The grandfather arrived at night in the back of a truck, one of a dozen new campers. Out of a rip in the canvas that enclosed them he could see ahead the barbed wire of the outer fence. A series of guard towers, deep snow piled around their wooden legs, loomed in between that fence and the next fence inside it. Searchlights from the towers slowly swept the snow from barracks to forest. Soldiers with dogs walked in the darkness between the two fences. It was so cold that breathing was painful.

Welcome, grandfather, to your final resting place—a place devoid of rest.

Anatoly Ivanovich Aslanov was now (and had been for a long time) a number—"Shch-232." He was a zek, the name that inmates gave themselves, an abbreviation for "imprisoned." The guards had another name for them—pyl—meaning "dust," which summed up nicely the official attitude toward them.

It didn't take long for the others in his barrack to discover that he was a priest—Father Sergius by name, but no one had called him that for a long time. He wore the same clothes as everyone else, and no one ever asked a new prisoner about his past, but the grandfather gave himself away in ways large and small. Most obviously, he crossed himself frequently, but that only revealed he was a believer, as were some others. Then it got out that a few were coming to him for confession. They could see it in the fields when out on work detail. He would be huddled together with another prisoner, their heads bowed, foreheads almost touching. After a few minutes, the grandfather would put his hand on the man's shoulder and make the sign of the cross over him.

Most of the prisoners thought nothing of this. Once they discovered he was a priest, they knew why he was here. Lenin had made clear that priests were maggots, eating the flesh of a long-dead Jesus. He compared religion to syphilis and promised it would be cured by the antibiotics of materialistic atheism. And all of Russia had found that Lenin was a man who kept his promises. Bishops had been executed by the hundreds, priests by the thousands, and monks and nuns by the tens of thousands. This priest was lucky not to be already lying in his grave with a hole in his head—if being in a Special camp could ever be considered lucky. Which it couldn't.

There were many different species in the camp zoo—criminals, politicals, and ex-soldiers being the largest collections. But there were also subgroups defined by ethnicity, language, class, profession, regional or religious affiliation, and so on. You didn't survive long if you didn't have someone who identified with you, who gave a damn whether you were sick or not, who had your back when the guards were in a bad mood, who would maybe even risk protecting you from the criminals. Not that most survived all that long even if they had such a group.

The majority in his barrack were indifferent to the grandfather's being a priest. But there were some in the zoo who drew conclusions—especially the intellectuals. They were the former professors, writers, artists, journalists, teachers, scientists, and the like, many of whom had enthusiastically supported the Revolution in '17 and were surprised and offended to find themselves sharing space with criminals, traitors, and the socially impure.

For the intellectuals, experts in classification, a priest was by definition a fool—assumed to be uneducated, assumed to be superstitious, assumed to be a counterweight against progress. And therefore deserving of ridicule, an occasional kick, and maybe even having his tin cup of rancid soup stolen at supper.

Later that winter the grandfather had an encounter with such a one. A new arrival, he let everyone know that he had been a department chair at Moscow University. Mathematics. He also let everyone know that, unlike with them, his presence in the camp was a mistake. He suspected he had been accused falsely by a colleague who wanted his position, or maybe only his windowed office. Yes, certainly a mistake that would soon be corrected. He was sure of that.

Father Sergius was released early each afternoon from the outside work detail to go start fires in the stoves in the barrack. Without his doing so, the temperature would be the same as outside, minus 10 F today, only moderately cold. (The zeks could estimate the cold without a thermometer. If it was painful to inhale, it meant one temperature, and if your spit froze in mid-air, it meant it might be cold enough to avoid being sent out to work.)

The mathematician was sent with him this time—each to light two stoves.

They first had to split the wood. It was already piled outside the barrack in proper lengths, but the logs were too big to put into the stove. Standing before the pile, the mathematician established his superiority immediately.

"So, silly priest, where are the axes?"

"There are no axes. As you might guess, our hosts are not enthusiastic about providing prisoners with axes."

Embarrassed, the mathematician added anger to his condescension.

"Well, how do they expect us to split these logs?"

"They only expect us to die, sir. They do not worry about how we are to split the logs."

"This is absurd."

"Now you're catching on."

The grandfather regretted his sarcasm and silently asked God to forgive him. This new prisoner had not yet adapted to his changed reality. Absurd was the mildest thing one could say about a Special camp.

"I will show you, sir. I have made a wedge out of a piece of wood that I keep hidden near the pile."

Father Sergius stepped away and returned with the wooden wedge.

"Now we find a log that already has a crack in the sawn end, and we put the wedge in that crack."

He stood a log up on its end and placed the wedge.

"Then we take a smaller log, one we can . . . ."

The mathematician interrupted.

"Quit using the word 'we,' imbecile priest. You are not my equal. There is no 'we' between us."

The grandfather ignored him.

". . . one we can use to hit the wedge, which will, God willing, split the log."

He regretted using the expression, "God willing," knowing it would only irritate his coworker, but it just came out, as little spurts of faith often did.

The blow from the smaller log did not split the bigger one. Nor did the second, nor the third. But the crack got bigger and eventually the log split. Which only meant, of course, that the procedure had to be repeated to get four to six small pieces of wood out of one sawn log. They had to prepare enough wood to keep four stoves going for at least ten hours. (If they didn't, which was often, you could wake up with your hair frozen to your pillow—if you had hair, which few did, a head shaving being the standard greeting to camp.)

By the time they had enough wood, they were sweating heavily even in the cold, meaning that for their own survival they needed to get a fire burning quickly.

They carried the wood inside the barrack, stacking a portion beside each stove. They worked separately to start their fires. The mathematician stuffed each of his stoves. He looked over at the grandfather, who had yet to open the door of his first stove, and laughed.

"What are you waiting for, little priest. Do you think God is going to fill your stove for you?"

Father Sergius did not answer.

The mathematician did not know much about lighting fires. In Moscow, his servant made the fires, or his wife. He was an academic, not a serf. "From each according to his ability, to each according to his needs." So said Marx, so said he. His abilities were great—he was, after all, department head—but they did not, and should not, include starting fires.

And, alas, he did not. Match after match, but the wood did not catch. The work crew would be back soon. The guards will be angry if the barrack is not warm. Worse yet, the criminals will be angry, and they are notoriously unimpressed with intellectuals who cannot start a fire. (Contempt for the intelligentsia was common in the labor camps, often referred to as the "Ivan Ivanoviches." Superior attitudes and all. And the authorities knew they'd get little work out of them.)

When the criminals were unhappy, they made other people unhappy. They silently announced themselves by their tattoos and unusually long fingernails on the little finger—a flourish that enhanced their image as clawed predators. They also favored bronze-capped teeth (appearing gold), and aluminum crosses (being criminal and appearing religious offering no apparent contradiction for anyone).

The criminals of course had no monopoly on meanness. Cruelty and mercilessness were the common currency of camp life. Living in a camp didn't *make* you cruel or indifferent to the suffering of others; it simply brought out what you already were or were ready to be. Human nature was as human nature is—the camp was simply the catalyst.

The mathematician cursed the man he suspected of having informed on him. He cursed the makers of the matches, of which he had left only a few. He cursed the God he knew does not exist, who he accused of making the logs fireproof.

Cursing God reminded him of the priest. He looked across the barracks to see the grandfather closing the stove door on a roaring fire. He longed for his servant or his wife. But he had to settle for the grandfather priest.

"Okay priest, I'm guessing you come from peasant stock—a thousand years of starting domestic fires, no doubt. What am I doing insufficiently?"

He didn't really have to ask for help. Father Sergius was already heading his way without a petition. He came to the mathematician's cold stove and opened the door.

"You have too much wood in here, sir. And no kindling."

"How can a fire have too much wood?"

"The same way a man can have too much confidence."

The grandfather pulled out the logs.

"We are lucky these are birch. They provide their own kindling. Help me peel off the bark."

They did so and put the white bark on the bottom inside the stove, then put back only half the logs.

"You light it, sir."

The mathematician used one of his last matches and lit the bark. It slowly caught fire, then spread to the other kindling, then began working its way up the logs. They did the same with the other stove. Soon the barracks were comfortably warm.

Which was a problem.

A guard came in. He hated the priest and made trouble for him whenever he could.

Walking up to the grandfather, he said. "What is the meaning of this? It is far too warm in here. These logs belong to the state. You are using the people's logs to comfort the enemies of the people. You will be written up for this, priest."

With that he punched the grandfather in the face.

CHAPTER 4

August 1941

THE DOCENT LIVED IN AN APARTMENT BUILDING NEAR GOSTINY DVOR, the great market building that looked more like a palace than a place of commerce. His office, where he was a clerk, was ten minutes away by tram and thirty minutes by foot. He counted his time there as a daily visit to a waste land, as intellectually and spiritually sterile as a frozen Siberian steppe. As a quite intelligent young man, he had hoped for a different life work, but his lack of university education determined everything.

He was about the same distance from the place where he was most fully alive—the Hermitage, in his mind the holy of holies of the faith of art. He had first volunteered over a decade ago, and since then had spent as many hours there as possible, leading tours mostly, but also sometimes cataloguing, organizing schedules, whatever needed doing. Since the death of Sofia, it was one of the few sources of significance left in his life.

Daniil also spent time with a handful of friends, the most entertaining of whom was Aleksandr Andreevich Balakan, the neighbor the docent had been with when they listened to Stalin's radio speech in July. Aleksandr lived with his family two floors above Daniil. Once an engineer, he lost his position for being too free with his thoughts, a condition that did not abate thereafter. He was given to satire, a dangerous gift when living among authoritarians. Lie, steal, and cheat if you must, but do not, above all, make fun of the people in charge—in charge of anything, at any level. (There were lots of such levels, and lots of such people.)

Whenever anyone pompously spoke of loving the Motherland or loving the Supreme Leader, he liked to quote a Russian proverb: "Love is evil—it will make you fall in love with a goat." Yana, his wife, always pretended to take offense.

"Are you speaking of me, Aleksandr?"

"Not at all, my dearest. You are much prettier than any goat."

"Your loose tongue will get you in trouble, sir."

"You may be right, dear."

The last was also a favorite line of his. He finished most every disagreement with her that way, "You may be right, dear." Followed by a smile and rapidly blinking eyes.

Aleksandr was also a rare source of humor in grim times, often sharing jokes and proverbs that flashed a piercing light on dark things. Such as the joke he repeated about the Soviet penchant for revisionist history: "We Russians are certain about the future. It is the past that is so unpredictable," adding, "we change it all the time."

Or his joke on the Soviet claim to be a freely elected democracy based on the will of the people: "When was the first Soviet-style election? The time that God put Eve in front of Adam and said to him, 'Go ahead, choose your wife.'" These jokes more often elicited a grim nod rather than laughter, but Aleksandr saw them as a small form of resistance.

Yana never laughed at his jokes and grew positively angry when he told them in front of the children. She was not a dedicated Bolshevik, Party member, or lover of Stalin, but tried her best to keep the rules, stay positive about the system (which she sometimes defended), and, most importantly, keep herself and her family out of trouble.

She even tried to play the "march of history" card with Aleksandr from time to time, offering up the Party line that present economic suffering was just a down payment on a glorious and prosperous socialist future. To which her husband replied, "Ah yes, the ever-receding future—a place in time that by definition one never reaches. Very convenient for the propagandist."

Aleksandr and Yana had two children—Luka, seven, and Yulia, five. Luka was already developing his father's sarcastic wit. He also liked to draw—mostly dinosaurs and battle scenes. He had shown one of the latter to his father recently.

"Who's fighting here, Luka?"

"The Red Army. They're crushing the dirty Finns in the war."

"The Finns aren't dirty, Luka."

"Well, they are our enemies."

"We wanted their land."

Luka paused.

"Well, my teacher says it was our land once. Besides, he says we needed that land. To protect Leningrad."

Aleksandr could see that Luka was getting upset.

"Perhaps he's right, Luka. Wanted, needed. Sometimes it's difficult to tell the difference."

If Daniil and Aleksandr were friends, Sofia and Yana had been like twins separated at birth. Each had made the life of the other bearable. They shared strategies for surviving their husbands and for raising their children. Both assignments required patience and wisdom and endurance. Especially endurance.

Aleksandr and Daniil played chess most every Thursday evening. The Russians love chess the way the English love football. (In the labor camps, chess pieces were formed out of chewed bread.) Of course the Russians also love football, but they take great pride in excelling at chess. The two men would defend their favorites and sometimes even try to employ their strategies.

Chigorin, Alekhine, Menchik—famous throughout the world. Okay, so Alekhine defected to France in '21, but it was Russia that fathered and trained him. And Vera Menchik—no woman in the world had ever succeeded at chess like her. It was a testimony to the benefit of socialism for the New Soviet Woman.

Sometimes Aleksandr would play a game within the game. Daniil once noticed that his neighbor was not taking pieces that were available for capture, including important ones. At the same time, he was skillfully keeping Daniil from taking many pieces of his own.

"What are you doing, Aleksandr? Why are you not capturing any pieces?"

"I am playing pacifist chess, Daniil."

"What is pacifist chess?"

"Look at the board. Use your eyes."

Daniil studied the board for a moment. Aleksandr's two knights were out in the same position on either side of the board. As were his bishops. The pawns were likewise spread symmetrically.

"You are making patterns."

"That's right. Order. I am protecting and extending order across the board. A kind of shalom. You took two of my pawns, but I am adapting. I will restore order within two moves."

"Why are you doing this, Aleksandr?"

"The world needs order at the moment, Daniil. I am trying to save the world."

With that, Aleksandr smiled and blinked rapidly.

CHAPTER 5

Summer 1908

THE GRANDFATHER TRIED TO HIDE THE FACT, OBVIOUS TO EVERYONE, that Daniil was his favorite grandchild. He was drawn to his gentleness and quiet curiosity. His older brother, in contrast, was all movement and bombastic energy. Maxim was no doubt likable, but hard for the grandfather to keep up with. Maxim wanted to kick the ball with him, to play tag, even to arm wrestle. Daniil wanted his grandfather to read him fairy tales, to play the balalaika, to see and critique his drawings.

The docent's love for Rembrandt—and for the *Prodigal* painting—began, as mentioned earlier, with his grandfather. Anatoly Aslanov made his living as a history professor, but he was also a fine amateur painter, including, from time to time, religious icons. When the docent was seven or so, he visited his grandfather's small studio and saw for the first time a print of *The Return of the Prodigal Son.*

Young Daniil was not impressed. He liked action in pictures—sword fighting, a horse rearing, even a boat sailing. And he said so.

"Nothing is happening here, Grandfather. Just people standing and sitting and kneeling."

The grandfather answered quietly.

"Oh, something is happening, Daniil. Something very powerful is happening. The painting captures perhaps the most powerful event in the universe."

Daniil cocked his head, searching for this "most powerful event."

"What is it? I don't see it."

"Love, my boy. Forgiveness, mercy, love. The father is forgiving the son he loves who has wounded him. Mercy rooted in love—grace—the most powerful thing in the universe."

"I don't see any wounds. I don't get it."

"Someday you will, Daniil. Someday."

CHAPTER 6

September 1941

If the late summer of 1941 was full of dread, September brought dread's fulfillment. The worst fears were realized and then surpassed. Hitler had made it known that he did not want Leningrad conquered and occupied, he wanted it leveled and its people destroyed. A conquest and occupation, he said, would cost too many German lives and make Germany responsible for feeding people, something he had no interest in. They were instead to be surrounded, bombed, shelled, and starved. Afterward the city would be flattened—"erased from the face of the earth" said Hitler in the time-honored cliché of butchers. The birthplace of hated Communism would thereby become a mere footnote in history.

German scientists, always ones for precision, did calculations, estimating it would take three weeks after a blockade for starvation to begin. By January it would be complete. Then the Panzers would roll in, the whole strategy saving the lives of thousands of German soldiers and allowing German forces to move on ahead of time to Stalingrad. Hitler summed it up neatly: "Leningrad must die of starvation."

The docent himself witnessed from a distance an early example of the plan. The Badayev warehouses—made up of some forty wooden buildings—were the site of the largest collection of food resources for the city—grain, meat, butter, lard, flour, sugar. In early September, the Germans bombed them. Hundreds of tons of food went up in flames. Great quantities of sugar melted into the ground, later to be dug up and sold, soil and all, to desperate women hoping to feed their families.

The docent was returning from the home of a colleague near Zabalkansky Prospekt that evening and saw the smoke in the distance. He asked a man on the street what he thought was burning and got this answer.

"Our lives, sir. Our future. Our hope. It's the food warehouses at Badayev. Don't ask me why the officials kept most of the food in one place."

The man then flinched, afraid he had said too much to a stranger, and walked quickly away.

CHAPTER 7

September 1941

IN A TIME OF DISINTEGRATION, ONE OF THE FEW UNIFYING FORCES in the city was Radio Leningrad. It was a voice of encouragement and defiance as well as news and music. (When the news became almost exclusively bad in the winter, the authorities shut all programming down for long stretches.) Before the war Radio Leningrad broadcast both through private radios and ubiquitous loudspeakers in apartment hallways and public squares and street corners. As the Germans rolled toward Leningrad, the authorities dictated that all private radios be turned in—to better control what people heard. Having one's own radio was one of a long list of capital offenses.

Early on the repeated refrain went out over all of Russia—"This is Radio Leningrad, the city of Lenin calling the Country!" The fully intended message: If we are still broadcasting, then Leningrad has not fallen, and there is hope for the nation in these menacing times. The voice of Lazar Magrachev, the omnipresent host, was a much-needed salve to his distraught listeners, a balm to wounded hearts. Even when he was announcing an impending air raid, at least it was a familiar and calming voice bringing the warning.

Among the others speakers were the cultural elite—writers, artists, musicians—recruited to play their role, just as factory workers and soldiers played theirs. No matter how dire the situation, the people must be encouraged. Which is exactly what Dmitri Shostakovich, the celebrated composer and son of Leningrad, set out to do in his radio speech in early September. He explained that he had completed the first two movements of a new work, which, when completed, would be called his Seventh Symphony.

He asked a rhetorical question—"Why am I telling you this?"—and then gave a rather incredible answer: "I am telling you so that listeners tuned in to me now should know that life in our city is normal." Surely he did not believe that life in Leningrad in September of 1941 was normal. Perhaps he meant only that his fellow citizens were responding to the horrible situation with their normal courage and resolve.

He went on to say, "All of us are soldiers today, and those who work in the field of culture and the arts are doing their duty on a par with all the other citizens of Leningrad." In the months ahead, Leningraders will murder people for their ration cards, grab other people's daily bread ration from their hand and stuff it in their mouths, and, yes, even eat their own dead, but at this moment, as the siege began, it was important to be upbeat. "I assure you in the name of all Leningraders, in the name of all those working in the field of culture and the arts, that we are invincible and that we are ever at our posts."

After all, all of Russia is listening. And its rulers.

Shostakovich had good reason to be upbeat. The arts had long been expected to fall in line with every other part of Soviet life. He had erred in his opera *Lady Macbeth* by being both too avant-garde—"formalist" was the standard epithet—and too erotic for the prudish Stalin, who walked out. A Pravda reviewer knew his role and called it "musical noise" and "vulgar," and warned ominously, "This game can only end badly." Shostakovich understood, as would anyone, that the reviewer was referring to much more than his music career.

So yes, "We are invincible."

A few days later the Germans, together with the Finns, completed the encirclement of the city, and the full-blown siege began. It would last for almost 900 days.

CHAPTER 8

Over The Years

Daniil always said that Sofia was more intelligent than he was. And she always agreed.

"It's simply true," she said whenever he mentioned it, "and there is nothing to be gained from denying what is true."

When she said that one time in front of Aleksandr, he had remarked, "Try to tell that to Mickey Mustache and his Little Apparatchiks."

Sofia reprimanded him—as Yana often did—for being so flippant when mere cheekiness could be considered felonious.

"Your cleverness will get you a change of address some day, Aleksandr. And the rest of us as well for not reporting you."

Sofia had been on her way to being a working scientist at one time, but her career got spiked for sticking to her own principle regarding simple truth. She learned the hard way the difference between experiential truth and Party Truth. Like medieval Jesuits in their total obedience to the Pope, the Soviet citizen was expected to call black white if the Party said so. The Party often said so and most people agreed.

Sofia was studying at university to be a biologist. Her mentor and professor, a woman in her thirties, was deeply into Mendel and genetics at the university. Unfortunately, a highly influential Soviet scientist of the time, Trofim Lysenko, didn't believe in genes. He believed an organism's environment determined all, a nice fit with Marxist ideology—and a requirement for all intellectual and artistic endeavors.

But a bad fit with reality. Millions starved because of his foolishness. Sofia's mentor was fired for "anti-Soviet thought," and Sofia herself quit the university in frustration. She got a job as a dental assistant instead and spent her time picking at people's teeth. She claimed not to regret it.

"Yes, being a scientist would have been interesting. But I would never have met Daniil. My first meeting with him involved his lower right third molar—a cavity the size of Lake Ladoga. I could see even with his mouth wide open and wearing a bib that he was cute."

This always got a laugh, not least from Daniil. Sofia was three years older. They discovered at that first meeting that they were both Dynamo football fans, and he asked her to a game not long after. Daniil was unusually in love with his wife. Most husband-wife relationships go from passion to affection to acceptance, and sometimes on to boredom, tolerance, and, in some cases, hostility. Daniil, on the contrary, loved her more after nearly twenty years than ever before. He considered her the great blessing of his life, though he didn't have a clue how one could defend the concept of blessing while holding an acceptable materialist view of the world. His family had used the word "blessing" a lot in his childhood, but it was not one he ever heard at work or at the Hermitage, unless it was in the title of a painting.

Sofia was indifferent to Daniil's longtime job—clerking—but was proud of his volunteer work at the Hermitage. The museum wouldn't take just anyone, certainly not anyone approved to lead tours. He had to know as much as the paid guides, and he did. His grandfather had initiated his love for art, and it was his passion thereafter. He studied for weeks before first offering himself as a volunteer, and he had continued studying ever since.

At first the staff guides belittled him. He was restricted to guiding school children and sewing clubs. A senior guide was assigned to monitor his tours from time to time to see if he was up to snuff. They were impressed, particularly with his knowledge of Rembrandt. The leading Rembrandt guide retired in Daniil's third year, and more and more often Daniil was assigned groups that would have gone to her. Sometimes the other guides would even ask him questions.

Sofia also admired him for his kindness.

"Daniil is the kindest man I know. It's not typical of men, you understand. Soviet men are trained to be tough and unsentimental and to follow orders. They see kindness as weakness, as do the authorities. 'The People understand an iron fist,' they say, 'but kindness only confuses them.'"

She even used her biology background to expand her point.

"'Kind' is a quasi-biological term as well as an ethical one. It refers to organisms that share common traits. The word originates in the Bible and biologists prefer 'species,' but they are related and neither is precise. When we say people are kind, we mean they recognize that others are like them and deserve to be treated as one would wish to be treated because one shares a similar nature. It's the Golden Rule hidden inside science."

Daniil loved when Sofia went on these little jags. Sometimes he tried to repeat them to others, but he seldom got them entirely right. As Aleksandr would remind him.

"Now you're just repeating something Sofia told you. Confess it, Daniil. You haven't had an original thought since you married her."

"Guilty," the docent would say with a smile. "Originality is so overrated. Better simply to acknowledge wisdom when you hear it."

For such an intelligent woman, Sofia took very readily to motherhood. Some bright women consider a filling womb the enemy of a filled mind. Not Sofia.

"Why not pass on one's intelligence? That's where genes come in. Reproducing is a form of kindness. It says, 'I have been blessed with life. I will bless others.'"

That word again.

Not that they made a conscious decision to bless the world with another life. In fact Sofia discovered she was pregnant only a few months after they met. It was the primary factor in their deciding to get married as soon as feasible. Daniil was an honorable man and, more importantly, he found Sofia easy to love and was wholly pleased by the idea of spending a life with her.

When Yuri was born, the marriage got deeper. It wasn't "we have less time for each other," it was "loving the same child increases our love for each other." Like young Yuri later sharing the family love for Dynamo football.

CHAPTER 9

October 1932

From time to time poetry broke out in the labor camps. Poetry is more highly prized in Russian culture than elsewhere. A great poet is seen as a natural resource, more significant than copper or tin deposits. Mandelstam once observed, "Only in Russia is poetry respected. It gets people killed." And in the dangerous late 1930s, he proved the observation true with his own life.

Reciting poetry, though not common in the camps, was, when it happened, often a group activity. It normally started with the intellectuals during one of their frequent barrack discussions of big ideas with big passions. They used poems like battering rams to pierce their antagonists' defenses. But it could spread even to the peasants and the proletariat. Different zeks contributed different poems, sometimes only in bits and pieces. Surprisingly perhaps, one of the criminals had memorized the most. He could move from Blok to Esinin to Pasternak, but the poem that paralyzed everyone one night was by Simonov. The title explains everything: "Wait for Me, I Shall Return."

The thief began it unannounced after lights were out at the end of a particularly difficult day. One of the men, having reached the end of his endurance, had exercised his last free act as a human being, choosing to liberate himself in what the zeks called "escape by death." All you had to do while marching out to work or back was break ranks and run toward the woods. The guards were instructed to fire a warning shot and then to shoot to kill. (And if they successfully shot to kill first, they always fired a second shot into the air, just to appear to follow the rules.)

Most of the time, they simply chased after the man, knowing what he was hoping for. They didn't want to reward his hopes by killing him (or, as the zeks called it, "being sent to the moon"). That would mean paperwork, because even though death was commonplace in the camps, every death still had to be recorded and explained. Not justified, just explained—which is to say, made to fit the rules. It was easier to run him down, beat him, and drag him back into line.

But today, a young guard, new to the camp and not understanding the protocol, raised his rifle, called out a warning, and then shot the man dead—a man most of the zeks liked. The other guards shook their heads and the zeks sagged. Some were a bit envious, but most were angry.

So the barrack was in a somber mood when the lights went out. Of course the barrack was never actually dark. Tall poles with powerful lights surrounded it. And the searchlights from the guard tower regularly swept over it. That was one of many reasons why the nights were not a time of rest in the camp. Sleeping was difficult. In addition to the lack of darkness, there were always the groans of the sleeping and loud cries from men struggling through a nightmare of the night that mirrored the nightmare of the day.

The poem began while most were still awake. It rose into the air like a mist and spread around the room. The thief spoke it, slowly and reverently, but it felt like the poem was speaking itself, a kind of condensation into sound from a distant reality.

Wait for me, I shall return
But wait and wait well.
Wait, when yellow rains
Bring sadness,
Wait when snows are blowing,
Wait when it is very hot,
Wait when many are no longer awaited,
And are forgotten.

As the poem unfolded, the zeks changed. The sleepers awoke. The awake awakened even further. Some lay on their bunk, staring through the ceiling. Others propped themselves on their elbows to better face the poem as it flowed toward them. A few, Father Sergius among them, stood up beside their bunk at attention, a way of honoring the poem and the poet. And, in a sense, honoring themselves and their loved ones.

The poem goes on to speak of letters not received, of people who no longer wait; and then it makes a seemingly impossible promise:

Wait for me. I shall return,
Against all and any odds.
Let the ones who did not wait for me
Think that it was luck.

Yes, luck, chance, coincidence, randomness—the only possible explanation for wild good fortune in a flat, materially determined world.

But the poet knows otherwise. His explanation is simple:

. . . *in the midst of fire you saved me*
by waiting for me.

The poet is saved, he concludes, because the one he loves knew how to "*wait and wait well.*" So were the prisoners heartened by the poem or further saddened? A bit of both, most likely. Heartened that a poet's words could express their longings, saddened that there was no logical reason for anyone to wait. Then again, if logic offers only misery, then logic be damned.

CHAPTER 10

September 1941

After the Finns and Germans closed the circle around Leningrad in early September, the docent's office closed. There was no point to doing their particular business when the most relevant business in the city was trying to stay alive.

The good part was that he could now go to the Hermitage almost every day. The museum never officially closed, but of course with much of the great art gone or stored in the basements, there was no reason for the public to come.

And the basements were more than a dark place to store the art. They were also huge bomb shelters—twelve in all—and places where around two thousand people moved in to live. Much of the staff took up residence, including scholars who continued their research, hidden away, their desks amidst the forests of statuary, huge collections of coins, ancient vases, and every kind of artistic expression of the human imagination. Their desks piled high with books and manuscripts, they kept at their work as though the Nazi hordes encircling their city were merely an annoyance, like mosquitoes in July. Later, in starvation time, they began dying at their desks, their bodies unable to keep up with their minds.

The Germans made sure there was plenty of reason for the Hermitage to be attended to. Between incendiary artillery shells and bombs through the roof, the great museum was itself in constant danger. Piles of sand dotted the galleries and entrance halls to be used to put out fires. Watchers—including Shostakovich—patrolled the roofs to do the same. In the late summer and fall there were acres of shattered glass to sweep and windows to board up. Orbeli held regular staff meetings to hand out assignments of all kinds.

The docent had always enjoyed his walk to and from the museum along the great boulevard running through the heart of the city—Nevsky Prospekt. (Blok had called it "the most lyric, poetic street in the world.")

It is named after the famous Nevksy Lavra Monastery at its eastern end, itself named after Prince Aleksandr Nevsky, who defeated the German and Swedish invaders in the thirteenth century, preserving Orthodoxy and being sainted three hundred years later. (After the 1917 Revolution it was officially renamed Avenue of the 25th of October, but it takes more than a political revolution to change people's habits, and they continued to use the traditional name.)

Nevsky Prospekt is also a literary character, found in the works of Gogol, Dostoevsky, Gorky, and Tolstoy, all of whom frequented a favorite restaurant, The Literary Cafe. It runs to its western end at the Winter Palace and the Neva river. In between are great edifices like the neo-classical Gostiny Dvor and the magnificent Kazan Cathedral, the latter turned into a museum of atheism in 1932. The docent walked past the former cathedral most every day, never without a pang. He tried not to look at it.

In summer he walked on the odd-numbered side of the boulevard for the shade. In the winter he walked on the even side of the street for the sun, a merely pleasant habit that in the first winter of siege time became a small survival trick.

To get to the museum he walked along the great square behind the Winter Palace. In its middle, the focal point of Leningrad and at one time of the old Russian Empire, was the red granite Alexander Column, 155 feet high, raised after the defeat of Napoleon. On top stands an angel, its arm around a tall cross. The docent wondered how an angel and a cross had survived the antipathy of Soviet humanism to all things religious. Maybe the focus of the authorities is so earthbound that they've never looked up.

More to be expected are the sculptures of the charging horses not far away atop the triumphal arch of the sweeping General Staff building at the formal entrance to the square. The straining horses are under the command of the Goddess of Glory in her Chariot of Victory, images that any Soviet dictator worth his salt can admire.

Though it was not the most direct route to his work entrance, he usually walked past the Palace garden on one end of the Winter

Palace in order to take a brief look where the great avenue ended at the Neva River. There was something about moving water that fascinated him. The shortest major river in Europe at less than fifty miles long, the Neva runs from the largest lake in Europe, Lake Ladoga, to the Baltic sea, magical miles to every Leningrader.

Daniil did not know why he was so attracted to bodies of water. Perhaps it was the use of water in poetry and paintings. Perhaps it was, as with Heraclitus, because it was a symbol of transience and change. No river is ever the same from moment to moment, the ancient Greek informed us, and neither is any life. Seeming routine is merely the mask of unceasing alteration.

Whenever walking along the Winter Palace on the river side, the docent no longer looked up at the many statues of mythic gods and heroes, each around ten feet tall, that were spaced along the roof line. They had become invisible to him, just as someone raised on a mountainside might eventually become immune to the view.

But he still found himself looking often at the statues of writers and artists atop the New Hermitage. Perhaps because while he never yearned to be a Greek god or hero, he had often daydreamed about being an artist, a magician who could turn tubes of paint into worlds—both immanent and transcendent. He knew where each of the statues was located on the roof perimeter: Leonardo, Raphael, Correggio, but also Daedalus and Onatas. And of course Rembrandt—especially Rembrandt.

Once he was walking with a fellow Hermitage worker, a man who had spent time in the labor camps before being rehabilitated. The docent pointed out his favorite statues above. The man only glanced at them and his face grew solemn.

"I am sorry, Daniil, I cannot appreciate them as you do. They remind me of the sentries standing in the guard towers in the camps. I always imagine each of these statues holding a rifle."

It was a painful memory for the man and a painful allusion for the docent.

CHAPTER 11

January 1918

DANIIL HAD HEARD THAT THE SECURITY AGENTS DID INTERROGATIONS at his high school. His friend Boris had been through one and said the interrogator was intimidating but polite—an exaggerated and unsettling politeness, in fact—and also quite vague. The agent indicated it was just a "get-acquainted chat," something he hoped to do with all the boys at the school eventually. He added that the government was always on the lookout for talented students, especially those headed for university, and that such chats were useful for identifying the most promising. "There are many ways to serve the people in the new People's state, and we want to help you find a way."

The NKVD agent called it an interview, but all Daniil's friends knew it was an interrogation. And they also knew there were a dozen different ways to answer any question wrongly. Facial expressions and body language counted as much as words. An experienced investigator could unmask an enemy of the people by a twitch of the eyelid as easily as by the slip of the tongue. All the students knew of Alexi, who was interviewed one day and disappeared the next, never coming back to school—apparently so "talented" that the authorities put him to work immediately somewhere serving the people.

Daniil was reluctant to tell his parents about such things. They would only worry, especially his mother. At the same time, he knew he needed help to be ready. He decided that if an interview was arranged, he would tell them of it in advance and accept any advice they gave him. No need to worry anyone needlessly. Maybe he would never be called.

He was called. No prearrangement. A small man in a dark suit simply walked into his classroom one day and handed the teacher a note. The students were silent. Some looked down, as though they wouldn't be called if they weren't looking. The teacher read his name—"Daniil Mikhailovich"—and told him to come forward.

As he did, the man in the dark suit pointed to the door and walked out. Daniil followed.

He was led to a small room with only a bare table and two wooden chairs, one on each side. The man gestured for Daniil to sit and himself sat down opposite. He smiled tightly, appearing to Daniil like the fixed "smile" of a snake.

In the beginning it was as Boris had said.

"Hello, Mr. Aslanov. My name is agent Karlovsky. I am a member of The People's Commissariat for Internal Affairs. I am talking to all the boys in the school. It is just for a chat, so please relax. We are looking for talented students who can be of service to the people, especially those going to university. Your record shows you are, for the most part, an excellent student. We wish to congratulate you on that and offer any help we can so that you make the best use of your talents."

Daniil nodded. He felt sweat trickling down his spine.

The man inquired about Daniil's plans for university. What university was he going to? (Daniil didn't know if he had a choice—the issue was still two years away. A trick question perhaps.) In what area of study did he anticipate concentrating? (Was an answer here potentially dangerous or at least regrettable?)

"Engineering, sir. Perhaps."

"A good choice. Why 'perhaps'?"

Daniil realized his mistake. He tried to make up for it.

"Well, I like mathematics as well, sir."

He didn't like mathematics, but the first lie committed him to a second.

"Perhaps you could do both. They're related."

"Yes, sir. Related. Perhaps both."

In fact, Daniil did not want to be an engineer, but that had seemed like a safe answer. Better than art history or literature—too many dangerous ideas, too many free-thinking people. Daniil was learning early to tell Authority what Authority wanted to hear.

The man asked a few more questions about Daniil's future education and then went silent, drummed his fingers for a while, and finally leaned his small head across the table, trying on his smile once again.

"Tell me about your family, Mr. Aslanov."

"What would you like to know, sir?"

"Just talk about them. Tell me anything you think I ought to know. Really, anything. Anything at all."

Suddenly, Daniil heard his mother's voice in his head. It came to him from a conversation he overheard between her and his older sister. His sister had told their mother that a woman at her work was asking strange questions, wanting to know about their family history, whether anyone in the family was in the military, what they thought when the royal family disappeared.

Their mother had taken his sister's face in her hands and drawn her close.

"Whatever you say, Kira, say nothing."

Daniil understood for the first time that this admonition was meant as a survival principle. If his mother said this to Kira, she was saying it to him.

"I have an older sister and brother. My parents are in their fifties. We live together on the Petrograd side of the river.

"And what do your parents do for work?"

"My father works at a store. My mother mostly works at home."

The man did not look pleased. He stared at Daniil for a long time, then spoke in a clipped monotone.

"Your father owns that store. It is a furniture store on Bolshoy Prospekt. Your mother works part-time at Sunrise Bakery on Ulsita Lenina. And you all live at 3866 Polosova. We know these things, Mr. Aslanov. I would advise you not to try to hide from us the things we already know. Which, in case you're wondering, is everything."

He let this sink in for a while. Daniil's lower lip started to tremble.

"I would ask you whether your family is religious and whether they go to church. Except I know that they are and that they do—that you all do. And I know where. And I know you are about to cry, which I find tiresome."

He made a dismissive flick with the fingers of his left hand.

"Return to your classroom."

The man did not stand. As Daniil reached for the door, the interrogator added a final word.

"One more thing, Mr. Aslanov. About your interest in engineering and mathematics. Your record indicates you got a 3 in advanced algebra, average at best. You might want to work a bit harder in that area before—or I should say *if*—you get to university."

He then flashed one last snaky smile.

CHAPTER 12

October 1941

One of the more memorable events in the docent's career at the Hermitage was the day Shostakovich visited, not long before his evacuation in October. He was with General Mikhail Krzyzewsky, who was that rarest of individuals—an intelligent, well-educated, highly competent Soviet military leader (later to be executed for being a threat to inferior rivals).

The General was not only a brilliant military strategist; he was also very knowledgeable about the arts. When word spread quickly that both Shostakovich and Krzyzewsky were on a tour in the Winter Palace, Daniil joined the growing crowd that followed the tour.

Unfortunately, the guide for the tour, a notably arrogant senior guide, recognized Shostakovich but not the general, who was not in uniform. From time to time the general would ask penetrating questions, then started making even more penetrating remarks correcting or adding to what the guide was saying.

This did not sit well with the guide. After the general found fault with his comments about the colossal Statue of Jupiter, the guide turned to Shostakovich, who had been smiling throughout the general's comments. Pointing to his antagonist, he asked Shostakovich angrily, "Who is this guy?"

The composer raised his eyebrows and widened his smile.

"Why this is General Mikhail Krzyzewsky, hero of World War I and chief advisor to General Zhukov, military commander of Leningrad and beyond."

There was an audible gasp from the surrounding crowd. The guide's face turned ashen. His manner went instantly from petulant to obsequious.

"Yes, of course. I apologize, General, for not having recognized you without your uniform. My deepest apologies, sir. And I want to thank you for your very helpful questions and insightful commentary. It is a privilege to have such a knowledgeable personage on one of my humble tours."

All the time rubbing his hands and offering repeated small bows of the head, he finished weakly.

"Yes, an honor as well as a privilege. I think I join everyone here—all of Leningrad in fact—in thanking you for your service to us during this trying time."

Then it got worse.

"I think we all gathered here should give a round of applause to express our gratitude to General Krzyzewsky, should we not?"

With that he began applauding enthusiastically, looking from face to face. No one joined him. His claps echoed off the Statue of Jupiter like pebbles bouncing off a mountain. Mercifully, one of the staff walked up and led him away, and another guide took over.

CHAPTER 13

Summer 1906

NEITHER THE GRANDFATHER NOR THE GRANDSON FORGOT THE OTHER during the long years of separation. The grandfather often prayed for Daniil and for his family, and Daniil often thought about his grandfather and where he might be—if he was alive at all. In the first few years of his incarceration, the family received occasional letters and could even send food packages. Then, as the grandfather sank deeper into the abyss, all communication ceased. "Without rights to correspond" was stamped on the returned letters, which often was camp code indicating the prisoner was dead. "Without rights," indeed.

A recurring theme in Daniil's memories of his grandfather was Daniil's being taught by him. Being taught to draw, to read, to ask good questions. A favorite memory was his grandfather teaching him how to ride a bicycle. The grandfather tended to make any specific teaching a lesson in virtue and the nature of cosmic reality.

Daniil's first bike was a used one—big balloon tires, single gear, rubber grips at the end of the upright handlebars, front fender missing. Maybe once red.

The grandfather gave a speech before the first launch.

"As with everything, Daniil, the activity of bike riding is a collaboration with the nature of reality as God has created it. Without gravity there is no bike riding. Without torque there is no bike riding. Without angular momentum there is no bike riding."

And then he moved from physics to psychology.

"And then there is the God-created nature of the rider. A rider must have courage, especially at first. A rider must have confidence. A rider must have trust. A rider must persevere, getting back on the bike after a fall. All things necessary to ride a bike; all things necessary to live a good life. Align your life with the way things are, Daniil, which is the way God has made them, and things will go well with you. Set your life in opposition and you miss the blessing."

Daniil remembered these words with affection, but as an adult he had always thought them naïve. "Blessing?" he later thought. "Your faith led you to prison and to the camps. Where is the blessing in that?"

Actually that first lesson in bike riding was something of a failure. The grandfather ran along steadying the bike as Daniil first began to pedal. But as soon as the grandfather took his hand away, Daniil crashed. And then he cried. And then he quit.

"This is stupid. I don't want to do this anymore."

A sensitive boy, given to dark moods, Daniil often felt himself a failure. Sometimes he blamed the cosmos—"This is stupid!"—but often he blamed himself—"I am stupid!" On this occasion, the grandfather tried to encourage him.

He emphasized the pleasure riding was going to give him when he mastered it.

"You're going to love bike riding, Daniil. Gliding around the streets, the wind in your face, joining your friends for rides in the country. You just need to keep at it. You'll learn."

But Daniil would have none of it.

"This is stupid, Grandfather. I don't want to do it. Everything is stupid."

This prompted a short speech, of the kind for which the grandfather was known.

"No, Daniil, everything is not stupid. Everything has the potential to be wonderful. The universe shouts out wonder and meaning. The Bible says the rocks and hills cry out in celebration of the Creator. We must learn to listen—and join the shouting."

The grandfather still believed this, even in the camps.

CHAPTER 14

October 1941

THERE WAS ONLY ONE CONVINCING REASON TO GET OUT OF BED each morning—to get one's daily bread ration. All other reasons became increasingly less relevant beginning in October of 1941. Go to work? Fewer and fewer workplaces were open. Take care of your family? The best way to take care of your family was to get the daily bread ration. See your friends? Why? To discuss the many ways of dying in Leningrad? To find which friends had done so in the night?

No, one got up in order to eat, and the most available thing to eat was the daily bread ration. The only way to get that was to go every morning to your assigned shop with your coupon book (and perhaps the coupon books of your dependents). *Early* every morning, because sometimes they ran out of bread. The shops opened at six, but in the worst of times people were lining up by five, often sooner.

Which gets us to what some have called "the psychology of the queue." It should be a subject for advanced study in philosophy and the social sciences, for it includes many of the fundamental qualities of human nature. As the docent discovered each day.

Because bread had stayed available all morning the last week, Daniil did not rise until 5:30. It would not be light for hours. If Leningrad is famous for its White Nights of summer, when the sun barely sets, it should also be famous for its Dark Days of winter when the sun only reluctantly rises. Leningrad is the closest to the Arctic Circle of any big city in the world. By December and January the sun will show itself, grudgingly, for only six hours a day.

With nothing with which to make breakfast, the only thing he had to do was empty his bladder. He took the slop pail with him on his way down the stairs. He will dump and then hide it and retrieve it when he returns. If he doesn't, his apartment will stink when he comes back.

As he walked, Daniil could not help thinking of what had happened yesterday. The woman handing out the bread had forgotten to detach his coupon from his ration book. When she looked away from him and said, "Next," he froze. Should he tell her she had forgotten to take his coupon, or should he simply consider it a bit of luck and hurry on?

His mind, as minds will do, went directly to a scene from his childhood. He had gotten a perfect score on his spelling test. But he had cheated, copying the word "piano" from the red-headed girl sitting next to him. He couldn't help it. He had earned a perfect score on spelling tests all year and he couldn't bear to ruin his record.

Being sensitive of conscience, he was tortured with guilt and finally confessed to his grandfather. His grandfather both admonished and commended him.

"That was a sin, Daniil."

"But it didn't hurt anyone, Grandfather."

"You hurt only yourself, true, but it was still a sin. But telling me was a good thing, because it was the right thing. Those things go together, my grandson. What is right is good and what is good is right. And anyone who cheats in little things, will eventually cheat in big things, including the biggest of things."

The grandfather paused.

"It's good you told me. Now you must tell God and ask for forgiveness. Confess it to your priest at church. Then tell your teacher."

Those were the docent's thoughts as he approached the bread shop. He hadn't said anything yesterday, but he also hadn't reused the coupon. He would give it more thought.

For now, he was glad to see that the line at the shop was not long, only about half a block, not even to the corner yet. Still, he found himself stepping up his pace as he got close to its end. He spotted others arriving, including a few small groups, and he wanted to get his place before they beat him to it. He had missed getting bread by just a handful of people more than once, so it paid not to dawdle.

What does one do while waiting in a queue? Talk with others? In the early days perhaps, but no longer. What is there to talk about? Death? Disease? Destruction? How the Zenits are doing in football? (They shut down last summer.) People are irritable. That's the definition of a queue these days: compelled gatherings of people with a common purpose who annoy each other.

Perhaps a person in a queue should spend the time thinking. No, same problem as talking: What is there to think about that isn't depressing?

The docent's chosen strategy for waiting in a line was to mark his progress toward the entrance by observing the markings on buildings or the various displays he passed within a shop window. (He avoided looking at *himself* in a window—too disconcerting.)

Today, for instance, he found a cruel sign painted across the large picture window of the closed meat market in front of which he was standing: "Fresh Meat of All Kinds: Beef, Chicken, Lamb, Wild Game." Clearly an outdated lure. He first stood by the word "Fresh." Within ten minutes he got up to word "Kinds," another ten minutes and he got to "Chicken." And then things slowed down. It took twenty more minutes to get to "Wild," and after that he looked for a new marker on the next building. When things were moving this slowly, he suspected people were butting in line somewhere up ahead.

The people in a bread queue not only irritate each other, they also compete. You would think that once you had your place in line, the only competition would be with luck—as in lucky enough for there to be bread left when you got to the front. But that would not account for human nature, including cheaters.

The biggest cheaters by far were men. They were the most likely to cut in line in the first place, and the most likely to try to jump ahead a few places if someone wasn't paying attention. Daniil watched it happen today.

As they approached the door into the shop, the line now stretching back around the corner, a large man walked up and wedged in. The woman he pushed in front of protested, as any good Russian matriarch would.

"Hey, pig! What are you doing? You can't just push in here."

The man first responded with a rationalization.

"I've got to get to work."

Which was met with a much more rational response.

"You think other people in this queue don't have to get to work? Get to the back of the line."

Then the invader played his trump card.

"Listen, woman. I am twice your size and three times your strength and I will break your nose if you speak another word."

With no answer to that logic and no reason to think he wouldn't do exactly what he asserted, the woman fell silent, though grumbles passed back down the line like falling dominoes.

Daniil was about ten people back. The woman in front of him said to nobody in particular, "He's been trained to think that as a man his time is more valuable than the time of a woman. His mother started him thinking that way. His father reinforced it. Now we all pay for it."

Daniil had long ago noted that these bread lines—in fact most lines in Leningrad, even before the invasion—were made up of women, often with children. He recalled, with a hint of shame, that when Sofia was alive, she did most of the queueing for them. The only reason he was in line at the moment was because he now lived alone.

Irritation, impatience, anger, petty immorality—all these things and more abounded in a typical bread queue. The "more" include avarice and craving and self-pity. As people get closer to the front of a bread line, they begin to look at the cutting and distribution of the bread itself. (Sometimes the portions were preformed lumps, sometimes cut on the spot.) This is not helpful. When you are severely malnourished—spending much of both your waking and dreaming time obsessed with food—it is not comforting to see stacks of freshly baked bread behind the two women at the counter—one cutting and one distributing. Stacks and stacks of bread and you are to get only one slice—perhaps thick, perhaps not.

Daniil's practice was not to look. But it was impossible not to smell. And practically impossible not to salivate. Your body is playing games with you, and you with it. It salivates as though a fine meal awaits you, rather than a single chunk of bread. And you, once you have your bread—if you are wise—break it up into smaller pieces to eat throughout the day and evening, fooling your body into thinking it's getting more than it is.

When it's finally your turn in a bread line, you can't help watching the slicing off of your piece of the loaf. Some cry out when the knife is place on top, before it even cuts.

"That's too small. That's not fair. You're cheating me."

If the cutter doesn't adjust, the pleading woman ups the ante.

"You are killing my children."

Sometimes it works, sometimes it doesn't. Often the women further back in line yell out for the complainer to shut up and quit wasting time.

The scene today was even more interesting. The cheater—the man who threatened to break the woman's nose—was next to be served. He handed the dispensing woman his coupon book. The store will not take a coupon that has already been torn out—who knows how the person got it. Nor will they give you two days' ration for two coupons on the same day. One day, one long wait, one coupon, one ration. Come back tomorrow and start over.

Then she said something that delighted the queue.

"Your ration book. You're not registered for this shop. We can't give you bread. You have to go to your registered shop."

The man was instantly furious.

"What are you saying? I've been standing in line."

The women behind him laughed.

"He's lying. He butted in at the door."

Others jeered. The man ignored them.

"You must give me my bread! I demand it!"

He shook his fist at the woman holding his coupon book.

The woman threw his book on the counter. The slicer stepped over with her large knife and waved it in the man's face.

"Demand this, you bastard."

The man snatched up his coupons and stormed away, chased after by applause and hoots.

The docent thought, "Perhaps there are fragments of justice in the world after all."

Now that was something worth thinking about.

CHAPTER 15

October 1941

THERE WAS NO BETTER GAUGE OF THE STATE OF THE BLOCKADE than the docent's walks between home and the Hermitage. At first it was an opportunity to judge the mood of the people, later it was an opportunity to observe the desperation of the people, and later still it was a requirement to step over the bodies of the people.

Today in late October, for instance, a time when people were routinely hungry but not yet despairing, he was walking past Gostiny Dvor. There was a long line coming out one of the doors, stretching into the distance, composed, as usual, mostly of women. It had long been a practice in Stalin's Russia to join any queue one saw and ask questions after. It might be a line for something you needed, or something rarely available even if you didn't need it. (And if it was shoes for your kids, you always made sure to buy them one size too big, in case another opportunity was slow in coming.)

As the docent walked along beside the queue, he wondered if he should join it. Finally he asked a young woman what the line was for. She merely shrugged.

"Not sure."

An older lady behind her solved the mystery.

"A rumor of onions, sir. A strong rumor of onions."

"Aha. Onions. Thank you."

He didn't join the line, but for the sake of those in it, he hoped the rumor was true.

On the same day, walking home from the Hermitage at around five in the afternoon, Daniil discovered that bombs and shells weren't the only things the Germans dropped from the sky. It was suddenly raining leaflets of different sizes and colors. Like those around him, the docent picked some of them up.

Each was a piece of psychological warfare, all in perfect Russian. One was a pamphlet containing an antisemitic rant—almost as likely to find an audience in Leningrad as in Berlin, the Nazis were hoping. Another was a fake ration card. A third was Russian currency, not well counterfeited, but perhaps well enough. All designed to undermine the system, all designed with human nature in mind.

In minutes the streets were bare of leaflets, thanks undoubtedly to the Soviet-inspired neatness of the citizens who snatched them up.

A few hundred yards later, Daniil heard music coming from an empty storefront. It was a haunting music, melancholy and slow. Russian folk music has songs that are melancholy and slow, but this was different. It wasn't nostalgic, it was, well, just sad.

Daniil knew exactly what kind of music it was, and though the music was sad his spirits were lifted. He had first heard it as a young man in the 1920s. He once owned Sidney Bechet and Ma Rainey records and had even heard her in person. The records were long gone but the memories were still fresh.

He looked through the window. He could see five players on different instruments—piano, drums, guitar, trumpet with a mute, and saxophone. They formed a circle, sometimes looking at each other, sometimes looking far away.

The music was highly repetitious, the same chords over and over, with slight variations. The docent found he couldn't walk past. The music told him to stop, to listen, to dialogue with it. It made him regret having traded Sofia's clarinet earlier in the month for food, not that he could play the clarinet himself.

He listened for quite a long time. Actually, the music told him to forget time. It told him the things it was speaking of were timeless, as old as the human experience, maybe older. Sadness, melancholy, disappointment, regret—the infinite permutations of human suffering, of creation's suffering.

Why the attraction to such expressions of pain? Why stick yourself with needles? Because the articulation of the suffering somehow lessened it—gave it a shape, named it, made it less random, clarified its sources, commended endurance, suggested, even if faintly, the possibilities for survival, perhaps even overcoming.

Eventually, the docent sensed he was not alone. He turned and found another man listening as well. They smiled cautiously at each other and nodded. Neither said anything.

Nothing needed to be said.

CHAPTER 16

February 1939

CAMP AUTHORITIES WERE NOT ENTIRELY INHUMANE, ONLY MOSTLY so. You were allowed to be sick in the camps, as much as you wished, actually. Then again, you were only allowed to go to the infirmary if your temperature was above 103 degrees. Even at that the rule was, "If you can stand, you can work." So everyone knew that if you could get your temperature up, you best also claim to be unable to walk.

There was, in fact, a camp doctor. Or someone who passed for a doctor. If you were an actual doctor assigned to practice at a labor camp, you were either at the bottom of your class or had offended a local official and were yourself a prisoner. The only equipment likely at your disposal was a thermometer, a bed, and a bed pan, and the only medicine was aspirin—a socialist cure-all.

The grandfather often tended to the sick and dying. The zeks preferred him to the doctor. Something about his quiet manner and hopeful words were better than medicine—even than aspirin.

Believers died more peacefully if they could first confess. Any and all religious practices were of course banned. Technically they could get you sent to the punishment cell. But the guards knew that Father Sergius was good for order in the camp. If every barrack had such a one, their job would be easier. And they were not completely indifferent to the dying of another human being, or at least some of them were not. So when the grandfather was hearing the confession of a dying zek, they tended to look away.

The grandfather was never fully at ease listening to the confession of another. He had a heightened sense of his own failings, and anyone's confessing of sins reminded him of his own. Among them was the guilt he felt at the failures of the Church. When asked why Russia had fallen so completely for Lenin's lies (something only asked in private by the brave), he had a ready answer.

"It's our fault—we priests. We did not guide the people properly. We did not teach them the truth convincingly. We did not live our own story faithfully. The Communists did not overthrow the Church. We overthrew ourselves. They just filled the vacuum, as nature always will."

Among the people whose dying confessions he heard was that of the judge who had originally sentenced him. Such ironies were not uncommon in Stalin's Russia, or Lenin's either. Everyone walked a narrow plank high above a fiery pit, rotten in some places, gaps in others. The higher up you were, the more threatening you were to the next person up from you. And the more the next person down from you wanted your spot. You walked without seeing your next step. One minute a judge sending people to the camps, the next minute sharing a bunk with those you had sent.

The judge was already in the Special camp when the grandfather first arrived from his previous incarceration. Although assigned to another barrack, the grandfather had run into him not long after. The grandfather took no pleasure in seeing his former tormentor brought low. He considered the judge no worse than himself—and told him as much.

"You were required to do a job, sir. You did it efficiently. I am grateful that I was not offered your job. I am weak. I might have taken it."

In his early days the judge was frightened to be in a camp where he might easily run into people whose lives he had ruined. But he was unrepentant. In fact, he was offended. Not long after his own arrival, the grandfather witnessed a vicious argument the judge had with a White Russian, the losers in the Civil War that followed the 2017 Revolution.

The White Russian grabbed the judge by the collar.

"You scum. You murderer. You destroyer of men and families and country. You don't deserve to breathe another breath."

The judge tore himself away, almost falling down. He straightened his padded jacket and struck as dignified a pose as he could muster.

"I have served the Motherland faithfully. I sent its enemies to places like this. Many I sent to the firing squad. There are endless enemies of the Revolution. People like you. They must die if the Revolution is to live. I only wish I had put away more. My only regret, traitor, is that you did not appear before me. If you had, I can assure you that you would not be in this camp. No, you would be in a shallow grave. And the Motherland would be better for it."

His antagonist made a leap for him, but the judge nimbly stepped behind the grandfather and continued his sentencing speech.

"If I am ashamed of anything, it is that I now have to share life with people like you—traitors, criminals, religious freaks. I should not be here."

Yes, the sincere sentiment of many. "I should not be here." "It is not right." "A mistake has been made." The mistake was being alive in Russia in the twentieth century. All other mistakes flowed from that one.

You may wonder that a man who has unjustly ruined or ended the lives of so many could be this brazen about it. If so, you do not understand that mass injustice, mass killing, requires an ideology. A man can kill a handful out of anger or spite or other personal reasons, but to kill countless people—people one doesn't even know—demands a theory, a broad way of seeing the world, with values attached, a theory that requires the elimination of impurities—unwanted things and unwanted people.

And you may wonder also that I said that the grandfather heard the dying confession of this judge. How can that be, when he had such an attitude?

Well, the camps are a great attitude changer. Haughtiness was his attitude in years one, two, and three. It was less so in years four, five and six. By years seven, eight and nine, he could no longer remember his wife's face. And when, in year ten, the last year of his sentence, he was told that his sentence had been extended for another ten years, he broke completely.

Because the judge was in a different barrack, the grandfather had few exchanges with him over the years. But in the eleventh year, now an old man, the judge came down with his final illness. As sometimes happens, it made him contemplate eternity seriously for the first time.

He even returned to the faith of his childhood, something he had first hidden and then cast violently away as he rose through the legal ranks toward his judgeship. The grandfather had nothing to do with his transformation. Another zek, not himself a priest, had led the judge slowly back. But that man had died, and as the judge himself was dying, he called for the grandfather to hear his last confession.

Father Sergius talked to him for hours over two days. The judge did not want blanket forgiveness. He wanted to enumerate each sin, each misdeed, only some of which involved the courts. He included a personal apology as well as a formal confession for having sent the grandfather away.

"You know, Father, when I gave you your sentence, when I gave every sentence I ever gave, I always was confident that I was doing what a good person should do, what was good for the Party, good for the nation, good for the Revolution, good for humanity. I knew myself to be right, always right, and now, before you and God, I think that confidence was perhaps my greatest sin. Or at least my most persistent sin."

Father Sergius answered as he always did to one confessing.

"Yours is a sin God has seen and forgiven before. And he does so again for you."

It was a bitterly cold night. Father Sergius was allowed to stay with the judge as he slipped away. No one else paid him any attention. The judge was known and hated in the camp, even after his late change of heart. When he died in his bunk an inmate called the guard.

One of the zeks spat when he saw that the judge was dead.

The grandfather simply said, "He was a human being made by God. He fought a great battle. In the end, he won."

A sledge arrived outside the door and a worker came in. He felt for a pulse, then shouted to the man outside.

"We got a stiff—number Shch-158."

CHAPTER 17

October 1941

"THE BEST LAID SCHEMES O' MICE AN' MEN . . . ." YOU KNOW the rest. A blockade example of the Scottish poet's insight was the German pilot whose plane was shot down and who had parachuted not to safety, but to execution. He was first captured by civilians who watched him floating down from the sky as a hungry dog watches the piece of meat waving in his owner's hand.

They beat and abused him even as he was trying to untangle himself from the lines of his chute, but the police showed up soon enough to rescue him from significant harm. He was destined for a more ceremonial dispatching.

Mayor Zhdanov decided it would improve the morale of the people if they dealt with this war criminal in public. A small propaganda coup for the sake of morale. They brought him to the great square behind the Winter Palace and made sure a large crowd was gathered. To maximize its potential propaganda impact, they had newsreel cameras there and broadcast it live on the radio. Microphones were stationed close to where the pilot was to be shot by a firing squad. The hope was that he would snivel and cower and, if things went well, even weep, perhaps bellow.

Daniil did not know of this show execution, but discovered the scene as he left the Winter Palace to walk home from his volunteering at the Hermitage. He asked a man what was going on.

"They're shooting a German pilot."

Unlike many around him, the man did not seem very enthusiastic. A woman nearby set him straight.

"Dispensing Soviet justice to a killer of children."

Things did not go as hoped. The microphones picked up the German's words, spoken in very tolerable Russian, as the firing squad marched into place.

"Yes, please shoot me. I am happy to die for the Führer. All of you will soon join me. The plan is to starve you. We have agents everywhere in your city. You are starving already. Your precious Red Army has not saved you. We have taken Tikhvin, cutting your last supply route. We have been victorious everywhere. We stopped and surrounded you on purpose, so that you could be bombed and starved while my comrades go on to destroy Moscow and Stalingrad. I laugh at you. You are all going to die. Every one of you. I laugh."

Which he did.

The speakers went dead. The firing squad raised their rifles and shot him. The man beside the docent pronounced a quiet requiem.

"Yes, one less Nazi killer. But unlike us, he dies with a full stomach."

CHAPTER 18

November 1941

THE SIEGE CHANGED THINKING FOR EVERYONE AND EXTINGUISHED it for some. The main causes for this were fear and starvation. As pointed out at the beginning, engines run on fuel and, to a materialist—Marxist or otherwise—the brain is essentially a meat engine. If it is not adequately fueled, it does not run. And fear, while a stimulant, is also a deranger. It makes the mind race in place, like gunning a car engine while in neutral, lots of noise and smoke, but no forward motion, and, eventually, neither noise nor smoke.

One of the things people thought differently about was their homes. Most lived in large, sterile apartment buildings, aesthetic nullities but highly efficient for packing great numbers of people into a small space. Some enjoyed living on upper floors—for the views and the breezes—and were willing to put up with climbing stairs. Stair climbing was once thought healthy, like a good walk in the mountains.

But the blockade changed that. Now an upper floor apartment was the most vulnerable to bombs and shelling. You had to think differently.

Not that lower floors were significantly safer. Everyone had seen buildings that had completely collapsed—top floors sitting on crushed lower floors. There were whispers that they had been poorly built, but no building is constructed with the idea of a five-hundred-pound bomb coming through the roof—and a half-dozen floors—before exploding. If a building is going to collapse, do you want to be living on the bottom floor?

In sum, how many floors do you want above you for protection from shells and bombs versus how many floors do you want crashing down on you if the building collapses?

And then you had to think about stairs. Climbing them took you up and away from the chaos and noise of the streets. On the other hand, climbing stairs burned calories. If you are living on one thick slice of bread a day and boiled wallpaper paste, how many calories can you afford for climbing stairs? Every step was a test of heart, lungs, and legs. The siege introduced a new mathematics, or at least a new calculation. Was it possible that the walk to the bread shop and back, combined with the expense of climbing stairs, actually cost more calories than the adulterated bread—as much sawdust as flour—provided?

Upper floor or lower floor? The deciding factor for many was fire. The Nazis were excellent fire starters, dropping firefalls of incendiary bombs designed expressly for that hellish purpose. And there was less and less water in Leningrad's pipes, the pumping stations and electrical system being systematically destroyed. So every fire bomb gave birth to an omnivorous, devouring creature with an indefinite lifespan. Bombed buildings could burn for days at a time, often spreading to the buildings next door.

The greatest fear was that a fire would reach the stairwells early on. If you were on the first or second, or maybe even third, floors, you could possibly escape through a window. Any higher and your death was a foregone conclusion—the only question being mode. If by fire, you were lucky if you died of smoke inhalation before the flames could taste you. As with a well-built martyr's pyre in medieval times, smoke was more merciful than flames, though the end result was the same.

One morning the docent was walking to the Hermitage. The punctual first shelling of the morning had just concluded. At the time, you could count on four sets of artillery shellings per day: two morning shellings from 8 to 9 and 11 to 12, a going-home-from-work shelling between 5 and 6, and a nightcap shelling between 8 and 10, the first three timed for when the most people would be on the street and the last as folks prepared for bed. You could set your watch by them.

In the early days, the docent was worried that he would get to his apartment after a day at the museum and find his building either collapsed or ablaze. But then he got used to it, as the citizens of Leningrad got used to daily atrocities they could never have imagined. Perhaps that is a silver lining—evil numbs the mind, making the shocking merely disturbing, then only irritating, then hardly noticed. (Does not a man working in a slaughterhouse eventually stop noticing the blood?)

Today the docent saw the crowd and smoke from two blocks away. Why a crowd? he wondered. Fires no longer attracted crowds in Leningrad. As he got closer, he heard shouts and cries. People were not just gawking, they were agitated. He soon saw why.

On the sixth or seventh floor, there were three children at a window. The oldest, a girl, was maybe ten. Next to her were two younger boys, maybe six and then one that looked to be a toddler. They were frighteningly silent, too terrorized to yell out.

The docent wanted to hurry by, but his legs stopped working. He joined the crowd, witnesses to the unthinkable. Smoke was coming out around the children. Some people were holding out a pathetically small blanket and shouting for the children to jump. The only choice really—burn alive or jump to your death, body shattered on the pavement.

Then it got worse.

A woman ran screaming through the crowd to where the blanket was being held.

"My children! My children! Save my children!"

She tried to run into the building but was held back. The whole first floor, and yes, the stairs, were aflame.

"I was just getting our bread! The lines, the lines! They are too long. I had no choice! I had to get their bread!"

Seeing their mother awakened the children. All three began to cry, stretching out their arms.

"Mother! Mother! Save us!"

The mother now jumped up and down, her own arms outstretched, as though she could jump all the way to them.

The men held her and the women tried to console her. But there is no consolation. She is Rachel weeping for her children, refusing to be comforted, for her children are soon no more.

The docent wished he could pray, or believed such a thing useful.

Daniil could not take it. Why, with suffering so omnipresent, should he volunteer for more? Some things are so unspeakable that they must be driven from the mind, lest it shred. He turned away from the crowd, and continued his walk to work, shedding his own useless tears.

CHAPTER 19

May 1926

Maxim knew early on that Daniil was his parents' favorite, his grandfather's favorite—everyone's favorite. And he thought it unfair.

Just because Daniil was the youngest and still cute, whereas Maxim had outgrown cuteness. (And sister Polina wasn't a consideration, because girls are a separate category.) Just because Daniil was compliant whereas Maxim had developed a mind of his own. Just because Daniil asked so many clever questions, especially of his grandfather.

Such as this one.

"Why, Grandpa, doesn't God just make everyone happy?"

The grandfather had smiled.

"That's a good question, Daniil. A very good question. Smart people have been asking it for a long time. I would say this—God has made it *possible* for everyone to be happy—in the long run. I think that is the thing we should focus on. God has made it *possible.* We are responsible to act on that possibility."

"I don't understand."

"Think of it like this. The Psalmist tells us to 'taste and see that the Lord is good.' If I give you a sweet, you have the chance to be happy, but only if you taste the sweet, Daniil, only if you taste it. The Lord is good, but we must taste him."

"Yes, clever boy," Maxim remembered. "Ask your religious grandfather a question about God. A sure way to make yourself the favorite."

All this bothered Maxim when they were children, and it still bothered him when they became adults. The fact is the brothers did not much like each other. Now something had alienated Daniil from their parents too. Maxim didn't know what. The parents refused to talk about it. It was taboo. It seemed Daniil was the one who minimized contact. For some reason, the lifelong favorite chose to mostly stay away.

His parents were old now, but the memory of their favoring Daniil was still fresh for Maxim.

"He is physically absent, but psychologically ever-present," Maxim ruminated. "He is the child they talk about, worry about, obsess over."

After their father was injured in the accident at work, Maxim was the one who looked out for both parents. Daniil made occasional visits, sent money here and there, but Maxim was the one on duty day to day. He was the one who took his father to doctor visits, who fixed anything in the house that needed fixing, who talked to his mother when she grew depressed.

"But who do they talk about? Daniil. Whose rare letters light up their faces? Daniil's. Who do they pray for constantly? Yes, exactly."

When Maxim visited Leningrad once on business, he met Daniil for lunch and they talked.

"How come we never see you back home?"

"What do you mean? I was there just . . . when was it? . . . I was there not that long ago."

"Eighteen months, Daniil. Eighteen months. You didn't even make it for Christmas."

"Christmas was banned years ago."

"Okay, you didn't make it for the New Year celebrations."

"Life is busy, Maxim."

"Too busy for your family?"

"I have my own family now. A wife and a son. It's not easy to travel with a five-year-old."

"A son of yours who needs to know his larger family, Daniil. It's more than that. What is it? You have always been the favorite and now you're a ghost.

"I wasn't 'always the favorite.' I was just the youngest. When you were a toddler, you were the favorite."

"When I was a toddler, I was the only one."

Daniil realized there was no adequate defense against envy—it is a self-propelling emotion. Denial from the one envied only fed the fire. He decided to play a bit of offense.

"I may have been favored for a while in the family, but you made sure I was not favored in the neighborhood and among our friends."

"What does that mean?"

"It means the games we played and you directed."

"What games?"

"'The Civil War game—'Whites and Reds.' You always assigned me to the Whites and yourself to the Reds. I was always with the bad guys, you were always with the winners. And winning was usually violent. We Whites—always the smaller kids—had to be not only beaten, but beaten—with fists and kicks. And your own victorious blows were always reserved for me."

"Really, Daniil, kids' games. You are going to bring up kids' games?"

Daniil did not respond to Maxim's response. He moved on to the next example.

"Then there was 'Search and Requisition.' You would burst into my room, yell 'Search and Requisition,' and then empty the drawers of my dresser and pull my clothes off the hangar and pretend to find contraband and run out laughing with my favorite possessions."

A smirk cracked Maxim's face as he responded.

"Ah yes, your framed print of that painting that grandfather gave you."

Daniil was not done. And he was getting angry.

"And how about 'Interrogation,' Maxim? How about 'Interrogation'? That was your favorite game, wasn't it? You were a loyal Pioneer—joining over our parents' objections. They couldn't stop you for fear you would denounce them. You were determined to progress to the Komsomol when old enough, and eventually become a member of the Party, where the games would grow more serious.

"Do you remember the day you called for a game of 'Interrogation' amongst the kids on the vacant lot?"

"Of course I don't remember a particular game on a vacant lot, Daniil. Why are you getting angry?"

Again, Daniil does not answer his question. He is back on that vacant lot.

"'Hey kids, let's play Interrogation,' you said. The kids cheered and asked, 'Who shall we interrogate?' You swung your arm around and pointed at me. 'Let's interrogate Daniil. He's an enemy of the people!'"

The smirk disappeared from Maxim's face. He was remembering.

"Everyone formed a circle around me. You began, 'You, lice, are accused of being a counter-revolutionary. Give us the evidence of your crime.' I said nothing, too scared to speak. You continued, 'Your father is a vermin kulak, an exploiter of the poor, an owner of land that rightfully belongs to the people. He has resisted collectivization and is an enemy of the Revolution. Your biography is spoiled. Your father is a self-seeker and you are his self-seeking son.'

"The game got out of hand, didn't it Maxim? You were a skilled interrogator—a natural. The other kids got into it. They started spitting on me. You tried to stop the game but it was too late. You couldn't stop the game then, just as no one can stop the game now. One kid threw a rock, then another. They started to punch and kick me. A kid yelled, 'I saw him coming out of a church. His family goes to church.' That's when you ran, Maxim. That's when you ran away. I limped home, a bloody mess. And you complain that I was favored as a child."

"That's enough, Daniil. I came here to woo you back to the family, but apparently you don't want to come back. Have it your way."

Daniil felt ashamed for bringing up the past, but Maxim was gone before he could formulate an apology. In his mind, he heard the sound of a closing door.

CHAPTER 20

November 1941

DIFFERENT FRIENDS PLAY DIFFERENT ROLES IN ONE'S LIFE—AND excavate different strata of one's nature. One who dug deeper than most was Leonid the artist, three floors up, who everyone except his wife called Lev. With Aleksandr he could talk politics, sports, and daily life, with Lev he could talk art and ideas and other risky things. (At one time he had talked all these with Sofia.)

Daniil had not seen his friend for a couple of weeks when he labored his way upstairs to Lev's door. When Lev opened it, the docent was stunned at his deterioration. He was greeted by a skeleton. Though only in his early fifties, Lev looked ancient. Most of his hair had fallen out. His skin was gray. His hand shook. The docent wondered if he himself looked this bad, but he had long stopped checking.

The small apartment Lev shared with his wife, Mila, had been transformed into an artist's studio. His previous studio nearby had burned in an early air raid. Some of his work had been lost, but many paintings now leaned against walls or were stacked in corners.

Daniil had trouble judging the quality of Leonid's art. It leaned modernist, not as steeply as Malevich and Kandinsky, but enough so that the docent, immersed as he was in Renaissance art, didn't feel he had the visual vocabulary to judge it. A number of the subjects were architectural—staircases, grouped buildings, stylized cityscapes. But they usually projected some kind of emotional content, often brooding or haunting.

He recalled a rather acerbic response to a hypothetical question posed by a fellow guide at the Hermitage recently, given in private, of course. "What is the difference between painters of the naturalist, impressionist, and Socialist Realism schools? The naturalists paint as they see, the impressionists as they feel, the socialist realists as they are told." The docent saw both "see" and "feel" in Lev's paintings, but not much of "told," which put him at risk.

Lev sat at his table drinking what passed for tea. At least the liquid was dark. In today's Leningrad one accepted anything that seemed even an echo of food or drink. (Leather belts were boiled to make a kind of gelatinous soup, or were cut into chunks and boiled for something to chew on.) While Lev sipped, Daniil sifted through some of the frames leaning against the wall. He came across a painting of a train—more a suggestion of a train than a realistic portrayal, capturing its movement and speed in its thrust from the upper left of the canvas to the lower right, smoke streaming back to convey rapidity.

"What's this?"

"What's it look like? More important, what does it feel like?"

"It feels like a screaming artillery shell just before impact."

"Good. That's what it should feel like. Have you ever stood near the tracks when a high-speed train whizzes past? It's a visceral experience—all the senses provoked. There was nothing equivalent in human history before the Industrial Revolution."

"Maybe standing at the lip of an active volcano."

"Not loud enough."

"Outside in a lightning storm?"

"Closer."

Daniil flipped through a few more, then froze.

"Lev. This one. This one."

"This one what? What have you found?"

Daniil pulled it out, his hand shaking a bit. The painting seemed to frighten him.

Lev laughed.

"Oh, that one. The traditional mother and child."

"Not just any mother and child, Lev. Mary and the baby Jesus. Remember, I did go to church as a boy and I spend my days at a place with hundreds, maybe thousands of paintings of these two. They stare at me every day."

And stare was the right word for Lev's depiction. It was painted on cardboard. Painting supplies had disappeared in blockade time. For a while he had painted on plywood, but with winter cold beginning, any kind of wood was becoming almost as precious as food. "Can you imagine a Raphael or Bruegel painted on cardboard?" the docent thought. It made him hate the Nazis even more.

Lev had made use of the traditional Mary and Christ Child theme so omnipresent in Western art. But at the same time, he made it new. Both Mary and the Child look shell-shocked. Both stare directly at the viewer, but in a more profound sense they are staring at and appalled by evil. For in the pupils of Mary's eyes is the tiny reflection of a window with flames leaping behind it. The window is askew, suggesting that reality had been knocked off center. The wood molding in the middle of the window frame is broken and hanging, forming an upside-down cross, an allusion to their future—the Christ Child hanging on it, she standing beneath it. Nothing is as it should be. Mary's tense face and pursed lips suggest the first moments of witnessing the apocalypse that is Leningrad under siege. The blankness of the face of the infant Jesus looks too much like the blank expressions of starving children Daniil saw too often on the city streets.

Daniil questioned Lev.

"Is this an icon, my friend?"

Lev smiled.

"Mila asked me the same question. It is and it isn't."

"Well, it certainly looks like one."

"Yes, but appearance does not make an icon an icon. Only God can make it an icon."

"I know. I know. The ancient saying: 'The hand of the icon painter is guided by an angel.' Isn't that how it goes?"

"Something like that. The paintings I'm doing these days have some of the features of traditional icons, but not some other necessary features. Icons carry the memories of the people—including memories of their experiences with God. They are a resource; they help us live. I hope the same for my paintings. I will let others decide what they are."

Daniil replied with alarm.

"Which others, Lev? Which others? Surely you know how a commissar would judge it. And what the consequences of that judgment might be."

"Of course. He would call it religious art."

"Yes, and it is dangerous to be associated with anything religious in our time. I know this personally, in my own family."

"Art *should* be dangerous, Daniil. A danger to the status quo, a danger to conformity and convention, a danger to cant and propaganda, a danger to dictators. And if it is, then for the artist it carries the danger of not having enough to eat, and, yes, sometimes, as now, a danger to one's body. And yet, it is even more dangerous to stifle oneself, for then you shrivel up inside. You become not an artist but a parrot."

Daniil admired his friend, but could not help a rejoinder.

"The labor camps are full of people with admirable principles, Lev. You must be careful."

"It's impossible to be careful enough, as you know. They've sent people to Kolyma for wrapping fish in newspaper that had a photograph of the Leader. And for not applauding his speeches vigorously enough. Or these days in Leningrad, for having a private radio. Even that painting of the train could get me in trouble. It smacks of Goncharova and the Futurists, who were squashed not long after the Revolution."

Daniil nodded. To himself he thought, "And now *I* am in danger, friend. Because having seen this, I should report you. I might even get extra food for it. But if I did, I would not be a parrot, I would be a Judas."

The unspoken word—"Judas"—made him twitch.

Lev continued.

"Besides, my public art is more or less acceptable to the boundary-keepers. I even painted set designs for one of Shostakovich's operas. I do much of my work for the community. I do these for someone else."

"For God, I suppose."

"Maybe for God. Maybe not. He will have to decide. I think people should be careful about claiming to do things for God."

"We can agree on that."

"So given this conversation, it is appointed that I show you a painting I am working on now, almost finished with in fact."

With that he rose and walked to an easel and lifted the cloth covering the work beneath. The docent's eyes widened. He was silent before it.

If the painting on cardboard was perhaps an icon, this was a palladium—an image that offers protection. A wooden depiction of Athena was said to protect ancient Troy, and a statue of Constantine the Christianizer was thought to do the same for Byzantium turned Constantinople. It stood on a hundred-foot pillar, and in the statue's hand was an image of the goddess the Romans called Fortuna—an interesting hedging of bets by mixing Christian and pagan superstition (within the column itself was said to be, among other things, an axe used by Noah, bread pieces from the feeding of the five thousand, and even the original Athena palladium).

The palladium in Lev's painting followed the icon tradition of Mary spreading her veil over those needing protection. In this case, she is spreading it over a city—Leningrad, no doubt—with a look of disbelief and horror at what she is seeing. Her huge eyes are staring, open wide, and her mouth is gaping. Her head tilts severely down. Her hands, while holding the veil, are raised over her head, palms out—perhaps a suggestion of prayer, or of deep grief and lament, or even of Jesus on the cross.

In a recent speech on the radio, Stalin himself had invoked the idea of a palladium, giving it a contemporary twist. "May the unconquerable banner of the great Lenin," he intoned, "o'erspread you! Onward to victory under the banner of Lenin!" A smart rhetorical move, given that the people still have the idea of a protecting palladium in their bones, if not in their hearts. Not that either Mary or Lenin seemed to be offering Leningrad much protection at the moment.

Lev's painting is an icon but not an icon. Missing are the traditional calm and control of the Theotokos. The painting suggests it may be too late for protection—the devastation is already far along. The background of red clouds implies an inferno of fire. The windows of buildings below are black and empty, like the eye-sockets of skulls. The city—the country, the modern world—has waited too long to turn to the Holy Mother, to God, for protection. Evil is not only loosed in the world; at this moment it reigns.

On Mary's vestment is the faint outline of a church, perhaps representing *the* Church. Faint because almost obliterated in Soviet Russia? Or suggesting the Church is the medium through which God speaks, the only hope of Leningrad, of Russia, of the world?

"It's entrancing, Lev. I can't take my eyes away from it. I don't know whether it's an icon or simply a painting with a religious theme."

The artist seemed to enjoy the docent's ambivalence.

"Maybe the question is determined by the impact it has on you. If it moves you in a certain direction, it is an icon. If not, not."

"This is the most powerful work of yours I have ever seen, Lev. But like I said, you could never sell or even show these paintings. It's dangerous even to have this kind of thing in your apartment, to let people like me see it. What are you thinking?"

"I'm thinking that I am not painting these for buyers, or for curators, or even for myself. I will be dead soon, and so, most likely, will you, Daniil. Maybe I am painting these, as you suggest, for my next Landlord after all. And to leave a little piece of my true self behind."

CHAPTER 21

June 1933

YOU WERE MORE LIKELY TO BE SENT TO THE CAMPS FOR IDEAS and attitudes than for deeds, including ones you never entertained. The intelligentsia are brimming always with both ideas and attitudes and therefore were well represented in the gulag. Especially so since under the horizon-wide expanse of Article 58 of the penal code, even the most innocuous idea or act could be deemed an offense if a prosecutor had a quota to fill.

One academic, for instance, was sent to the camps because a student reported that while he often quoted Marx and Lenin, he didn't as often quote Stalin. Another fellow was there because he was seen smiling while reading Pravda, implying skepticism. Similarly, it was dangerous to be seen shaking the hand on the street of someone under surveillance, likely not knowing they were being surveilled. Guilt by the slimmest of associations.

Article 58, instigated in 1927 and expanded in 1934, was the trawler net of all laws, indiscriminately capturing everything and everyone in the sea of suspicion. Its expansive subcategories explicitly named traitors, saboteurs, spies, terrorists, agitators, shirkers, and those who associated with "international bourgeoisie," but it also included any activity or idea or attitude that could be deemed—by anyone with power—to be "counter-revolutionary," including giving religious instruction to children (article 58-10). It also covered people, including family members, who failed to report offenders—imagined or real. And Article 58 could be useful for the common folk. It was quicker for a woman wanting to get rid of a bad husband to denounce him than to divorce him. And for anyone angling to get a better apartment or promotion.

And it was often, when convenient, turned against those in power who had previously used it against others. Article 58 filled up the Soviet incarceration system like a river fills a reservoir behind a dam.

The zone was filled with superstitions as well as ideas. If you were released, for instance, you were advised to take your spoon with you. Otherwise the spoon would call you back; you were destined to return to the camp and to the spoon you left behind. And it was bad luck to whistle indoors, not that there was much to whistle about in the camps (and one's luck was already proven "bad").

The intellectuals imagined their own superstitions to be instead "ideas," equally fanciful but presented as simply rational. In the grandfather's barrack, for instance, the intellectuals often debated questions related to the nature and spirit of Marxism. "Spirit," in fact, was a word central to the exchange on one occasion. It started innocuously with a comment emanating from a discussion about football while the zeks prepared for lights out.

Igor: "In football, the more skilled team is often beaten by the team with greater spirit."

Nikolai: "What do you mean by 'spirit,' comrade? Marx taught us that reality is entirely physical. Are you trying to introduce an anti-Soviet concept by way of sports? No wonder you are serving a tenner."

Igor was both insulted and delighted. The match was on.

Igor: "Not at all, you provocateur. 'Spirit' simply refers to mental strength. 'Spirit' is the driving force of the Revolution."

Nikolai: "But the word 'spirit' is a cognate of 'spiritual,' which is not at all a Soviet concept."

Igor: "Marx explicitly endorses the need for spirituality among the masses. You can read it."

Nikolai: "Yes, but what did he mean by it? Is it a reference to something beyond the material? I'm sure not, comrade."

(Beware of someone calling you "comrade" twice within the same conversation. It doesn't usually bode well.)

This drew in Rodion, known for his attempts, whenever possible, to muddy the waters in any discussion.

Rodion: "So, what do people mean when they speak of 'the spiritual' in art? Is that merely a mental or psychological quality? Is that 'anti-Soviet'?"

That brought in Matvey, a onetime landscape painter.

Matvey: "The 'spiritual' as it refers to the arts is simply a synonym for the imagination. It is purely a function of the brain, an ability to envision multiple possibilities—speculations, you could say—some of which are subject to physical embodiment—as in architecture, for instance; some of which can be embodied in words and metaphors—as in poetry; some in musical notes; and some of which remain vague and undefined. But nothing in this understanding of 'spiritual' suggests a reality beyond the material."

Rodion indicated his concurrence with a nod of the head. But Alexei, already twenty years in the camps and very likely to die there soon, exercised the freedom of thought camps provided for those with nothing else to lose.

Alexei: "I see no reason why a world shaped by Marxist thought has to be incompatible with a parallel reality beyond the physical. Why not two kingdoms—the kingdom of God and the kingdom of Marx and Lenin?"

This brought a howl of protest from Nikolai.

Nikolai: "Two kingdoms? What foolishness. Even your vocabulary betrays you—or I should say, 'reveals you'—as anti-Soviet. 'Kingdoms' require kings—the ancient and continuing oppressors of the proletariat. And 'God' and gods are simply notions to keep the people sedated and compliant, blind to their oppression."

Alexei persisted.

Alexei: "Not at all. Or at least not necessarily. Jesus was a Communist, perhaps the first. The early Christians shared everything in common. They were an early expression of 'from each according to his ability, to each according to his needs.' They couldn't have been more Marxist."

Nikolai had moved beyond debate earnestness to anger.

Nikolai: "Rubbish, comrade. Rubbish."

But Alexei was on a roll.

Alexei: "It's Hegelian, my friend. Christianity is the thesis. Communism is the antithesis. And a possible fusion of the two is the synthesis. Spirituality is more than the psychological, and more than imagination—it is a genuine transphysical reality. And it is entirely compatible with Marxist economic and social thought."

Nikolai dismissed this with a wave of the hand.

Nikolai: "More rubbish. Pure mysticism. Straight from Blok. Incorrigible, anti-Soviet thinking. I will report you to the authorities for this. I . . . I . . . I . . . ."

One of the criminals—who usually stayed out of such debates—laughed.

"Report him, will you? Look where we are. We are already in the place the authorities would send him, you fool. Your reporting days are over. Someone no doubt reported you for something, likely a lie."

The criminal walked toward Nikolai flourishing a clenched fist.

"Don't you understand what happens to people around here who 'report' things? Shut your trap or I'll break your neck."

The criminal then turned to the grandfather, who had listened to it all from a distance.

"So what do you think, priest?'

The grandfather gave a reply that confused them all.

"For my thoughts are not your thoughts, neither are your ways my ways."

To himself he added, "saith the Lord."

CHAPTER 22

December 1941

It was generally considered bad form to talk to others about hunger in starvation time. Think about it obsessively, okay, but talking about it showed a lack of strength, even a lack of patriotism, implying that the authorities and the system were letting the people down.

But you could think anything you liked. And Daniil thought that the hunger of starvation was not like the normal desire to eat. That was merely appetite, the periodic desire to put something in your mouth, preferably something tasty. The hunger of starvation, on the other hand, made you begin to tremble before a bowl of soup, or even the thought of one. It was the difference between an itch and a laceration, between irritation and rage.

Furthermore, this hunger was not like being hungry because you were poor and couldn't afford the food all around you. In that case you at least knew the possibility of food was near at hand, even if you had to steal it. When food no longer exists, anywhere, there is nothing to scheme for. There is only deepest despair.

A despair that can sometimes be masked with a joke, such as the one Aleksandr told at a Thursday evening chess match.

"Have you heard, Daniil, the one about the man who walked into the shop?"

"No, but I suspect I'm going to soon."

Aleksandr smiled and told his joke.

"A man walks into a shop and sees bare shelves. He asks the clerk, 'Don't you have any meat?' The clerk says, 'No, here we don't have any fish. The shop that doesn't have any meat is across the street.'"

Daniil tried to laugh, but couldn't quite get it out.

"I liked that one so much, I put it in my diary."

Daniil admonished him.

"Your diary, Aleksandr? Surely you don't keep a diary. It's the first thing the NKVD look for when they invade a home."

Aleksandr did not retreat.

"I have to lie at work. I have to lie in our apartment building meetings. I have to lie to my children. I need one place where I don't have to lie. I whisper in my diary, but I whisper the truth. Besides, they don't need evidence to arrest and shoot you. If they don't find a diary, they'll torture you until you agree to write one that they will dictate. Or they'll write one for you—retrospectively."

The conversation then took a statistical turn.

Aleksandr was an engineer. You know the stereotype—all numbers and analysis. Engineers reputedly like not only formulas and equations, but also grids, rows, columns, graphs, charts, databases—ancient and modern—the Universal Decimal Classification system, constellations, peg boards behind work benches with each hanging tool outlined in white, and closets arranged by function, sleeve length, and color. In short, they seek out order everywhere and impose it where it is not found.

Large scale disintegration, such as was happening everywhere in Leningrad, puts particular pressures on such a mind. Aleksandr applied his engineering predilections to the subject of death generally and starvation in particular.

"Death is a slave to life," he declaimed to Daniil one day over their weekly chess board. "It cannot exist without it. No life, no death. So, as the English poet said long ago, death should not be proud. It is less than a parasite, merely the absence of something, not something in itself. The excess of death in these days is, from one perspective, a testimony to its futility. So many can die only because so many are alive."

Daniil responded without looking up from the chess board.

"This is whistling past the graveyard, Aleksandr Andreovich. Surely you do not find it assuaging even yourself."

"Of course I do not. But I do find it interesting."

"Next you will be telling me that death is the great problem solver. There is no problem that death does not remove, at least for the dying."

"Except for the problem of what comes after death."

Daniil picked up his bishop and waved it above the board, looking for a place to land.

"Yes, there's that. But let's stick to what we can know."

"Okay, then, let's do the math on malnutrition."

Daniil played along.

"Let's."

Ironically perhaps, given the stated topic, Aleksandr fished from his pocket a small pouch of tobacco and rolled a papirosa, put the cardboard holder in his mouth and struck a match. Smoking suppresses hunger for a moment. Every little bit helps.

"The ration at present is 125 grams of bread—a block about the width and thickness of two fingers together and the length of your hand."

"Yes, I know what a bread ration looks like."

"That's for most people and their dependents. Factory workers and soldiers get a little more. And, of course, top officials get a lot more—because they have so much thinking to do. And, oh yes, because they're thieves."

Aleksandr added cynical asides to his observations as other people add salt to their food (back when they had food).

"That much bread ought to provide around 300 calories, but, of course, that assumes that it's all bread. We know they add sawdust to make the dough stretch."

Daniil helped out.

"Among other things."

"That's right—among other things. So, since sawdust is not digestible, that supposed 300 calories is probably more like 200 calories. Let's say one manages to find another 250 calories from other sources. No, let's be generous—after all, everyone's hungry. Let's say we find another 350 calories from other sources—an impossible number, but let's fantasize in good Soviet fashion."

Daniil chipped in.

"Yes, when reality is this grim, who would not prefer a fantasy."

"So that's at most 600 calories a day—less than what a child needs to stay alive and half of what a man needs, with women somewhere in between."

"Telling us what?"

"That eventually death will result."

"How soon?"

"Depends on many things—initial body size and composition, for instance. Women and overweight men will last longer because they have a higher percentage of fat deposits to be converted."

"Lucky them. I should have eaten more baklava back in the day."

Aleksandr ignored Daniil's witty asides. He was on an analytic roll.

"The body fights hard, Daniil. Human bodies have had hundreds of thousands of years of experience with too little food. Immediately after completing the digestion of its last meal, the body starts its hunt. The goal is glucose for the brain and nervous system. Initially it searches out carbohydrate stores, especially hepatic glycogen. These sources last for about twenty-four hours. It then goes to work on fatty deposits. In time the body, realizing the seriousness of its situation, alters its whole strategy for finding and producing the raw material for the energy it needs. Fatty acids, for instance, are converted to ketones in the liver and used for fuel.

"When these strategies prove inadequate, the body gets desperate and starts consuming its muscles, including the lungs and heart muscle. At this point the body is cannibalizing itself. It is buying time while waiting for the next influx of raw material from the outside."

"And if it doesn't get it?"

"The organs continue to shrink, the heart muscle weakens, brain function deteriorates, the body can no longer control its temperature or fight off germs. It dies either of disease or dehydration or the heart simply stops."

"Brilliant, Aleksandr. How does knowing this help us?"

"It helps us be realistic."

"How does realism help?"

This stumped Aleksandr for a moment.

"Normally, I would say realism helps us to plan. But I see your point."

"Yes, planning implies resources and choices."

"And something called the future."

"Correct. We have none of these. So why do the math? Why calculate? Why plan?"

Usually it was Aleksandr who punctured balloons. Today it was Daniil. And he felt sorry for having done so. After a long pause, Aleksandr answers slowly.

"Because I have children, Daniil. Because I have children. I am beyond desperate to believe that I can save Yulia and Luka. I cannot stop thinking about it. I cannot stop looking for a way out. Starvation is awful for anyone, Daniil. For a father or mother with young children, it breaks both your heart and your mind."

CHAPTER 23

December 1920

DANIIL FOUND HIMSELF NO LONGER A BELIEVER WELL BEFORE he found himself no longer in church. And "found himself" is the appropriate phrasing. It was something he discovered more than something he decided. He was both surprised to realize he no longer believed in God and not surprised. After all, it's what everyone with standing around him—from teachers to officials to journalists to artists and intellectuals—had been saying all his life was simple common sense.

Furthermore religion was dangerous—to society in general and to one's self in particular. And to those one loved. It was difficult enough to believe in a good and powerful God in a supportive society, so why work so hard to believe it when the belief itself also put you at risk? A no-brainer.

Not that he announced his disbelief. For one thing, no one was asking. And for another, Sofia was still holding on. She didn't put it that way—holding on. She actually was quite comfortable believing in God in the twentieth century. It even felt natural, like breathing or resting. They once, early in their marriage, had a conversation along those lines.

"Why do you find it so difficult, Daniil—believing in God and goodness and all that?"

"Because it can't be proven. I want to be rational, and it's irrational to affirm things that can't be proven."

"Can you prove that you love me, Daniil?"

"Of course I love you. I tell you so all the time."

"How do I know you're not faking love?"

"Because I show you, by my actions."

"How do I know your actions are not motivated by self-interest rather than by genuine love?"

"Oh, Sofia, let's not argue about this."

"No, let's do argue about this. Can you prove—scientifically—that Tolstoy is a better writer than Gorky? Can you prove that there's a genuine basis in a Darwinian world for justice as opposed to power? Or is all our fairness, justice, classless society talk just hot air and sentimentality?"

"Okay, okay. I see your point. Many important things are not subject to proof. Maybe insisting on proof in some areas is itself not rational. Let me put it another way, then. I cannot prove that God does not exist or that the story Christians tell about the world is not true, but I can say without any doubt whatsoever that I find that story irrelevant to my life. It does not draw me. It is not compelling to me. I see that it is so for others, including my parents and grandfather, and, of course, including you. But it is not so to me. The whole story strikes me as of another era, another time in the human experience. I do not find it credible. Literally, not something I can believe."

Sofia looked at him in silence, a deep sadness on her face, her eyes wet.

"That is wounding news, Daniil. It is a truth I have tried to hide from."

"What truth, Sofia."

"The truth that we do not share our most profound convictions. The truth that we have radically different foundations for our lives. That our greatest hopes are in different things."

"My greatest hope is in our love for each other, Sofia. Why isn't that enough?"

"Because purely human love is based in emotion and desires and perceptions and pledges and the whims of fate—all changeable, all too often transient, all here today and potentially gone tomorrow."

"That's simply the human condition, Sofia. We have to accept it."

"I believe otherwise, Daniil. I believe the human condition works itself out in the context of the divine condition. We are not self-created. And we are not blindly created by natural forces. We are God-created, and so love is real—as is justice and mercy and all good things. If there is no God, we are just making it all up as we go, fooling ourselves, pretending, actually. That's not enough for me, Daniil. I don't find it compelling. I don't find, literally, that it's something I can believe."

Now they shared the deeply sad look. Sofia reached out her hand and took his.

"But I still love you, Daniil. God tells me to love you, and I find it easy to do so. I love you, I love our son, I love the life God has given us together."

They did not talk often of the different foundations for their lives. But it came up not long after that conversation in a pointed way. Sofia wanted Yuri baptized. Daniil did not object philosophically, but it worried him pragmatically. He had hoped before their marriage that life would wean Sofia away from religion. Not arguments for and against, not antagonism from him (for he had none), not pressure from authorities, but simply the busyness and practicalities of everyday living.

Baptism was simply not practical—not in Soviet Russia. It marked one as a believer. It was something the state, sooner or later, would make its business to know. It would get in the way of getting ahead. It was possible, but it was not practical. It was even dangerous. He tried to say so. It didn't go well.

"Is it really necessary, Sofia?"

He made the mistake of asking the question in earshot of his grandfather, who Sofia wanted to perform the baptism. The grandfather answered the question before Sofia could.

"Is it necessary? Is baptism necessary? Really, Daniil. Such a question. Is breathing necessary? Is the sun necessary? Is gravity necessary?"

Daniil did not want to argue with his grandfather. He didn't even want him to know that he was no longer a believer himself. He not only loved his grandfather, he respected him. And he respected his decision after his grandmother's untimely death to become a priest instead of continuing as an academic. Daniil understood the risk his grandfather had taken. But he also wanted to be honest with him.

"But a baby, Grandfather. A newborn baby. What does Yuri know of anything regarding God or belief or the Church or anything else? Why baptize a baby?"

"Why ought we to inoculate Yuri against smallpox? He knows nothing of disease. Inoculation is something we do for a child, not something a child chooses himself. The same with baptism. Baptism is an acceptance of what God has already done and will do. It accepts Christ's death, burial, and resurrection as an atonement for our sins, which the immersion into and raising from the water symbolize. It demonstrates God's love for the child even before the child knows enough to love God. It joins the child to the Church, which God established as the community of believers who will guide Yuri in the ways he should go. It is not a ticket to heaven; it is a promise that must be accepted by Yuri when he is old enough to understand and to make a decision for God."

So, thought Daniil, *what of me? I was baptized. Does that stamp me and get me to heaven if there is one? Or must I, as grandfather says, now embrace the promise?*

Daniil was happy enough to leave it at that. Yuri was clearly going to get baptized, no matter the consequences, so he was not going to fight it. Sofia nodded when the grandfather had concluded. Case closed. Daniil smiled.

"Thank you, Grandfather."

The baptism also threw light on another tension in the family. An Orthodox baptism requires a godparent, a member of the Church in good standing. It is a legacy from the early Church in Roman times when the parents of children in a believing family would sometimes be martyred. A godparent was assigned early in a child's life to identify another adult who would take responsibility for the spiritual welfare of the child if the parents died. The godparent in an Orthodox baptism is not a ceremonial role only—he or she is expected to participate actively in the spiritual formation of a child. It is a serious responsibility.

A godparent is expected to be the same sex as the child. Sofia and the grandfather both thought Daniil's older brother, Maxim, was an appropriate choice. Maxim accepted, but let Daniil know how he felt about his new role.

"I am happy to be Yuri's godparent, but it is unfortunate that I will be looking out for Yuri's spiritual development when his own father is not."

Daniil was used to veiled barbs from Maxim, though this one was not so veiled.

"I value things of the spirit, Maxim. I just do not think of them in religious terms."

"The theological brought to heel by the philosophical, eh, Daniil. Like the Marxists have taught you."

"Perhaps. But more in aesthetic than in material terms."

"Ah yes. Artist as priest. The rhyme and the paintbrush rather than the bread and the wine."

Daniil simply smiled—again.

The baptism itself was a performance worthy of Diaghilev. Sofia was anxious before the service, afraid she might have forgotten something.

"Let's see now. One large new white towel, one small new white towel, one new white baptismal gown, one gold cross, one white taper candle."

Daniil was feeling playful.

"And don't forget. One newborn baby, also in this case white."

"Very funny, father of the child." But she liked that he broke the tension a bit.

"Why so much white? Why is everything white?"

"Symbolism, my boy. Symbolism. Everything Orthodox is saturated in symbolism. The white symbolizes innocence and forgiveness of sin."

"Oh, yes. Yuri is a big-time sinner."

Sofia ignored him and went on.

"The water symbolizes purification. Immersion symbolizes death to self and sin, and the raising symbolizes resurrection—*the* Resurrection. The font itself symbolizes the womb from which emerges new life. The priest blows three times on the child to symbolize the imparting of the Holy Spirit. The baby is held toward the west, which symbolizes death and the devil (because the sun sets in the west), and then is pivoted to the east to symbolize, I think, Easter and the light of Christ associated with the dawn, or something like that. And on and on."

"Why not just straightforward action without all the baggage?"

"Like Soviet realism, I suppose. I thought you were skeptical of Soviet realism in art? Symbolism is a way of pointing to a more profound reality. It employs a tangible, surface reality to suggest a deeper, intangible truth. You like Rembrandt. He's full of symbolism."

"Touché. Symbolism it is."

The baptism lasted almost an hour. Symbolism takes time, apparently. Even Daniil was pleased to see his grandfather holding Yuri and performing the rituals.

This feels significant, Daniil thought, *even if its significance is mostly lost on me.*

CHAPTER 24

December 1941

DANGER ENGENDERS BOTH FEAR AND APATHY—IN THAT ORDER. At first fear, then when danger never ends, apathy—especially when combined with starvation. The first bombing and shelling arrived in July. When the sirens sounded, people scattered for their lives. Simple common sense. They ran for the shelters, they ducked into the closest building, they headed for basements. This continued in August, September, and much of October. By November, not so much. By December, hardly at all.

After all, death is an abstraction (until it happens to you or one you love). It's very difficult for human beings to imagine their personal nonexistence. It requires an excellent imagination to be properly afraid. Repetition and starvation give one a kind of protective indifference. In times of great suffering, death can even seem attractive, hence the growing number of suicides. As Tyutchev says in his poem, it's "so easy not to be."

Daniil, for instance, was one morning walking to the Hermitage. The day had started well. He had gotten his bread ration at the shop in only an hour. His feet were less swollen than usual; his gums had stopped bleeding. There hadn't been an overnight air raid, so he hoped to not have to spend the day sweeping up broken glass. And amazingly enough, as he neared the museum, the lights were actually on in Orbeli's office and a few other rooms. The former czarist yacht, *Polar Star*, was docked in the nearby Neva. Lines had been run from it to the Hermitage to provide, for a time, electricity. Daniil had never realized how pleasant it was to have light on command—until there was none.

And then the banshee scream of an incoming shell. He had heard the sound so often that often it hardly registered—something like the sound of a bird in the distance, detectable but not notable. But this one was close. It exploded in the block ahead of him, throwing up a white cloud of debris mixed with snow. His only thought: "Glad I didn't start out three minutes earlier."

It seemed advisable to stop until the shelling was over, and so he did. He recalled that sometimes shells land repeatedly in one place, but at other times their landing places travel—farther on or farther back. He considered the possibility that his block would be next, but not with any great concern. He was too weak and hungry to have great concern about much of anything.

He then noticed the sign on the store front he stood next to—"Motherland Beauty Parlor: Look Your Best to Be Your Best." Amazingly, it was open. Two women and a man sat in its three chairs, hair being shampooed or trimmed or put in curlers. At one an attendant labored over the fingers of an extended hand. Despite his condition, the docent managed to be shocked, an emotion he hadn't felt in a long time.

"How can this be? How is such a place open in blockade time? Why do none of these people react to the sound of explosions?"

Understanding that the next shell might be in this block, he stepped inside for the illusion of protection. A woman sat at a small table near the door.

"Do you have an appointment, sir?"

"Of course not. Did you not hear that explosion?"

"Why yes, sir. It is the eight o'clock shelling. It happens every day. You know the Germans like their schedules."

"How is it that you are open? Who possibly comes to have their hair and nails done during times such as ours?"

The woman just looked at him, then glanced around and lowered her voice.

"These are not charwomen, sir. They are the wives and daughters of our officials. The mayor himself comes in for pedicures."

The docent is shocked again, twice in one day. But then he understands that there is nothing to be shocked about. The siege experience, as Aleksandr frequently points out, is not evenly distributed, even in a classless society. Some are hungrier than others. Some are not hungry at all.

"They must pay a lot of money for your services."

The woman again said nothing, and then she whispered.

"Money, sir? Money is useless. They pay us with food."

CHAPTER 25

December 1941

THE DOCENT DIDN'T SEE THEM ARRIVE HIMSELF. HE WAS SWEEPING up snow that had fallen through the hole in the roof that was not yet repaired from the shelling a few days before. They had been hit a number of times, both by artillery shells and by bombs from the Nazi planes. So far, no one had been injured.

The entry doors were closed. One of the staff heard a faint knocking, like that of a child. He opened the door and found three young soldiers standing in the cold, rifles slung on their shoulders but peaceful smiles on their faces—a tall one, a short one, and a fat one.

"Is this the Hermitage?" the short one asked.

"Yes it is. Can I help you?"

"We would like to see the paintings, please."

Imagine—knocking on the front door of the great Hermitage and asking to see the paintings, like children begging for candy. During a war. During a siege. During starving time.

"The paintings are no longer here."

"Where did they go?"

"Away. We sent them away. To keep them from the Nazis."

The fat one piped up.

"We soldiers are here in Leningrad to see that the dirty swine don't take nothing."

The staff person bowed slightly at the waist.

"And we appreciate that greatly. We thank you for your defense of the Motherland and our city. But I'm afraid the paintings were removed before you arrived. When you have pushed the enemy away, the great masterpieces will return and we will welcome you to see them."

Now it was the tall one's turn.

"We are from small places far away. We have always heard of the Hermitage—from our teachers, from our parents, from everybody. We thought we were very lucky to be sent to Leningrad.

We thought we would finally be able to see the greatest paintings in the greatest museum in the world. Is there nothing at all, then, to see?"

"There are only the frames on the walls where the paintings use to be, I'm afraid."

The three soldiers turned to each other and exchanged words, then looked back at the man.

"Could we then please see the frames?"

By this time, a half-dozen employees, including guides, had gathered round, the docent among them. When they heard this request they all smiled—both at its innocence and because they were moved by it. Simple Russian citizens, from far away, defending the city, full of hope for a great cultural experience. These men deserved to be taken seriously.

And therefore they took them seriously.

After talking among themselves, the senior guide in the group spoke to the soldiers.

"You gentlemen encourage us that, even in this darkest of times, civilization is not dead. We are glad you know of the Hermitage and that you wish to see it. It will be our honor to show you our great rooms and the frames of the great works of art that once hung in them and, thanks to soldiers like you, will soon hang in them again."

With that he pointed to three of the guides—including the docent—and tasked them with conducting perhaps the strangest tour in the history of art.

The Winter Palace alone has over a thousand rooms. It is estimated that a walk of the magnificent galleries of the multiple buildings of the Hermitage would cover fifteen miles. The soldiers indicated they had two hours. Time only for a handful of masterpieces. Which is to say, for their frames.

The tour started with a walk up the famed Jordan Staircase, itself a major artwork of Baroque extravagance. The mid-eighteenth-century creation of Francesco Rastrelli, restored after the great fire of 1837 by Stasov—with the double stairs surrounded by majestic, opulent walls of white and gold, massive windows looking out to the Neva, with tall, gray-blue marble columns, and ceilinged by a massive painting of the Olympus gods spread across the clouds—the staircase alone creates the sense of awe appropriate for the entry of worshippers into a cathedral of art.

With their priest-guides, the three soldiers ascended to the holy chambers.

In ordinary time, to use a religious term for the time before the invasion, each Hermitage guide had his or her specialties—favorite rooms, favorite periods, favorite artists, favorite paintings, or other works of art. And each had a number of spiels—about a period, about an artist, about a particular work. The spiels didn't much vary. They were given multiple times a day. They didn't require that the speaker even look at the work. Another group, another performance of the spiel.

Because no one had ever conducted an art tour with no art, the docent and his colleagues had no plan. As it turned out, they started with the frames of more modern works—Picasso, Cezanne, and Matisse—and worked backwards chronologically. The Picasso stops included the "Absinthe Drinker," "Portrait of Soler," and "Woman Playing the Mandolin." The guide was careful in what he said. Picasso was not a Soviet favorite—too much bourgeois ennui and too little heroic realism. But he was too famous, and his paintings too valuable, to dismiss.

Earlier masters were safer—like the Bruegel family, for instance. Painters of the people—people working, people dancing, people fighting. Women with big shanks, men with beer bellies, dogs scratching themselves. The guide wisely skipped talking about Jan's *Adoration of the Magi* and spent most of his time in front of the frame for Pieter the Younger's *Fair with a Theatrical Presentation*. He described what the soldiers would have seen had the painting been on the wall—people eating, drinking, arguing, gambling, kissing, selling, buying, performing—people even climbing trees, for goodness' sake. In short, a fine cross-section of proletarian life.

Since none of these characters were there to be seen—only a frame—it was the guide's job to make them visible to the soldiers' minds and imaginations—an appeal to their inner sight: difficult enough with paintings of a single figure or small grouping, impossible with a panorama of a village square filled with dozens of people and animals doing all the different things that people and animals do.

Along the way, they took in the frames of paintings by Vermeer, Uccello, and that great flayer of oppressors, Goya. The docent walked along with the soldiers, enjoying the commentary on artists and works he did not himself ever tour.

Eventually, near the end of the time, it was his turn. They came to the Rembrandt Room. The docent loved Rembrandt the way his grandfather loved God—deeply, humbly, with awe and devotion. If art is a religion—and for many it is—then Rembrandt was his Jesus. No, his Christ.

And of all the wonderful Rembrandt paintings in the Hermitage's astounding collection, none was more iconic—in the Orthodox sense of an icon as a depiction of a being worthy of veneration—than *The Return of the Prodigal Son*. This massive painting both mesmerized and disturbed him.

He stood in front of the frame and began his spiel.

"Rembrandt van Rijn, as perhaps you well know, was a Dutch Baroque painter who was born in 1606 and died in 1669. He is widely considered one of the greatest painters of all time, and this painting, *The Return of the Prodigal Son*, is considered one of the world's greatest paintings.

"Rembrandt created this masterwork late in his life, right at the end in fact. Some have speculated that it may not even be finished. It is, as you can see . . ."

The docent paused and started again.

"It is, as you can see by the size of the frame, an enormous painting. It measures 8.6 feet wide and 6.7 feet tall. Materially, it is oil on canvas. The painting depicts a myth from the Bible: A younger son asks his father for his inheritance, which is explicitly insulting, because it suggests he wishes his father dead so he can get his share of the money; he goes off and wastes all the money with profligate living, eventually ending up hungry and tending pigs; he returns to his home, and his father, rather than rejecting him, welcomes him, despite the protests of the young wastrel's older brother.

"The theme of the story is obvious—one should respect authority and work hard, otherwise one's life will fall to tatters, as has the clothing of the returning son."

The soldiers nod.

"As the painting is not here to see, let me describe it to you. The main figures, left of center, occupy the viewer's attention. The returning son, called the prodigal, is kneeling in front of the father. His clothes are in rags, his partially bare feet are cracked and filthy, his head is dirty and appears shaven. We can see only an angled view of his face, buried as it is in the father's robes.

"The father has his hands on the son's shoulders and upper back, in a gesture of welcome and tenderness. He is dressed in rich robes with an ochre mantle. He is looking to the side, the depiction of his eyes suggesting he might have compromised vision. He is bending over his returned son.

"There are four additional figures in the painting. On the right side is a man standing on a low platform and a man sitting. Deeper in the scene and in the shadows are two women, one barely visible. Scholars have for centuries debated who these four people are. A common view is that the man standing is the older brother of the prodigal, the man sitting is a family friend or advisor. The two women are the prodigal's mother in the dark shadows and a servant, perhaps bringing fine clothes in which to dress the young returner.

"Scholars have also waxed eloquent over the years on various meanings the subject and its rendering may have. When you someday see this painting—here in person or in a book—you can decide on any larger meaning for yourself.

"From a stylistic standpoint, *The Return of the Prodigal Son* is a striking example of Rembrandt's late style. You would see his use of impasto—thick paint, often applied with a pallet knife that gives the painting a kind of three-dimensionality that is lifelike. This rough texture reinforces the emotion of the moment—a failed son coming home to a waiting household, both son and household with divided emotions.

"You would also see Rembrandt's skillful use of light, illuminating not only the face of the father and the head and body of the prodigal, but also the face of the older brother, tying each of the main characters of the story together. Each one plays a part; each one displays an emotion, in a psychologically complex depiction of an important moment."

The docent went on a little longer, pointing out other technical details, also noting such things as the contrast between the open hands of blessing of the father and the folded hands of judgment of the older brother. Looking at his watch, he then stopped.

"Do you have any questions?"

The short soldier raised his hand.

"Yes."

"My mother once showed me a picture of this painting in a book. She said the father is a picture of God. Is that true?"

The docent looked at the other guides and then back at the soldier.

"As I said before, if you are fortunate enough to come back to the Hermitage when all the paintings have returned, you can study it and decide for yourself."

With that the tour was over. The three staff members walked the three soldiers to the main entrance and shook their hands and wished them well. They agreed it was an unprecedented event—an art tour with no art. A once in a lifetime kind of occurrence. Something to remember.

CHAPTER 26

August 1930

EVERYONE KNEW IT WAS BAD IF YOU WERE SUMMONED AT NIGHT. It meant either an interrogation—usually accompanied by a beating—or an extension of your sentence, which happened so regularly that only the naive were surprised. "Another tenner" was the common phrase, ten years being the standard extension. One was never to ask a zek about his interrogation. (Unnecessary curiosity could be costly in Soviet Russia.) Asking suggested you were trying to discover if he had informed on anyone (the common verb being "to blow" on another). But sometimes a zek returned to the barrack and just flashed all ten fingers as he headed back to his bunk. Everyone knew. When summoned, all hoped it was merely for an interrogation and beating.

(And they hoped it wasn't a form of torture disguised as interrogation called "the conveyor"—continuous interrogation without sleep that could go on for days, sometimes resulting in insanity.)

When Father Sergius was called one night, he assumed the beating because he had a history of never giving the information an interrogator wanted. He was in this Special camp because he had been labeled an "incorrigible," meaning they'd given up hope that he would renounce his faith and become a good citizen (or inform on other citizens). Therefore his sentence lacked even an ending date as far as he knew. No, this would be an interrogation and a beating. The only mystery was what the topic might be.

The commander that night was in a hurry. He was also already angry. Sitting at his desk, head down, studying a stack of papers when the grandfather approached and stood in front of him, he spoke without looking up.

"I have written out the report summarizing our interview and your confession. Sign it and you can return to the barrack."

"To what, sir, have I confessed?"

The commander looked up, shocked by the question.

"Impudent priest! You know that we do not have to reveal what you are charged with. Everyone knows that. The charges are our business, confession is yours."

Father Sergius did know this. Simple curiosity—and principle—had prompted the question. And the commander decided to satisfy that curiosity.

"You have confessed to having briefly withheld your discovery of a conspiracy in the camp to assassinate General Secretary Stalin."

In Stalin's Soviet Union it was imperative that deviant behavior be continually found and eliminated. If it could not be found factually, it had to be manufactured, like tanks and tractors. Paranoia was necessarily a growth industry. More important than inventing new medicines or technology was inventing new crimes. A saying of the Organs went as follows: "Just give us a person—we will create a case." A quota of plots had to be met in the same way as a quota of wheat or steel. The commander expected the priest, a veteran of the camps, to understand this.

Father Sergius, for his part, expected the commander to understand that bringing harm to others with a lie was impossible for him as a priest.

"But, sir, I have no ill will toward the General Secretary. In fact, I pray for him regularly."

The commander stood, reached across the desk, and slapped the priest, knocking him to the ground. He came from around and stood over him.

"Fool. The General Secretary loathes your prayers. Save them for yourself. I did not say *you* were conspiring to kill our leader. I said you were confessing to hesitating to report a plot to do so. You have named names. It's in my report on our conversation. You might yet be rewarded for having reported the plot—even though not reporting it as immediately as you should have."

The commander was red in the face and shouting.

"If you do not sign this, I will amend the report and offer it to the next prisoner in this office to sign. In that report, you will be the ringleader of the plot. If you will not sign, I assure you that the next one in here will."

Now he began kicking the priest, screaming the standard line of every interrogation throughout the eleven time zones of the vast worker's paradise. It was the last thing Father Sergius heard before passing out.

"We know everything! We know everything! You stupid, stupid fool. We know everything!"

Father Sergius awoke two days later in the infirmary. The doctor was peering into his face. He smiled when he saw the grandfather's eyes open.

"Hello, Father. I am glad you have come back to us. We were worried about you, but I think you will be fine. I will keep you here as long as I am able."

Only in a Special camp is a long stay in a sickbed considered a blessing.

CHAPTER 27

December 1941

THE DOCENT SAW A CROWD GATHERED AHEAD. ANY CROWD IN Leningrad during the blockade, like any line in front of a store, was a magnet for passersby. Since it was directly in his path to the Hermitage, the docent had no choice but to join it. He did not expect the reason for it to be anything but tragic. And he was right.

He first saw the gallows—a thick beam resting on two posts from which hung three ropes over a platform. A hand-scrawled sign nailed to one of the posts said, "Deserters—Traitors to the Motherland." Then he saw three young soldiers, one little more than a boy, standing below the platform, their hands tied behind their backs.

The crowd was not convinced. They knew from long experience how easy it is to be considered a traitor in Soviet Russia. The docent heard mutterings from the people around him.

"They're so young."

"Probably refused a foolish order."

"The Germans don't kill enough of us, we have to kill our own?"

The three were led up onto the platform, executioners holding both arms of each one. A plump official shouted out a speech.

"These cowards have shamed themselves and the great Red Army. They are a disgrace to their families and to the nation. Let their deserved fate be a lesson to you all."

The youngest one began to tremble and cry as they put the rope around his neck. The other two were completely stoical, offering their heads to the noose.

The gallows, having been hastily constructed, had no trapdoors. Two soldiers stood behind each of the three. On signal they pushed them off the edge of the platform. The boy, being small and emaciated, was too slight for his neck to snap. He dangled at the end of the rope like a marionette, choking, legs kicking. The crowd groaned and some shouted protests. The official motioned to one of the soldiers standing on the ground, who walked up, raised his rifle upward, and shot the boy in the chest. Then the official and the soldiers marched away, leaving the three bodies hanging, emblems of Soviet justice.

Was the shooter troubled? In the camps, the executioners were given vodka both before and after an execution. On the outside, the executioners—if they felt the need—had to buy their own.

CHAPTER 28

December 1941

THE DOCENT HAD A SPECIAL PLACE IN HIS HEART FOR HERMITAGE director Orbeli. He was a genuine scholar as well as that rarest of things in Stalin's Russia, a competent bureaucrat. His specialty was medieval history, especially of the East, and the Hermitage was an important center of widespread archaeological research and exploration as well as an art museum. The docent looked to him as a private would look to his general.

And Orbeli could be as imperious as any general. He lacked the gold braids and billboard of medals, but he was confident, in charge, and insisted that others recognize it. Until weakening near the end of the blockade, he continued his daily rounds of the museum exhibition rooms like a general reviewing his troops, even though most of the troops—all the subjects in the great paintings—were gone.

But Orbeli could also be encouraging, even comforting. On the day of invasion, he pointed out to the assembled staff that Napoleon had attacked on almost precisely the same day of the year, suggesting that Hitler's impunity would suffer a similar fate. Especially in the first months, he would give pep talks, expressing confidence that both the city and the Hermitage would survive.

In December 1941, Orbeli went ahead with the annual St. Catherine's Day celebration of the founding of the museum in 1764. And even in the dead of that first winter, when things were most dire, and thousands of people were dying every day, he oversaw a scheduled archaeological conference based on the ancient warrior Tamerlane. His old teacher, Daniili Zhabelev, attended and greeted Orbeli with words that expressed the director's own conviction.

"I am so glad that science continues to develop with us even under such difficult conditions. This is the way we scholars fight Fascism."

Joseph Orbeli was not the only one who patrolled the empty galleries of the Hermitage. Daniil often did the same, though it was more wandering than patrolling. He would walk and think, think and walk. He eventually understood that unrequired walking came at a health cost, but he decided that he needed to find sustenance for his soul as well as his body.

He would stop before the frames of paintings now in the Ural mountains—or so the rumor went. He would think about the painting and the artist and the things he used to say about both while guiding. The painter was now dead and the painting was now gone. The painting still existed, but it was in another place. Was the same true of the artist? Was the artist still somehow in existence—not just in the work of art, but in some conscious state, bodily or otherwise?

That's what he thought as a child. That's what he was told. This life is just a prelude, a dress rehearsal, an appetizer—pick your metaphor. But it is critically important, because it determines the main event, which is to say, your eternity. The idea of heaven frightened him more than comforted him as a child. Failing to make it seemed so easy.

Although he had long since pushed aside any belief in either heaven or eternity, he still sometimes felt the afterglow of his childhood world. Recently, for instance, he had stopped in front of the empty frame for Rembrandt's *Haman Recognizes His Fate* and found himself whispering aloud his guiding spiel.

"This is a late Rembrandt—around 1665, within four years of his death. Like so many Rembrandt paintings, it is based on a Bible story, one of the myths invented by the Jews. But which myth? Rembrandt did not title his paintings. Scholars often do not agree on who or what event is being depicted here. The main figure in this painting is a man turning away from two others, a troubled, even haunted, look on his face. Many believe, as do I, that it is the myth of Haman, set in the time when the Jews were exiled in Babylon.

"Haman, a high court official, hates the Jews and devises a plan to kill them all throughout the country, but especially to execute

Mordecai, a Jew who has insulted him by refusing to bow when he passes. He has a gallows built for exactly that purpose. The plan backfires, however, and this painting depicts the moment that Haman learns that he himself is the one who will be executed on that gallows."

The docent goes on in his mind, pointing out the details that convey the character's inner emotions—as Rembrandt's late paintings typically do: the body leaning unsteadily to the right, the hand to the heart, dark shadows from his giant headpiece covering his forehead and eyes, the violent red of his clothes. This was Daniil's favorite part of guiding, helping people see not only the meaning and emotion of a painting, but identifying the artistic strategies used to convey them—the artist working *with* the viewer to co-create meaning and significance.

But there was something more in the docent's reaction to this painting. Here was a man who declared others guilty and now found he'd been declared guilty himself. Perhaps he thought his plan to kill the Jews was a good thing—for his king and kingdom. Undoubtedly he saw benefit in it for himself, revenge for certain, but perhaps advancement. But at the last moment, he realizes he has plotted his own downfall. The tables have turned. His reward is death.

This painting, as did so many of Rembrandt's, made the docent think of his own life, and it always left him troubled.

CHAPTER 29

July 1938

YANA AND MILA MISSED SOFIA ALMOST AS MUCH AS DANIIL AND Yuri did, which didn't speak to any deficiency in the men's grief, but only to their own deep sense of loss. The three women had been friends in ways that men usually are not with other men. The husbands liked each other and shared common interests; the women needed each other and shared their lives. The men talked for entertainment and information; the women talked for intimacy and mutual encouragement.

The wives tried to get together at least once a week, often when doing laundry. They would rotate apartments, two women bringing their empty metal tubs and washboards to the apartment of the third. They didn't like doing laundry, and talking while scrubbing made the time go more quickly.

One day, a few years ago, they were at Mila's apartment. They filled their tubs with hot water and added soap, then separated each of their piles of clothes into dark and light. Their first topic of conversation was the arrest of a neighbor three days prior.

Mila asked a question for which she knew there was no answer. "What was she accused of?"

Yana answered.

"It doesn't matter, neither to the officials nor to her. The only important thing is that she was arrested. Her fate is sealed. After being arrested it is not possible to be found innocent. That would be like a stream flowing uphill. It would cast doubt on the great system of Soviet justice."

It was unusual for Yana to speak so skeptically. That was Aleksandr's forte, and she was always shushing him, especially in front of the children. She tried her best to be a good Marxist citizen, but it was hard. You had to pretend so much—pretend not to see what you saw, hear what you heard, experience what you experienced.

Sofia and Yana usually avoided initiating any talk about children. Mila and Lev had none and it was painful for them. The other two women always said, "Children will come when they come, Mila. Don't worry about it." But the years were passing and Mila was beginning to use "God's will" talk about having no children. Sofia and Yana didn't object, but Sofia let Yana know in private that the issues were likely biological, not theological.

Today Mila asked about the other women's children. Sofia indicated they had a recent letter from Yuri, who had recently joined the army, but so much of it had been censored that there wasn't a lot to it. Yana talked about how she enjoyed the fact that schools were closed for the summer because it gave her more time with Luka.

"He's actually a pleasure to talk to. He asks me questions about my life. Unlike his father."

The other two smiled, but they knew it was a serious observation. Aleksandr was a good man, but not an easy man to live with. He always thought himself right about everything and expected others to recognize it. He would tolerate rebuttals from Daniil and Lev, but not so much from his own family.

Yana's comment about Aleksandr made Sofia inwardly thankful for Daniil. He respected her, even leaned on her. He shared with her what he was thinking and wanted to know what she was thinking too.

Today, the women talked not only about arrests and husbands, but also about the meaning of life. And of a practical question that grew out of that abstract one: What do you tell children about such things?

"In the early years," Sofia said, "children won't think about the meaning of life. Give them food and love and a toy to chew on and they are happy. But eventually, quite soon actually, they'll start asking meaning and significance questions."

Like Yana's report of Luka's question a day or two prior.

"Mother, does God know that we know he isn't real?"

All three women laughed. Sofia responded.

"Sounds like a trick question. Something the security folks might ask just to confuse you and see how you answer."

Mila, the most religious of the three, took the question seriously.

"There is great faith in that question. Good for Luka."

Sofia was more skeptical.

"Depends on whether you emphasize 'does God know' or 'he isn't real.' I suppose it's a question of tone. Is Luka tweaking believers or is he tweaking his teachers and mother?"

Yana laughed.

"He's good at both—an inheritance from his father."

Sofia nodded but took an opportunity to praise Luka.

"Luka is a good boy. He's very protective of Yulia, at an age when many children still see their siblings as competition."

Mila returned the conversation to the issue of how one answers the big 'meaning of life' questions that children ask.

"Children—everyone for that matter—need more than correct social and economic thinking to build a life on. What do we say to them about ultimate things?"

Both Sofia and Yana knew that Mila would be happy to answer her own question. The three women were more or less on a continuum. Mila was always prepared to spread a little propaganda for God. Yana, although raised in the Church, was quite happy to put it behind her and join the long march toward Progress. And Sofia was hedging her bets—holding on to as much faith as she could—even going sometimes to church—but also not wanting to be a sucker.

Mila and Sofia had been great friends for a long time, and each helped complete the other, as friends and spouses ought. Sofia was unusually rational, Mila unusually mystical. But each liked and respected the defining qualities of the other. Sofia summed up the three friends on these things this way: "Yana is too cautious. Mila is perhaps not cautious enough. Yana and I try to keep Mila from believing too much, and she tries to keep me and Yana from believing too little."

CHAPTER 30

December 1941

When one is under stress, words will slip and slide and change their meaning, both denotation and connotation. Sometimes they will retain a portion of their traditional sense, other times not at all. Two words that morphed under stress during the blockade were "normal" and "safe."

Normal is thought more or less boring during normal times. Same old, same old. Another day, another ruble. It is associated with rut and routine. But when normal disappeared in Leningrad, it became a state of things desperately wished for, the condition of life to which everyone wanted to return. One made vows, "I will never complain again when life returns to normal."

That hope for "when" lasted for months, then faded. At first "when" was assumed: "*when* life returns to normal." It always does, it always has. The Great Red Army will make it happen. Our Great Leader will make it happen. God will make it happen. By December it was clear that "when" was irrelevant, because by the time things returned to normal, most will be dead.

And if abnormal goes on long enough, it becomes the new normal. *It* becomes the same old, same old. *It* is the new rut. And when it happens in siege time, it means taking for granted the unthinkable. Like the daily starvation of thousands and callousness in the streets.

One victim of the loss of the normal was the scale of values. Things once highly valued were now worthless; things once of little value were now prized.

Money, for instance.

The Nazis had done what no Communist revolution could ever achieve: It made everyone equal, and capital—in monetary form—of no value. Money was less valuable than strips of wallpaper, because the latter, its glue having a potato base, could be boiled, as we have seen, and made into a kind of soup. One often saw signs offering to trade furniture or clothing or even jewelry for wallpaper. Or for a cat. The value of anything is determined by the context within which it exists. And the context in Leningrad during siege time was omnipresent and protean death. Death had more shifting shapes than Proteus, the Shape Shifter.

The new god, replacing money, was bartering. At first the most desired item was vodka. Tea, tobacco, and bread were considered hard currency, as they were in the labor camps. But later the obsessive question became this: What do I have that I can use or exchange for something that at least resembles food? And the terms of exchange were severe. What are a pair of dress shoes—especially with high heels—compared with the green stems of carrots? (Not the carrots themselves—who would part with those?—just the green stems.) You can boil and eat the carrot stems. Can you eat high heels? (Well, actually, if the shoes are made of leather, perhaps you can—and some people did.)

You had to be careful, however. Yana confessed that she had exchanged her favorite earrings for a stick of butter. It was carefully wrapped and tied. When she got home she discovered it was instead a bar of soap—useful, but not something you could serve for supper.

Wallpaper, bread filled with sawdust, boiled pine needles and leather—there was a quaint name for it all: siege cuisine.

And the once terrifying became mundane, hardly worth comment. Bodies in the street were simply litter. Bombs and artillery shells became mere background noise, one of the little-noticed sounds of everyday life. The common wisdom was that if you can hear a bomb or a shell in the air, it's not going to hit you. The one that will turn you to splattered jelly will be silent. So it did no good to run when you heard something coming. That one had someone else's name on it. Your name was on the next one, the quiet one.

"Safe" was really a self-cancelling, one-word oxymoron. There was no "safe" any longer in Leningrad. Nothing was safe. No place was safe. No strategy for living was safe. No relationship was safe. No way of believing was safe. "Safe" was the punch line to a bad joke.

The docent one day was walking to his assigned shop to pick up his bread ration. The walk took twenty minutes at the beginning, but now it was closer to sixty—in part because he was weaker and in part because the sidewalks were now small mountain ranges of ice and snow, nature's winter minefields. As with so many small daily practices, shoveling sidewalks stopped weeks ago. Because a fallen person was now likely to be ignored, the potential of deadly consequences of a fall had increased exponentially.

Calling it "walking" is being generous. He was shuffling to the store, both because of the conditions and because he had failed to get his bread ration for two days in a row—once when they ran out of bread just as he got to the head of the line, and once because he was too sick to try. If he doesn't make it today, he will likely not live to try tomorrow. Not that this bothers him—it is now normal.

As he made his way toward bread, shells began making their way toward his crowded street. About half the people kept walking, the other half ran into a building with a big "Shelter" sign over the door. They wished to be safe. The docent passed it by, hoping the artillery attack would make the bread line shorter. When he was about fifty yards past the shelter door, he heard a loud explosion, and small chunks of debris rained down around him. He looked back and saw that the shelter door was no longer there, only a great hole and a roaring fire. The building was already starting to collapse.

That's how "safe" worked in Leningrad. That was also "normal."

When he got to the store the lines were shorter, as hoped, and the docent did get his ration of bread. He knew enough to immediately bury it in his pants pocket and button his long coat from top to bottom. The woman ahead of him was not so wise. She was still stuck in the old normal.

When she left the store, she held the wrapped piece of bread in her hand. The docent saw two men come up to her. One grabbed the bread and the other pushed her down. The one with the bread unwrapped it and began stuffing it in his mouth. The other man shouted.

"You bastard, give me my share!" and began to beat him.

But the first man gladly absorbed the beating for the sake of eating. He covered his head with his arms while he chewed.

This too was now normal. The only thing abnormal was that the other man had trusted him in the first place.

CHAPTER 31

December 1941

HAVING LOST SOFIA TWO YEARS AGO, AND WITH YURI FIGHTING at the front, Daniil lived alone in his apartment, a rarity in socialist Russia. He had acclimated himself to being alone, but the apartment still felt unnaturally empty. And in blockade time, aloneness was risky. As the months passed, he started to feel not only alone, but lonely. And then not just alone and lonely, but isolated, increasingly cut off from the people and practices that help make one human. Daniil had friends—Aleksandr and his family for instance, and Lev and Mila—but he needed someone to share his private space. He had no interest in remarriage. (Was anyone in Leningrad getting married anymore?) And who had strength for even a new friendship?

And then it came to him—a pet. He would get a pet.

It was an absurd thought, actually, perhaps an evidence of the fogging effect of hunger on the mind. As with so many other words and concepts, the connotations of "pet" had changed. Once meaning "companion," it now meant "calories."

Take cats, for instance. Once ubiquitous in Leningrad, now they were a fading memory. And the reason was obvious. A cat was calories. A cat was protein. A cat was a rare meal of meat for an entire family. Only a few days ago, Luka, Aleksandr's boy, had described his dinner to the docent.

"Fried cat, Mr. Aslanov. Crisp and quite tasty."

The docent did not blame the boy—or the family—but the situation did make him sad. All the zoo animals and many of the horses had already been evacuated or eaten in Leningrad. On what grounds does one spare a pet? Eating animals both provides nourishment and also solves the problem of what to feed them.

Still, the docent had long believed that life should not be exclusively rational. That was too confining, timid actually. And he had always felt an affinity with cats. Like them, he preferred being left alone with his thoughts. Like cats, he watched the world warily, a bit jumpy, having seen what it could do to the overeager—dogs, for instance.

As it happened, there was a centuries-old tradition of cats at the Hermitage. Empress Elizabeth had introduced them in the eighteenth century to do combat with the mice. Cats became a Hermitage convention, better known than many of the works of art. Allowed to roam anywhere, they were well fed, and their numbers multiplied; eventually an employee was assigned the exclusive duty of providing for them. After the art was evacuated in July, the cats far outnumbered the visitors. But since October their numbers had declined precipitously, for a well-understood reason. The docent hadn't seen one in weeks.

Then one day he spotted something moving behind the huge statue of Jupiter. It was a cat. He decided to take it home, not for calories but for companionship. It wouldn't last much longer in the museum.

But how to capture it? Already significantly weakened, he couldn't hope to be quick enough to catch it. The only thing that might work was a lure. The only thing he had to lure the cat with was the small piece of bread in his pocket. He had allowed himself one piece when he had gotten it early this morning from his assigned shop. He had planned for a second piece midway home to increase his strength. And then a third and last piece later tonight before bed to help him sleep.

"Well," he said to himself, "I will sacrifice the second piece and hope for the best."

With that he pulled out the bread, broke some off, and with it placed on his open hand, approached Jupiter and the cat. The cat backed further behind the statue but poked its head out to watch the docent, now on his hands and knees—cat level. Daniil decided a soft entreaty might help.

"Come on, kitty. Come here, little prodigal. Have a bite to eat. Doesn't that look good?"

Now, everyone knows that cats do not eat bread. But not everyone has been around a cat during a blockade. A starving cat—like a starving person—will eat anything. Or at least inspect it.

And so the cat did, and so the docent was able to grab it as it nosed the bread.

"There we are, little prodigal. Yes, that shall be your name—Prodigal—for once you were lost, but now you are found."

CHAPTER 32

January 1942

ONE'S LIKELIHOOD OF SURVIVING HITLER'S VOW THAT "EVERYONE must die" in Leningrad depended on many interrelated contingencies—from luck to cunning to influences beyond our ken. One factor was the quality of one's neighbors. Friends and family were crucial in the early months of the blockade, but increasingly they were dying themselves or were effectively cut off from you by even short distances as travel became less and less possible. And phoning was a distant memory. For many the universe shrunk to the size of their apartment, from which they departed only upon necessity.

Daniil was blessed in this regard. Lev and Mila, and Aleksandr and his family, were people who would help a neighbor if they could. Sometimes they even invited you to a feast.

The invitation, shoved under his door, made the docent laugh. It was handwritten in a flowery script and in high diction.

> *Monsieur Leonid and Madame Mila request your presence at a banquet in honor of the arts and free thought in their almost penthouse apartment (only three floors from the top) near Nevsky Prospekt. The menu includes the highest quality wallpaper paste soup sprinkled with sawdust and deliciously prepared leg of rodent.*
>
> *Formal dress (i.e. clean boots) is requested but not required. Please indicate your acceptance of this invitation by showing up at our door at nineteen hundred hours on the morrow.*

How was it possible to laugh in a city where children are starving, where death comes punctually from the skies four times a day, where family pets become family dinner, where the only things in plenty are disease, death, and propaganda?

How was it possible to laugh?

How was it possible *not* to laugh?

A bit of laughter was one of the few remaining signs of humanity in Leningrad. Not lighthearted laughter, not superficial laughter, but profound and rebellious laughter.

Had all laughter ceased, the Nazis would have won for sure. If Leningraders could not outgun them, they could at least mock them. Laughter became an obscene gesture in their faces. "You kill us; we mock you." It displayed their superiority of spirit: "We will see you in hell."

Not of course that a good citizen believed in hell—or heaven either. It was an expression—of defiance—and defiance was about all they had left.

Of course Daniil did, in fact, show up at nineteen hundred hours on the morrow. He even brought a gift—a bottle of Sofia's perfume for Mila. (Though before walking out his door, he opened it and smelled the familiar scent one last time.)

As Daniil expected, Aleksandr and Yana were there too. Aleksandr had brought his French horn, perhaps at the hosts' request. He was actually a quite good amateur musician. The French horn, an exacting instrument, fit well his engineer's mind and personality.

The meal did consist of a soup of some kind and small chunks of something meat-like, though not, he hoped, the promised "leg of rodent." He knew enough not to ask for details. Mila served it on her best china, even the finest dinner plates and stemware having no barter value and therefore still in many people's cupboards.

It reminded Daniil of the old woman in the building—Natalia Borisovna—who went mad and smashed all her plates.

"I know there are crumbs in them. I just have to get them out," she whispered as she fingered the sharp fragments. They dragged her roughly away. Madness—even when reasonable—was bad for public morale and was dealt with rigorously by the authorities.

The faux feasting unfolded without the benefit of a dining room table. It had been sacrificed to the god of heat. Some people had turned their tables over and fill the bottom with soil and planted vegetables, usually with disappointing results. Because Lev and Mila had only two chairs left, nothing for guests, they all sat on the floor, amongst the necessary debris of Lev's art studio, forming a triangle of friendship. Mila placed the food in the space between them, a literal offering. When they finished eating—which only took minutes—they moved into the living room and leaned against the icy-cold walls.

What to talk about?

Does the docent mention the three Hermitage staff living in museum basements who did not survive the previous night? Or the two former staff members who were killed on the front the day before? Or does he speak of his recurring dreams of Sofia—both wonderful and searing—over the last few weeks?

Daniil decided to talk about art, Lev's art in particular.

"Did you finish that palladium painting, Lev?"

"I did. Or at least I think I did. One never knows."

"You need to be careful not to overwork it, Lev. Even Rembrandt sometimes forgot the difference between finishing and fussing."

"I know. One more brushstroke can be one too many, and it's difficult to undo."

"As I point out in my guiding, near the end of his life, Rembrandt's layers of paint got so thick they appear to have been applied with a palette knife."

"Like Van Gogh."

"Well, Van Gogh is like Rembrandt in that regard, not vice versa."

"Defending your man to the end, eh, Daniil?"

"Just pointing out who came first."

Mila jumped in, unapologetically changing the direction.

"Actually, God comes first. What are the first four words of the Bible? 'In the beginning God . . . .' Everything else flows from that. And back to that. God is the beginning and also the culmination—the Alpha and Omega. Miss that and you've missed everything."

Daniil smiled and exchanged looks with Aleksandr. He had been raised in the Church, was even formed by it, but Daniil quickly learned that religion was a career-ender and possibly worse. It was easy to believe what was said against it, and so he did. He had other reasons to flee faith as well.

Still, he enjoyed being sometimes around people who were believers, sort of the way one can take pleasure in reading fairy tales to children. He once said to Sofia, "Believers live in a bigger world—a world not exhausted by calculation and definition and explanation. I respect that. I do not understand how an artist or anyone who loves the arts—including literature and music—could believe that everything can be explained, even if you gave humanity an endless future to arrive at those explanations."

Sofia had replied, "And I do not understand, Daniil, why the stubborn myopia of human nature puzzles you. Once anyone is committed to a master story, they are reluctant to hear contrary evidence."

The docent retained his belief in something bigger, something simultaneously transcendent and foundational, something irremediably mysterious in reality. No, not a mystery—something eventually to be figured out—rather a Mystery—something beyond all our figuring. He found it in Rembrandt and other masters. He didn't find it in church, not that he ever went. And he certainly didn't find it in Marx or Lenin, though he kept that to himself.

The *Prodigal* painting, for instance. The docent cited it in his conversation with his wife.

"There's something there, Sofia, which can only be experienced, not explained. Van Gogh said, 'Rembrandt goes so deep into the mysterious that he says things for which there are no words in any language.' It goes beyond composition and pigment and the depiction of light. The painting gives off a spiritual light that illuminates one's soul—revealing what is there, for good and for ill. Nothing to do with religion of course, but the painting interrogates you in a way that goes far beyond the material. It is as unexplainable as reality itself."

Sofia had raised her eyebrows and nodded.

At Mila's request, Aleksandr produced his French horn. She asked him to play something relaxing. Knowing that Daniil was lost in some reverie initiated by Mila's assertion about God, he drew him back to the group with a question.

"Strauss's *French horn Concerto Number One* is a relaxing piece, don't you think, Daniil?"

They both knew that Daniil had no idea whether Strauss's *French horn Concerto No. 1* was relaxing or not, but Daniil played along.

"I have always thought so, Aleksandr. Would you please play a relaxing portion of it so that we can all relax."

And so Aleksandr did.

And so everyone did as the music suggested. The whole evening was an oasis in a parched and barren time.

CHAPTER 33

January 1942

In the first winter of the siege in Leningrad, every object and every activity offered resistance to living. Nothing was simple—not even putting on or taking off one's boots, which is why some people stopped doing it. Aleksandr claimed he hadn't seen his feet in weeks.

Think about it. Tying and untying requires agile fingers. With bitter cold outside and in, the fingers often stiffened in a contorted knot. You had to use one set of twisted fingers to pull straight the other set of twisted fingers.

And then there was bending over, even from a sitting position (assuming one hadn't already burned everything one could sit on). Your body was increasingly inflexible. The spine was becoming a single steel pole rather than an articulation of jointed disks. Lack of protein left muscles withered and knees cranky.

And don't even think about dipping your head to reach for your laces. You are dizzy at the best of times, and dipping your head between your knees to reach your boots is a recipe for passing out and falling off your perch. No, better to leave your shoes on.

And your clothes too, for that matter. Leaving your clothes in place, day and night, was a guard against shocking yourself by witnessing the state of your body. People foolish enough to look in mirrors or even store windows would often break into tears.

"What? Who is this person? That can't be me! Just look. So old. I'm not that old!"

And that's just from seeing your face. Imagine taking off your clothes and taking in your whole body.

The more logical reason for sleeping in your clothes was obvious. Survival depended on maintaining body temperature, something which increasingly the body could not do. Starving people were cold no matter the air or room temperature. The futile search for warmth meant entombing the body in as many barriers to the cold as possible. (Forgive "entombing," it just came out.) For men it began with long underwear, a shirt and pants, another shirt or padded jacket and a heavy coat. And of course boots and the thickest socks one could find. One commonly added a blanket, even when out on the streets. (People shuffling in the streets, hugging a blanket to themselves, heads popping out the top, looked like moths just emerging from a chrysalis.)

All this layering was enough to keep you alive in winter, but not enough to keep you warm, not even in bed with a mountain of blankets. For one thing, the mountain was bedeviled by slides, blankets ending up on the floor as likely as not. Sleeping was as much a struggle as being awake.

And sleeping was not to be confused with resting. You woke repeatedly in the night and were as exhausted in the morning as when you surrendered to bed at night. It didn't matter how long you had been there.

Competing to stay alive against the cold was something Leningraders shared with their neighbors and loved ones in the labor camps—commonly referred to as "the zone." In some ways the zeks had it slightly better. The camps were supposed to allow people to stay in the barracks with the stoves if the cold was ferocious enough (minus 40 F. officially, in some camps minus 70). And the camps, being often in the woods, and needing to keep the prisoners alive to get work out of them, usually had enough fuel for heat. In Leningrad, the availability of wood for the stove often fluctuated even more than the availability of bread for the stomach.

Therefore people burned their belongings. First completely wooden things, like tables and chairs, bookshelves, picture frames, and even pianos (if the latter hadn't already been bartered for horse meat or a bag of flour). Then things made from other forms of cellulose, such as books and old magazines. You burned anything flammable without much thought for the future, because a personal future seemed increasingly unlikely.

Life outside was even worse than life inside, adding unique tortures. Wind and ice for instance. Whereas the temperature stiffened the body, the wind serrated it. It penetrated your thickest coat like a knife blade. It made breathing painful and, by making your eyes water, froze your eyelashes shut.

It also multiplied the problem of distance.

When the siege was still in its childhood, automobiles disappeared from the streets for lack of fuel. Trams and buses eventually stopped running, and in winter even bicycles could not navigate the encrusted streets and sidewalks. Only walking remained, and, as people grew weak and icy sidewalks grew dangerous, even walking somewhere became a dangerous pilgrimage.

A short trip to a store or bakery became a journey. A trip to a hospital a couple miles away became an expedition. And a visit to a friend even further away became unthinkable. Phones had essentially become uninvented—and then forbidden—so even if you made it to a friend's house, you were likely to find that he or she had died a week or two (perhaps months) before.

The problems of distance were compounded by new geographical facts. The Neva river was now a part of military strategy—a defense for the Soviets, an obstacle for the Germans. A bridge became a military pawn, to be attacked or defended (or perhaps purposely destroyed to thwart an enemy advance). If you normally used a bridge to get somewhere, you had to account for this change in reality. You certainly didn't want to be on it when someone wanted it to disappear.

All of this argued persuasively for staying home, especially in the winter. Go out for food and perhaps for medical attention, stay inert at home for everything else. All in all, in that first winter the docent became convinced of Dante's wisdom in making the very center of hell a place of ice instead of fire. Fire is at least active; it accomplishes something, sometimes a desirable something. Absolute cold is the cessation of all activity. Even molecules stop vibrating.

And then there were the lice, another merciless enemy, whether one was awake or asleep. Aleksandr had a few questions regarding the lice.

"Why do we freeze and the lice do not? Why aren't they seasonal like other irritating creatures, around in the summer but gone in the winter? Why don't the authorities simply ban them? You know, a decree. Like they banned music on the radio a while back. And banned capitalizing the word god decades ago. They believe things will disappear if they are forbidden, so why not forbid lice?"

Aleksandr, of course, did not expect answers to these questions. He had a fondness for asking questions without good answers. Daniil was just supposed to smile and shrug, which he faithfully did.

The lice problem is a good example of how little things were often more worrisome to Leningraders during the siege than big things, as Aleksandr pointed out.

"Being killed by a bomb, Daniil, is a real but remote possibility. Being tortured by lice is a universal and constant certainty." Even a good thing, such as getting warm by the stove, had the lamentable consequence of activating the lice.

And the authorities did their part to make life miserable. The public speakers installed on the squares, street corners (about 1700), and in the factories, shops, and apartment hallways (460,000), were another example of nonlethal objects creating disproportionate misery. In June and July they had made announcements five times a day, mostly about the progress of the Germans toward the north. People would stop everything to listen. By November, December, and January they were considered largely a nuisance. The Nazis were here. The times of their shellings were largely predictable, even if the locations were not. The bulletins over the speakers were more irritating than a shelling because they were more constant and less consequential.

Besides, having restricted music and having little other programming, the authorities simply played the tick-tock of a metronome—tick-tock, tick-tock, tick-tock, tick-tock, tick-tock. Ad infinitum. The tick-tocking accelerated when an air raid was imminent. It was the new music of the blockade. Why? It was supposed to symbolize Leningrad's unrelenting and unchanging resistance, its continually beating heart, but it only reinforced the sense of debilitating monotony and doom. Even if the Nazis and the cold and the lice and the hunger and the boredom and the spiritual emptiness did not make you yearn for death, the metronome could—tick-tock, tick-tock, tick-tock, tick-tock, tick-tock, tick-tock, tick-tock, tick-tock, tick-tock, tick-tock . . . . . .

Aleksandr once pointed out, however, that there were advantages to all the deprivations that Leningraders endured.

"Think of the time saved every morning, Daniil. We do not have to dress because we have not undressed. We do not have to wash our face or shave because there is no water in the tap. We do not have to start the fire because often there is no wood. We do not have to eat breakfast because there is no food. We don't even have to switch on the lights because . . . well, you know why."

Time saved, yes, but for what end? Finding what to do with time was a problem that trailed only finding how to stay warm and fed.

This was a less recognized challenge of the winter, but perhaps as deadly as any of the others. What is one to do when staying home? The human mind requires something to occupy it. Otherwise it begins to dis-integrate—literally; one part of the brain stops cooperating with other parts. Extreme boredom breeds dysfunction. When book reading and conversations with friends and walks in the park and concerts and the challenges of work stop, brain rot sets in.

"It's not free time, Daniil, it's empty time. There's a big difference."

So said Lev one day.

"It's why I keep painting—even if it's on cardboard. Even if it's of subjects that can never be shown. Even if all of it will soon be destroyed. I wish to stay a human being until the end."

The problem of empty time, Lev argued, contributed to the mental and spiritual suffering that accompanied the purely physical suffering.

"The two are intimately intertwined. The body cannot suffer without affecting the spirit. And the spirit and mind cannot suffer without affecting the body."

At some point the question of "How do I stay alive?" becomes "Why should I stay alive?" Those questions are always present in the human experience, of course, but they become more pointed when physical existence is threatened and great suffering is added. Pain can be tolerated when one foresees its end. But if it seems to have no end, only the likelihood of growing worse, then why should one continue in it? And if death—the end of pain—seems inevitable sooner or later, why not sooner?

The "why live?" question had engaged the docent for much of his life. He had asked a form of the question of his grandfather even as a child.

"Why, Grandfather, did God make us? Was he bored? Like me when mother tells me to find something to do?"

The grandfather had raised his eyebrows, pleased with further evidence that he had an unusually reflective grandchild.

"Well, Daniil, I don't think he was bored. Maybe he was a bit lonely, but I don't think that was it either."

"Then what?"

"I think perhaps he wanted others to love. His love overflowed, and you and I were the result."

Young Daniil couldn't quite follow this thinking at the time, but over the years he remembered his grandfather saying so.

And it might have been enough—continuing with life despite suffering if the ones he loved most were still with him. But Sofia had died and his son Yuri was away at war. He now lived alone. He had a few friends. He had Prodigal the cat. He had his work at the museum.

But was that enough? So many had died already. So many were at the precipice of death. His own body was failing fast and fast failing. Simple existence was painful. Fighting to stay alive increased and prolonged the pain. What was the logic of eating his few grams of bread for another day? Why not lie down and wait for the inevitable? Leave a note for Aleksandr and Yuri just inside the door.

It wouldn't take long . . . tick-tock, tick-tock, tick-tock, tick-tock, tick-tock . . . not long at all.

CHAPTER 34

January 1921

Arrests in Lenin's and Stalin's Russia were performance art: highly choreographed, highly repetitive, highly effective. And also quite random. The Organs, as the security establishment called themselves, had production targets, like everyone else. They didn't require a cause to arrest you, only their own need to arrest you.

One of the zeks once passed along the following dark joke to the barrack, a joke he could tell to a group because he was already in the camps, giving him a freedom that the not-yet-arrested did not have. (Totalitarianism is the attempt to make every person, without exception, think and desire what the state wishes you to think and desire—and to punish those who don't. Ironically, that goal was frustrated when they put you away.)

The joke: "Did you hear the one about the sheep who tried to leave the USSR? They were stopped at the border by a guard. 'Why do you wish to leave Russia?' the guard asked. 'It's the secret police,' replied the sheep. 'Stalin has ordered them to arrest all the elephants.' 'But you aren't elephants.' 'Try telling that to the secret police.'"

There were an infinite number of things that could be considered "anti-Soviet," and there was also that wonderful crime officially called "crime by analogy"—meaning even if the thing you did was not specifically forbidden by law, it could be said to be analogous to something that was.

Lenin even made it quite clear that people need not be arrested for anything in particular they had done, but simply for the class to which they belonged. A member of the bourgeoisie could be arrested simply for being bourgeois. You own your own shop or farm, you are "an enemy of the people." (Stalin added an unacknowledged reason for arrest: the state's need for cheap labor, hunger for which grew ravenous over time.)

The grandfather belonged to such a suspect class—not only bourgeoisie, but also religious, a priest even—the syphilitic, maggot class. And a corrupter of the young with his assumed practice of giving religious instruction.

Arrests happened at all hours and in all places, but a middle-of-the-night arrest in the home was a favorite. People awakened with loud noise and stylized violence are both disoriented and afraid, therefore unlikely to resist.

The only one not afraid in this particular case was the one arrested. Father Sergius knew that his arrest was inevitable. In fact, he felt somewhat guilty for having delayed it by hiding. Being arrested was as much a part of his calling as performing the Eucharist. He had not become a priest until his wife had died, in the early years after the Revolution, but long enough after to understand the fate of priests in the new order. He had been trained and ordained secretly, but he had no illusions.

His only regret was that his family had to witness the arrest, and to fall under suspicion themselves. Not that anyone escaped suspicion in a state founded on it, as the later bloody purges of leading figures would prove. The earliest of the Soviet secret police—the Cheka—were followed by an alphabet soup of changing acronyms for the top security office—from GPU to OGPU to NKVD to MVD and so on. Of the murderous heads of these agencies—Dzherzhinsky, Yagoda, Yezhov (aka "the poison dwarf"), Beria—only the first had the good sense to die of natural causes. Each of the others was executed by his successor. And Stalin directed it all.

As Aleksandr once said, "Revolutions often eat their progeny, Daniil. They say a shark in a feeding frenzy, if its belly is ripped open, will eat its own guts. Stalin is the biggest shark in the sea—but blood in the water attracts many others."

Though arrests in the dark were a favorite, the grandfather's arrest happened in the afternoon of January 7, Orthodox Christmas Day, when Lenin was still in charge. Everyone was gathered at Daniil's parents' home, including baby Yuri.

They had all been to church, the most important part of the day. Now they were gathered to feast, exchange presents, and enjoy the family. The big meal the night before on Christmas Eve had consisted of twelve courses of vegetables of all kinds (including piroshki—a sauerkraut dumpling), to commemorate the twelve disciples, but today the meal would emphasize meat and pastries, with baked goose the headliner. A place was set in memory of Inessa Artemovna, their departed grandmother and grandfather Anatoly's much-loved wife.

All were sitting at the dinner table. The prayer had been offered and the food was being passed. The first noise was not a knock, but an explosive pounding accompanied by shouts.

"Open up! This is the security police. Open immediately or we will break down the door!"

Daniil's mother screamed. Daniil and his father jumped up. Father Sergius merely nodded his head and crossed himself. Before anyone could get to the door, the arresting agents smashed through, one holding a battering ram and three others with guns drawn. The woman from across the hall was led in by the arm, a terrified look on her face, the required civilian "witness" to the arrest to testify that everything had been done correctly (as though she could ever testify otherwise).

Baby Yuri began to cry. Sofia tried to soothe him.

"Everyone on the floor! Now!"

They all obeyed except the grandfather, who simply rose with his hands up.

"I am here."

The agents ignored him.

"Which of you is Anatoly Ivanovich Aslanov?" one shouted.

The grandfather repeated himself.

"I am here. I am the one you want."

One agent trained a gun on him while the others spread throughout the apartment. They began pulling out drawers everywhere, dumping the contents. They opened closets and tossed armloads of clothes into the air. They swept the plates of food onto the floor.

Baby Yuri was now howling. Daniil crawled over to Yuri and Sofia and put his arm around them. Daniil's parents held hands as they lay on their stomachs.

After a few minutes of random destruction, the agents gathered around grandfather Anatoly and made an official-sounding announcement.

"Anatoly Ivanovich Aslanov—you are under arrest as an enemy of the people. Any attempt to resist and you will be shot on the spot. As will anyone who attempts to aid you."

The grandfather nodded.

"As God wills."

Daniil's face was ashen. The others cried out to the grandfather as he was handcuffed. But he answered with words of comfort.

"Do not grieve for me, my pretties. This is good. My light will no longer be hidden under a bushel."

With that he was led out the door. It was the last time that anyone in the room would see him.

CHAPTER 35

January 1942

TOPICS OF DISCUSSION IN THE CAMPS WERE OFTEN PARALLELED by similar discussions on the outside. Daniil, for instance, puzzled from time to time over the concept of the spiritual and the possible spiritual effects of the blockade. Mila claimed that the spiritual sensitivity of the citizens actually rose during the siege—proximate death being an ancient spur to spiritual reflection.

Daniil had long wondered if the "spiritual" was only a subset of the psychological, part of the purely physical reality created by the brain, or whether it was something else altogether, even something "more." And he wondered how the suffering during the blockade was affecting his own spirit—not just his mood—and that of others.

He talked about it with both Aleksandr and Lev. Aleksandr, like some in the grandfather's camp barrack, was his usual skeptical self.

"The religious concept of 'spiritual' is as outdated as using leeches for treating disease, with a history just as bloody. It has no helpful function in the modern world. Start with a mystical conception of 'spiritual' and eventually you'll be believing in ghosts and Second Comings.

"And as far as the spiritual effects on Leningraders of this disaster, they are entirely negative. You've seen the increasing blankness in people's faces, the rising apathy of people whose humanity is bleeding out of them. Nothing good comes from sugarcoating it, Daniil—we are dying body and soul."

Interesting, thought Daniil, *Aleksandr used the word "soul" there. We can't seem to escape it.*

Lev thought differently.

"I am an artist. My direct experience tells me that there is something more than the material. I cannot prove it, of course, but there are many true—and important—things that I cannot prove. Proof is for the things that can be proved—which is many things, but not the most important things. Too much of what we rightfully call 'real' cannot be measured, or successfully categorized, analyzed, and systematized. Thinking so is reductive. It is also too risk-adverse. I believe in the spiritual because the richest life requires risk."

Daniil heard in this echoes of his own ruminations, and Sofia's convictions. Lev went on.

"And as for the effect of our suffering on the spirit, I believe it is a question of what is possible, not what is common. The lives of many, I would say most, will grow less and less as they physically and psychologically grow less and less. But there are also those, and you and I have both seen them, whose spirit grows as their bodies diminish. Trivial things pass away, and only the lasting things remain for them. A great work of art is still a great work of art even if the artist perishes. The truth remains the truth. The good remains good. Beauty remains beautiful. Love remains love."

Two very different understandings of the same conditions. Daniil wanted to believe Lev—for himself and for others—but he couldn't escape the possibility that Aleksandr was right.

Daniil knew that Lev included in his work icon-like paintings with religious themes, but he didn't know whether he was actually a believer. Maybe he just wanted to use some traditional forms in his quasi-modernist paintings as he investigated the so-called "spiritual." But then Lev invited him to go with him to church.

Daniil had mixed feelings about the invitation. He wanted to affirm his friend if this was something that would please him. And he had to admit to a blend of nostalgia and curiosity about Orthodox services. He had experienced them endlessly as a child, but hadn't been to one in decades. He was curious how things might have changed, but then laughed at himself, thinking, *The Orthodox never change—that's their main boast. I guess when you claim to deal in eternal things, change is not a major goal.*

And of course it was risky to go. Religion had derailed his education, which had derailed his hopes for a career. But even now his job—and most important of all, his place as a docent at the Hermitage—was in danger if he was thought to be a believer.

In fact, he had some close calls at the museum in the past. Because his great love, and much of his guiding, centered on the Renaissance, and especially on Rembrandt, he was constantly giving background to people about paintings of biblical and other religious scenes. Dozens of rooms were filled with annunciations, mangers, baptisms, miraculous healings, miraculous feedings, angels, devils, altars, and, most problematic of all, crucifixions, resurrections, and ascensions. Not to mention Aleksandr's warning about Second Comings.

After one of his early tours as a docent, he found that an informer had been in the group. Actually he was one of the assistant museum directors whom he hadn't yet met, checking up to see how the docent performed. The man came to Daniil afterward.

"You were fine with the data and the pacing and your articulation, Mr. Aslanov, but you were deficient in your references to subject matter. You kept using the phrase 'a story from the Bible.' The word is 'myth,' Mr. Aslanov, not 'story'—'story' sounds too much like 'history.' And you made multiple uses of the word 'Christ,' as in 'Christ on the cross.' That is discouraged. All references to the mythic figure are to be to 'Jesus' and only 'Jesus,' unless the artist has explicitly used 'Christ' in his title. 'Christ' is a religious term, used by the religious. The Hermitage is a place of art and knowledge, not a church. Is that clear?"

It was clear.

And it's still clear. If the Orthodox do not change, neither do the true-believer materialists. Fundamentalists are fundamentalists no matter what their ideology. So going even once, for any reason, to a religious service was risky. But he agreed with Lev that many good things involve risk, and friendship was a good thing.

What finally made Daniil accept Lev's invitation, however, was a lingering regret regarding Sofia. She had often asked him to accompany her to church, and he had always refused. He reasoned this way. She didn't enjoy fishing and didn't go fishing with him; he didn't enjoy church and thought it equitable that he be allowed not to go to church with her. Going with Lev this one time would be a way of honoring her memory. He fantasized that she would somehow know he was going and would be pleased. At least he told himself it was a fantasy.

There were only a handful of churches still operating in Leningrad in 1941, Orthodox or otherwise, and few priests left to serve them. The official Living Church still carried on, but only because it had, led by another Sergius—Metropolitan Sergius—sold its soul to the state in 1927 after the death of Patriarch Tikhon. Institutional survival trumped faithfulness, as for some it always does. But one of the biggest and most famous churches, St. Nicholas Naval Cathedral, still had its doors open, largely because it made major monetary contributions during the siege to the common good. A good bureaucrat is loath to cut off a source of funding, and the state was defined by bureaucracy. This church also had a history of faithfulness. They resisted the order to shut down in 1921, and when Archpriest Vladimir Rybakov died from state torture in 1934, over two thousand risked attending his funeral.

It was a cloudy Sunday, but Daniil chose to wear dark glasses. Lev was in good spirits as they walked.

"Relax, Daniil. You will not be infected. Consider it a cultural experience, seeing how other people live. A very Russian experience even if not a Soviet one. Besides, the building is beautiful."

Lev then asked a troubling question.

"Did you go to church as a kid? Pre-Revolution and all that?"

Daniil hesitated and then replied.

"No."

He immediately felt a pang and wanted to return home.

"Well, don't worry. I used to go a lot. I'll explain things to you."

His first explanation involved timing.

"We're going for the Divine Liturgy, but services will have been going on for a long time. There's a series of preliminary services but no break between them. Basically it's one long service, but people come and go. Originally they lasted five hours altogether, but over the centuries the church got more realistic about human nature. Now the Divine Liturgy is the main event and most people come only for that."

Daniil knew this but felt that feigned ignorance provided a kind of defense against outcomes he did not welcome.

When they entered the narthex, Lev first went to get a candle and then approached the icon of Mary to the left of the door into the nave. He crossed himself, bowed, and kissed the icon, as did others, standing before it and then moving on. An icon of Jesus Christ was on the other side of the door, with people doing the same.

Daniil stood behind Lev and watched—and found, unsettlingly, that Mary was looking back. She seemed alive to him, as she had done in his childhood—the Theotokos, the Mother of God. She seemed both welcoming and threatening at the same time. He felt her speaking to him: "Welcome back to worship, Daniil. I am glad that you are here. We have things between us to deal with."

And of course he could not enter the church and see the icon without thinking of his grandfather. Memories of his grandfather were both part of why he wanted to come and why he wanted to stay away.

During his years teaching at Leningrad University, his grandfather's specialty was early Russian history. When he became a priest, he took the name Father Sergius. The young Daniil, fifteen at the time, knew that Sergius was a famous saint from long ago—as well as the name adopted by the recent collaborator—but that's all he knew about him.

At the time he admired his grandfather's decision to be a priest, but later had reason to lament it. The rest of his family thought it a provision (for the widowed grandfather) and a blessing (for all of them).

Daniil followed Lev from the narthex into the nave. The scene reminded him of a crowded rail station. Nothing to sit on, people milling around, most moving from one icon to the next, stopping for veneration. Most of the icons hung on the carved wooden screen stretching across the far side of the room. A large icon of the Crucifixion hung on the wall to the left, and a richly decorated, woven depiction of Jesus's tomb hung on the opposite wall.

Some were singing, led by a small choir in a loft above. No hymnals. They all seemed to know the words. Daniil remembered that he once knew the words, too, but they had long since deserted him—or he them. There were three doors in the wooden screen. Through the middle one Daniil could see the altar, surrounded by busy priests. Acolytes and others went in and out through the two doors on the side, looked over by images of angels.

Daniil waited in the center of the room while Lev moved from icon to icon. Some were low on the screen so that children could kiss them. After a while his anxiety dissipated and he began to feel a kind of peace. He attributed it to nostalgia rather than devotion. He had always liked going to services as a child. The church seemed a refuge to him then. A place like no other place in his life. Not magical, as in a fairy tale, but in a sense of more real than any other place, more substantial, more right. He couldn't explain it then and he was not inclined to try now.

This went on for a long time. Lots of crossing and kissing and praying and singing. People around him greeted others with "Christ is in our midst." Daniil himself supplied the reply in his mind as others answered, "He is and shall be." He was starting to remember.

But one part of the service stabbed him. Over and over he heard the unison petition, "Lord Jesus Christ, Son of God, have mercy on me, a sinner." An admission of sin. An appeal for mercy. He resisted a memory of the former, but knew his need for the latter. It made him sorry he had come.

But also strangely hopeful. The possibility of mercy, of forgiveness. Was it conceivable? Did the nature of the universe allow for it?

And then the event for which everyone had come. Lev rejoined him. Everyone recited together a creed; he remembered doing this as a child, but did not recall the words. Basically it was a condensed telling of the Christian story—starting outside time but then entering history. Or what Christians believe to be history.

He and Lev watched through the middle door while the priest consecrated the elements of the Eucharist—bread and wine. The priests then came with the elements out the middle door. Lev whispered, "That's the Royal door. The priest is carrying the elements."

The people lined up. The bread had been broken into small pieces, then dipped in the wine. The priest presented each person a wine-soaked piece of bread on a spoon. It reminded Daniil of a mother bird feeding its young.

Lev got in line and received the elements in his turn. Daniil wandered to the back of the room. Lev came to him and said.

"Let's go. That's the important part. We can skip the sermon."

CHAPTER 36

May 1938

DEATH RESIDED IN LENINGRAD BEFORE THE NAZIS ARRIVED. (They simply made it omnipresent—a godlike attribute.)

Sofia's death, for instance.

It approached her slowly, even respectfully, but also inexorably. She was thankful for its measured pace. It allowed her to put things in order, including Daniil. It occurred during the great purges of the late 1930s, when death came very quickly for so many. But she lived long enough to see Yuri and Yelena married, which she considered a great blessing. ("God's final gift to me," she told Daniil, "and you were one of the first.")

Sofia worried much more about Daniil and Yuri's being without her than about herself being without a life. She shared a common woman's view that men are essentially incompetent. Loveable, often talented, good for some things, capable of courage and even kindness, but not really suited to get through the average day without the help of a woman. She expressed this to Daniil in ways both overt and subtle.

"When I am gone, Daniil, you must be sure to look at the work Yuri brings home from school and encourage him. Help him with his homework but do not do it for him. He'll be at university soon and has to learn to learn on his own. And be sure to meet his teachers. You need to know them. Some will be guides and some will be trolls, and you need to know what he's facing."

Daniil always protested any sentence that started with "When I am gone." He urged her to trust that the doctors would be able to save her. It made her laugh.

"Save me, is it? Science will save me? What would your grandfather say? I'm pretty sure neither he nor your parents believe that. And I'm not inclined to believe it myself."

Her talks with Yuri took a different tack. She decided he needed, among many things, some coaching on how to relate to women.

"You will soon find yourself dealing with women other than your mother, Yuri."

He protested, but she continued.

"No, listen to me. I likely will not be here when such matters get serious, so I need to tell you some things now."

And she did, everything from how to make a woman feel good about herself to what a woman most wants out of a man.

"She wants to know that she matters, Yuri. Not matters to God or society, but matters to you. And the best way you can show her that is by talking to her. And that means talking about what she thinks as well as about how she feels. And about what her hopes are. And then—don't miss this now—by telling her what *you* think and feel and hope. It's not enough to share the house and bed and children. You must share your lives."

Sofia was happy that she had made a point to speak with Yuri about death since he was quite young, possibly from a premonition of the future. One time death came up was during a visit the three of them made to the zoo, Yuri's first. He was then about seven.

"Look at that elephant, mama! It's not as big as the ones in the books."

"Yes, the sign says her name is Betty and that she's from Asia. She will be big someday, just as you will be big, Yuri."

"My teacher says elephants are very smart and live a long time."

"Yes, they live a long time. But all creatures die eventually, quite soon, really, compared to how long time is. So everyone needs to be ready to die."

"How do you get ready to die, Mama? It's not something you can practice, like you can practice music or football so that you know how to do it."

"You get ready for it by preparing yourself for the next thing after death."

"Is that heaven? Are you talking about heaven?"

"Yes, after this life is eternal life. That means living without ever stopping. God made this world for us to prepare ourselves for eternity."

Daniil was surprised, at the time, that Sofia spoke so confidently, knowing that she often struggled with God questions. But he was fine with it. Children should grow up hopeful, believing more than can be proved. They will learn about the harshness of life soon enough.

"My friend Sasha says there is no heaven. He says it's fake. He got a spanking once when he said he wanted to go to heaven."

Sofia kept up her catechism.

"Heaven is real, Yuri. God is real. God loves you and wants you to know him and love him back. And God also loves the people who don't believe he's real."

"So God loves everybody?"

"Everybody."

"Does God love animals?"

"I'm sure he does."

"Does God love Betty the elephant?"

"God loves Betty the elephant."

Yuri looked for a second opinion.

"What do you think, papa?"

"I think it is time for a treat. What do you say we find something to eat?"

That was when Yuri was a child and Sofia had every reason to expect a long life before the question of heaven or no heaven would be settled. When Yuri was a teenager she found out otherwise.

"Cancer," the doctor said.

"I thought so," she replied.

Not, "Why me, God?" Not, "I'm too young to die." Not, "This is so unfair." Rather, "I thought so," like it was an expectation. As in, "Yes, this is what life is like. It is why one must be ready."

But both Sofia and Daniil grieved what her loss would mean to Yuri. They didn't tell him immediately because there are no right words to tell a boy that his mother will be disappearing from his life. Forever in the ground or forever in heaven—either way, Yuri will have no mother making him breakfast, welcoming him at the door, offering him words of encouragement or admonition or wisdom. Nor touching his face and smoothing his hair.

Sofia went into the hospital knowing she was unlikely ever to come out. Daniil's parents came to see her and brought a priest to anoint and pray over her. She was grateful and encouraged.

And the last time Yuri saw her was sweet. He was not weepy, which allowed her not to be weepy. He even made a little speech, something he had clearly worked on.

"I want you to know, Mama, that I will try to be the person—the man—you have wanted me to be. I will believe in God if I can . . . so . . ."

He stumbled a bit.

". . . so that I can be with you . . . later."

Sofia smiled and touched his head.

"And I will help Papa. He will miss you a lot, and so I will be there to help him. We will talk about you and about football."

At that point Sofia did cry. And so did Yuri. And so did Daniil. But it was not a desperate cry. It was a goodbye-until-later cry. Daniil tried hard to believe it.

For all of Sofia's efforts to prepare Daniil for her death, he was not prepared. She had early on become the primary focus of his life, even more so after Yuri's birth and his own being expelled from university.

Being expelled erased his plans, so he had gone to work full time. Nothing that satisfied the soul, but the main goal at that point was to satisfy the stomach—three stomachs in fact. He told himself that he would not look to work to provide purpose for his life. He would find it in Sofia and Yuri and whoever else might join them. And he would take pleasure in his hobbies and other interests, such as concerts and galleries—and Dynamo football.

So when Sofia died, it not only meant the loss of a beloved one, it meant the loss of his primary reason for himself living, leaving only Yuri, which was, of course, reason enough.

Sofia's death made more distressing the long-term alienation from his own birth family. Sofia had never understood the reasons for it, and Daniil was reluctant to discuss it. But she brought it up from time to time.

"Your parents are distant and you rarely talk to your brother and sister. What's going on with your family? I'm your wife, Daniil. There's something you're not telling me."

Daniil tried to attribute it to his no longer going to church.

"You know how they are, Sofia. Love me, love my God. Essentially, they are White Russians—or at least sympathetic to them—and I'm more or less a Red Russian. Politics, religion—they've split many a family in our country. And throughout history. Not a lot can be done about it."

Sofia wasn't buying it.

"Of course, something can be done about it, Daniil. Love is bigger than politics, and it's supposed to be the defining quality of religion. Show people love and they will respond in kind."

Daniil thought this staggeringly naïve, but he admired Sofia for it. Her naïve faith—in God, in humanity, perhaps in him—counterbalanced his own grim skepticism. He couldn't muster such faith himself, but he knew he was better off for living in the same home with it.

Now he was no longer living with it. In fact, with Sofia gone and Yuri married and away, he was living only with his memories. And Daniil no longer trusted his memories of Sofia. Enough time had now passed since her death that he suspected his mind was filling in the gaps as it wished rather than as it was. But whether his memories of her were recall or new constructions, when he was resting in them he felt more pleasure than pain, and so he returned to them often.

CHAPTER 37

January 1942

It would be unfair to Leningraders, and to humankind generally, to suggest that the evil of the siege brought out only their own potential for selfishness and evil. Small acts of goodness were common in the beginning, and though declining, could be found to the very end. As the saying goes, "Darkness makes one more sensitive to the light."

Unknown to almost everyone, for instance, the staff of the Plant Genetics Institute guarded the giant seed bank with which they were entrusted. Which is to say *guarded* rather than *ate* the great store of seeds, some of them very rare, which could have kept them alive. Apparently they still believed in a future. More than a few of them starved.

Daniil witnessed more than one similar act. He was recently in the morning bread line. Ahead of him were a mother with two young children, and ahead of them was an old babushka. The children were not in good shape. Even with their layers of clothing, you could see that their bellies were swollen. Their faces were gray, their eyes sunken and glazed. They had the vacant stare of the condemned—little zombies.

A guard stood inside the door, opening it in turn for the next person in line. The old woman was next. She turned to the woman and children.

"You go ahead of me, mother. I am in no hurry."

The mother thanked her and they changed places.

In a moment the door opened and the three entered. The guard then faced the line and spoke.

"That's it, comrade citizens. No more today."

He stepped back inside and locked the door.

The line protested; the old woman did not.

Daniil was disappointed, but said nothing. He touched the woman on the shoulder.

"That was very kind of you."

She had tears in her eyes—whether for the children or herself was unclear.

"It was nothing. The little ones have more to live for."

Daniil reflected on this event as he returned home breadless.

"It was nothing," she said. Perhaps that's literally true. Perhaps goodness has no independent existence. Perhaps it's nothing more than a fleeting opinion, a mental affirmation of a behavior that gives one pleasure or satisfaction. Not much more than "this pleases me" and is therefore "good." Hence inescapably individual and transient. As in, "It is good my team won the game," which a fan of the other team thinks is not a good at all.

Or is goodness—as in the expression "the good"—an actual independent characteristic of reality—identifiable and doable? Are some acts and attitudes genuinely and universally "good" and some others genuinely and universally "evil"? Was it evil for the Nazis to invade us and bomb and starve us and our children? Or is that just our opinion?

Are they simply following on the nation level a version of nature's imperative to survive and flourish? They say they need "Lebensraum"*—living space—and so what is clearly evil to us is a necessary good to them. Do not our own leaders think similarly? Does not each of us?*

What would Tolstoy say? Is the servant Gerasim in the story genuinely selfless when he massages the dying Ivan Ilyich's legs? Or is there some underlying, self-serving motive?

As Daniil was walking home, thinking these thoughts, he noticed the outline of a human form under the fresh snow in the street just beyond the sidewalk. Winter had provided a coffin at a time when wooden coffins no longer existed. He could not help thinking that it was almost beautiful—white and crystalline, an emblem of rest.

He stopped for a moment and stared at it, incorporating it into his reflections. *That mound of snow there, clearly a body, clearly dead. Once a person—loved and loving, one hopes. Someone recently going somewhere, never now to return. Was this person missed? Did this person's life have value? Perhaps only if every life—throughout time—has had value. And how would one prove that? Very little evidence for it. Here today and gone tomorrow. A vapor.*

And what is my responsibility to this shape in the snow? To any family associated with it? To preserving some shreds of humanity and civilization in a time of moral and physical disintegration? Should I dust the snow off? Should I search for identification? Should I drag the body somewhere? Should I tell someone in authority? All of which would diminish my own chances for survival—an expenditure of rapidly dwindling resources.

What would Marx and Lenin say? That old woman giving her spot for the sake of the children she didn't know? Can one really get selflessness—such seeming goodness—out of philosophical materialism? Lots of noble words and phrases, to be sure, but over the long haul what chance does social engineering have against that strongest of natural forces: self-interest?

And then his thoughts turned to someone who he never thought of without a mix of strong emotions.

What would Grandfather say? Goodness—a fact of creation, no doubt. Built in by God, incarnated in Jesus. An available option for everyone—man, woman, and child—because it is part of the general creation. As real and as inherent in the nature of things as gravity. And evil—also available to everyone, and also a fact, not an opinion. And us? Free to choose. We do so every day, every moment.

His thoughts then shifted to whether goodness, if it truly exists at all, has a genuine opposite.

If goodness is just a name for what pleases us, is evil just a name for what I don't like? Is no act genuinely evil in any higher sense? Are good and evil simply out-of-date religious concepts—useful for social control, but neither absolutes nor universal? Cultural creations, like borscht?

Are we wrong to call the Nazis evil? Should we call their acts evil, but not they themselves? How about the fellow who came up with the idea of dropping booby-trapped toys into the city from the air—to blow off the hands of children? Was that idea and its execution evil, but the fellow himself just doing his duty? Or dropping booby traps onto the ice on Lake Lagoda disguised as cans of food, to kill starving folks fleeing the city (supposedly the very thing the Nazis desired)? Just part of the war effort?

And which is more potent—and more characteristic of human beings and our behavior: the little acts of goodness, such as the old woman giving up her place in the food line, or the gratuitous acts of evil like the booby-trapped toys?

As he stood there, batting at ideas as at mosquitoes in summer, a man approached. He carried a long, blue ribbon. He approached the mound and gently brushed off part of the snow. A woman's dress appeared. He moved up a few feet and uncovered a hand. He bent the arm—not yet frozen—at the elbow and tied the ribbon around the hand. He did not uncover the face. He crossed himself and turned away, nodding at the docent.

The daily body collectors would come by eventually. They would see the ribbon and take away the body. Some were not so lucky as this woman. They would sleep in the street until spring.

The docent woke himself from his reverie.

Why am I even juggling such questions in my mind when the only real question is where can I find a few more calories?

By the time he got home, he had forgotten both the body and the questions.

When Daniil walked into his apartment, he realized it was Thursday and that in an hour or so he was due at Aleksandr's for their weekly chess match. The Thursday evening chess matches had gone on long after they were practical. Everyone was husbanding their energy. His climbing up two flights of stairs was the equivalent of an ounce or two of bread, an expenditure few could afford. But playing chess with Aleksandr, like painting for Lev, kept him human.

Yulia and Luka used to watch them play chess, but now the children only sat on the floor, their backs against a wall. Yana looked on from what had once been the dining room, now bare. The table had been sacrificed to the stove god weeks before. She shuffled unsteadily to the kitchen and opened a cabinet door. There sat what was left of their daily ration of bread, sitting on two plates. Yana usually tried to save some for the children near bedtime.

She called to the children.

"Come, children, have something to eat."

The children did not move.

Yana brought the plates over to them. Each held only two small pieces the size of a thumb. Luka ate his and then stared at the floor.

Yulia looked up.

"I'm not hungry, Mother. You have mine."

A noble lie.

Yana broke into tears. Aleksandr came over to comfort her. Daniil stared at the chess pieces, pretending to be strategizing.

CHAPTER 38

January 1942

SINCE THE DOCENT HAD NEITHER SOFIA NOR YURI TO TALK TO IN HIS apartment, he talked to the cat. He found that he didn't need a reply from Prodigal, which was good, because Prodigal showed no inclination to give one. Nor even to pay attention. It was simply good for Daniil to hear a voice in his home, and at this time his own voice would have to do.

The main thing he talked to Prodigal about were the two people who were not there—Sofia and Yuri.

"You would have liked Sofia, Prodigal. She understood the cat-human relationship. She once said to me, 'Daniil, do not trust people who do not like cats. It shows them to be insecure. They know that the cat sees through them. The cat senses their weakness and its own superiority and acts accordingly—completely rational. People hate that.'"

When he had first brought Prodigal home, he had worried greatly about how to feed it. He shared everything he had himself, which was precious little, but the cat generally held the offers in contempt. It didn't maintain its weight, but it lost it more slowly than did Daniil. Apparently it was a moderately successful hunter.

Though Daniil tried to hide it, Prodigal's presence in the apartment did not go unnoticed. One day he ran into the building supervisor on the stairs. She was a formidable woman—in both size and temperament. She had a body like a tank and a face that would frighten Medusa. She was also mean. Residents were supposed to sign out when they left the apartment and sign in upon return. And to give both a reason and destination for all excursions. The security Organs often found such information useful.

Many apartment supervisors were casual about enforcement of this requirement—to their own peril, but a sign that all systems of control have cracks. This woman, however—Hulga Anatovna—took great pride in her punctilious attention to keeping the rules—

including the unwritten ones. She knew she held a low place in the pecking order, but she was determined to maximize it, as such people often are.

The 1930s were the zenith of the power of apartment supervisors. Housing was so short that two and even three families would often share one apartment. Privacy, long considered an outdated bourgeois value, was not expected and nonexistent. Arguments within and between families in the same apartment were common. A supervisor—sometimes called an "elder"—upon hearing one going on through the thin walls, would step into the apartment unannounced to be a "witness" to events should they later require adjudication. Needless to say, these crowded conditions were ideal for surveillance and informing.

Things were less crowded now, not least because so many had evacuated or died. But Hulga was a woman to keep an eye on, because she was definitely keeping an eye on you.

"I see you have a cat, Mr. Aslanov."

Daniil said nothing. Residents had been allowed cats before the siege and he had heard nothing that changed that. They had disappeared, of course, but that was for other reasons.

"It is not against the rules, but it could become so."

Daniil tried to stay calm.

"I like cats, Mr. Aslanov. I like them very much. They make good . . . good . . . let us say, good companions."

Daniil cleared his throat and tried to appear casual.

"What would you take for your cat, Mr. Aslanov? What would you like to barter? Perhaps a bag of flour? Just a small one, of course. But what do you say to your cat for small bag of flour?"

"I would not be interested, Hulga Anatovna."

Her face hardened.

"That is too bad, sir. Yes, too bad. As I say, cats are not against the rules, but, be careful, rules sometimes change. And then you might get nothing in return for your companion."

Yes, be careful. Always good advice in Leningrad, but never more so than now.

The docent had his companion in his lap one afternoon when there was a knock on his door. He opened to see Aleksandr with an anxious look on his face.

"It's about Lev. We were supposed to get together. I've knocked on his door three times in the last two hours. Neither he nor Mila is answering. They were both very weak the last time I saw them. I think we better check."

"Should we get the building supervisor?"

"Are you crazy, Daniil? She'll see the paintings. You know the ones I'm talking about. That's big trouble if they're still alive. It's also trouble if they're not, because the supervisor knows we are all friends and will ask why we didn't report the religious contraband. We need to handle this ourselves. Broken door locks can be repaired. Broken rules not so much."

They went up to Leonid and Mila's apartment. Only a few flights of stairs, but both men were wheezing when they got there. Aleksandr had a colorful past. He knew how to spring a lock without damaging the door frame.

When they went in the studio room was empty. The bedroom was not.

The bodies of Leonid and Mila lay on top of the bed, fully clothed. They were holding hands. There was no sign that they had taken their own lives. Lacking the minimum necessary to live, they had simply worn out together—or nearly so. It was a blessing. Leonid's off hand was touching her cheek, suggesting she was the first to pass.

The two icon-like paintings the docent had seen were propped on chairs next to the bed, the one on cardboard near Lev, the palladium of Mary spreading her veil next to Mila. Something to contemplate—perhaps venerate—as they waited for their new Landlord.

The docent remembered his friend's words when they were debating whether or not these were icons.

"Maybe the question is determined by the impact they have on you. If it moves you in a certain direction, it is an icon. If not, not."

The docent reflected for a moment and said into the air.

"They are icons."

The docent took the religious paintings—including one of a figure in a desert that was still on the easel—and Aleksandr took the rest. Otherwise the authorities would burn them. Or try to. Some things, as Bulgákov has taught us, do not burn.

CHAPTER 39

April 1938

FATHER SERGIUS WAS RARELY SICK, THOUGH HE DID DIE ONCE. He had a high fever and became very weak. It was big news in the barrack, even in the camp as a whole. Because of his care for so many over the years, he was the best-known prisoner in the camp. Many zeks came by his bunk in his days of sickness. Some asked for his blessing. Some brought him food. Others just stood silently, a show of respect.

But he did not get better. One night he fell into a coma. There was no doctor available at night. A former biologist zek boiled pine needles and tried to get him to drink it, but the priest was unresponsive.

When he died, Father Sergius felt his spirit lifting into the air. He also felt a great peace, unlike any peace he had ever felt in life. As his spirit rose, he looked back toward his bunk. A dozen men were standing around it, looking at his body. The biologist, inspecting him more closely, said, "He's gone. Father Sergius is gone."

A soft, collective groan went up from the men. A few began to weep. The spirit of Father Sergius paused. The sadness of the men made him sad. He lingered for some moments. Then he prayed.

"Oh God most merciful. I thank You for accepting me, an unworthy sinner. But I ask You to let me stay. These men have no one. Some are on the verge of suicide, some of turning to You. All of them need someone to give them hope. I believe I have more work to do. If You find it good, I ask that You allow me to return to my body, to my sheep."

In that moment he opened his eyes and saw the face of the biologist. They both smiled.

"Wait, he is not gone after all. No, he is still alive."

Father Sergius corrected him.

"Not quite, sir. Not still alive. Rather, alive again."

CHAPTER 40

January 1942

Daniil and Aleksandr did not have to discuss what to do with the bodies of Lev and Mila. They knew it was their duty—at the cost of their honor if they neglected it—to see that they were buried. Not properly buried of course, that was impossible. But at least buried. So many people were not. They were weeks in isolated rooms, frozen and undiscovered, no one inquiring of them. Or under the snow and ice somewhere, perhaps in the middle of a street, waiting to blossom in spring.

In the early days of the blockade, every death was a tragedy; now it was not even a statistic, because the authorities had more or less stopped counting. The registry bureau could not keep up with the demand for death certificates. People died these days as often on the street as they did at the hospital or at home, their bodies surrendering to the inevitable as they shuffled to the bread line or away from their burning apartment building.

In October or November of '41 people stopped to help if anyone collapsed. By December they hurried past. By January they stepped over the bodies or stopped only to go through pockets in hopes of a ration card. Or worse . . . No, I won't speak of that. . . .

As more and more people died—and they died by the thousands per day now, mostly related to starvation—there were fewer people in families or among friends to pay attention to anyone else's life. Or death. And paying attention could itself be deadly.

As in the case of getting Lev and Mila to the cemetery. The designated one for blockade deaths was Piskaryovskoye, about seven miles away—an easy two-hour walk in June of 1941, but no one did anything easily six months later. The trams and buses were moribund and cars were out of the question. People had taken to stacking bodies in courtyards or by the curb, awaiting the occasional city truck to pick them up. Adding Lev and Mila to a pile was unthinkable, even in a time when the unthinkable was commonplace.

Seven miles in the winter of 1941 and '42 in Leningrad were like seventy miles in any pre-war day—or seven hundred. Neither Daniil nor Aleksandr were yet as weak as Lev had been, but few would risk a long walk for anything but food. Still the two men knew this was exactly what must be done. After all, Lev and Mila were friends, and taking their bodies to the cemetery was the last act of friendship toward them that Daniil and Aleksandr would ever be allowed.

There was no coffin to be had, of course. Coffins were as rare as three-course meals. Anything wooden, including fences, ironing boards, and even the roller-coaster at the Leningrad amusement park—the Amerikanskye Gory—or what was left it after Nazi shelling, had long ago been burned for heat. No coffins, no individual graves or markers—neither for rich or poor, high or low, commissar or prisoner. Marx's classless society had finally arrived—the ultimate equality of being equally dead.

The standard method of private conveyance of a body to a cemetery these days was a child's sled. The sight was as common on the streets of Leningrad as a dog or cat had once been before they became prized for dinner. One saw it multiple times every day—a woman, usually, pulling a sled in the snow, a body wrapped in a sheet or sometimes curtains, especially heartbreaking when the load was two or three feet long.

Fortunately, Aleksandr had two children and therefore had two sleds. They set out early the next morning in the dark—part of the eighteen hours of darkness in a Leningrad January—before anyone official would see them leaving with two bodies. The bed the couple had died on had no sheets. Perhaps they had burned them for heat. But it had a bedspread, so they split it in two and wrapped each body. Both were already frozen before they were discovered.

Daniil and Aleksandr discussed how best to get them downstairs to the street. Almost skeletal, the bodies were not heavy. But Daniil and Aleksandr were also emaciated, so even carrying a bag on level ground was challenging. They decided to bring the sleds upstairs to the bodies rather than the other way around. They tied the corpses to the sleds, then tied long rope to the sleds and let them slide down the stairs slowly, step by step, floor by floor. That first stage took an hour.

Once in the street, they started out with their load. What was that load? Was it their friends? Were their souls still hovering nearby, as some superstitious people thought? Or were these just the residue of a certain configuration of atoms, even now breaking down into their constituent elements, a preliminary dissolution leading to a later recombining with other elements to form something new, not necessarily living, and certainly not Lev and Mila.

In the first hour of pulling, the men stopped to rest every three blocks. In the second hour, they stopped every other block. By late morning they were progressing only one block per stop, corner to corner, and the stops were less and less helpful.

They had been wise enough to bring bread with them. They agreed not to eat any until they estimated they were halfway to the cemetery. But starvation had weakened their power of estimation. Wandering off one's mental path had become increasingly common for them both. You suddenly didn't know what the next logical thought was, nor even remember the prior one. You had to go back to the beginning. Over and over.

Finally, Aleksandr said, "I have to eat."

He took out his handful of bread, the only thing he would eat today.

"Don't eat it all, Aleksandr. Save some for the walk back."

But it was too late. Aleksandr had already balled up the bread and shoved it in his mouth. Daniil sighed.

"Chew slowly," he said. "Make it last a bit."

Again too late. Aleksandr swallowed the lump quickly, then stuck his blackened finger in his mouth to dislodge any scraps clinging to his teeth.

"Sorry, Daniil. Couldn't help myself."

On their odyssey to Piskaryovskoye, they experienced Leningrad as it had become by January of 1942—the streets fit only for polar explorers, burned and bombed-out buildings in most blocks, haunted shades shuffling along the crusted sidewalks in a cold purgatory. Billboards advertised products that could no longer be purchased—or even imagined; most stores were closed, and money was worthless anyway.

Posters dotted walls with government exhortations, entreaties, and threats, including one obviously put up in pre-war days: "Life has become better. Life has become more cheerful." A newer one screamed, "Death to the Child-killers!" and showed a mother holding in her lap the body of her dead child, a siege pietà. A block later a billboard displayed a larger-than-life image of a mother and child shrinking melodramatically before the bayonet of a Nazi soldier. *The slaughter of the innocents*, thought the docent, amazed at how often Soviet visual propaganda played on biblical tropes of the kind found so often in the art at the Hermitage.

By late morning they had crossed Liteyniy Bridge spanning the Neva. A block from the trains of Finland Station, a favorite Nazi target, they could see between the buildings long lines of children being evacuated. Finland Station was also where the trains came in from Lake Ladoga, carrying whatever food had managed to make it across the ice road built on the lake.

Later, when grand rhetoric was back in style, they called the ice road the Road of Life, but for many of the drivers it was the Road of Death. Aleksandr knew a man who drove the route, dodging the Luftwaffe and the thin places in the ice.

"Kirill says dozens of trucks go through the ice every week. They drive with their doors open so they can leap out. They drive as fast as they can, truck nose to truck tailgate, knowing that death can come from above or below. He says, 'We are constant targets for strafing by the Luftwaffe. They seek us out like hungry predators seeking out rabbits.

"'On the way back out,' Kirill says, 'they take evacuees. Last week, they separated a family, the mother in his truck, the young children in the truck ahead of them. The truck with the children went through the ice. The mother screamed for him to stop, but he had to swerve and keep moving or his truck would go in too.

He stopped a hundred yards beyond. The mother leapt out and both of them ran back, she screaming all the way. They found only a gaping hole and bubbles, no other sign of life. Ladoga had exacted its toll.'"

"What happened?"

"What do you mean?"

"What happened to the mother?"

"She went mad."

Daniil and Aleksandr then heard a whistling in the air. It was time for the midday shelling. They were passing an unusually long bread queue at the time. The distribution must have been delayed, because bread at any shop had usually run out well before this time of day. The first shells hit a block behind them. Daniil and Aleksandr looked at each other, asking without words whether they should seek shelter. Both shrugged at the same time and continued walking. A safe place in Leningrad, as I pointed out earlier, was a contradiction in terms.

Then came the silent shell—the one most likely to kill you. It exploded fifty feet away, knocking them to the ground. Stunned, they called to each other.

"Aleksandr, are you hurt?"

"I'm okay, Daniil. How are you?"

Miraculously, neither of them had been hit by the shrapnel. Screams from across the street announced that others had not been so lucky. Thirty feet of shredded bodies punctuated the bread queue. A horse drawing a cart flailed and screeched on the ground, its driver dead. Daniil and Aleksandr waited for the inevitable next shell.

It never came.

What did come was something that made Aleksandr look away. First one, then two, then a half dozen people appeared with long knives. The horse was still quivering as they began cutting bloody hunks from its body—first the flanks and shoulders, then the belly. And the bread queue? People stepped over the bodies and reformed the line, now closer to their hoped-for slice.

A whistle sounded and the butchers ran, carrying their prizes with them. A policeman walked up. He looked all around, then reached under his coat and pulled out his own knife and a bag. Cutting off a piece for himself, he walked away, paying no attention to the confetti of bodies a few yards away.

Daniil and Aleksandr did the only thing they could. They continued.

Atrocity was too commonplace in Leningrad to alter anyone's plans. They got to their feet and started again toward the cemetery, pulling their silent cargo. Lev and Mila were beyond the carnage in the street. They were beyond further suffering. They had joined the lucky ones.

The two men made better time in the afternoon than they had in the morning. Perhaps the shelling had called up a last bit of adrenaline. They got confirmation that they were headed in the right direction and nearing the cemetery when a dump truck of bodies sped by. On top was a man frozen in a sitting position, looking as though he were lecturing the rest of the bodies.

As they approached the main gate, they experienced a bit of the dark humor that survived, even thrived, during the siege.

There, next to the gate, was propped the body of a naked woman, her frozen arm outstretched, pointing inside, a cigarette hanging from her lips. A moment reminiscent of medieval plague time, when whole towns and villages died together and the macabre was dominant.

As they passed through the gates, they heard an explosion. Daniil crouched low.

"Another shelling?" he asked.

Aleksandr remained standing.

"No, Daniil. Just the army sappers blowing holes in the frozen ground for the mass graves. Nothing to worry about."

It was true, as the docent soon saw. No one got their own grave—not in the camps, not in the city. But at least Daniil and Aleksandr got to place Lev and Mila themselves. While others were being slung off the trucks into the great hole, they walked the bodies of their companions a distance from the growing pile and placed them gently on the ground. They straightened Lev's tie—he had put on a tie before dying—and Mila's hair, then returned the bedspread over their faces.

They stood silently, hands folded, as if in prayer, but without prayer. Daniil spoke.

"I wish my grandfather was here. He would know the right words to say."

After a bit, he said the only thing he could think of.

"Rest in peace, friends. We will join you soon."

CHAPTER 41

February 1942

BY MIDWINTER, LENINGRAD HAD AS FEW RESOURCES AS A prehistoric cave dwelling—and was less safe. There was no water, no heat, no electricity, and only enough food to tease you before you died. And die they did, now by the tens of thousands each week, too many even to collect for the mass graves even if one could find the bodies, which often they couldn't.

As is the norm in human history, not everyone suffered equally. The ice road provided only a small portion of the food needed, and, unfortunately, too much of it never made it to the masses. Not "unfortunate," really, because the randomness of fortune had nothing to do with it. It was simply human nature at its most human. Given a choice between having as much as possible for myself and those I love, and sharing with people I don't personally know, the officials in charge of the city made the obvious choice. They fed themselves.

Andrei Zhdanov, the political boss of Leningrad (and Stalin's favored heir-apparent), managed to sport a near double chin even at the height of the starvation. His clothes fit him tightly, especially around the waist. Aleksandr speculated that he was the only person in Leningrad during the blockade to gain weight. His wife was spotted on a train feeding sweets to her plump children. People noticed. They hated them for it. But they also hated being fired from their jobs, or having their children barred from school, or even being sent to one of the camps. So they said nothing—at least not publicly. In private they referred to Zhdanov as "the pig."

Publicly, the authorities told the citizenry to buck up, be heroic, like the soldiers always were. The *Leningradskaya Pravda* printed an official warning that people had become unacceptably grim. "Because of the reduction in the bread ration, there has been a significant expansion of negative attitudes." Negative attitudes, huh? Wonder why that is. The newspaper offered the apparent antidote to negativity with a large dose of heroic rhetoric: "Citizens, be worthy of the Motherland which you represent and of the courageous Red Army which protects you!"

Letters to the outside world (they went out in the trucks going back across the lake) were censored if they painted too bleak a picture of the situation. Doctors could not speak of "starvation." The acceptable term was "nutritional dystrophy" or some equally euphemistic formulation. A rule was established that no photograph of life in Leningrad could show more than three dead bodies (unless they were German soldiers). All aimed at countering what was grandly called "counter-revolutionary defeatist agitation."

If reality itself cannot be sanitized, the reporting on reality certainly can be.

So, if there is not water in the tap, or in the bathtub spigot, or in the fire hose, where can you get water? You get it wherever you can—from the lake, from the river, from the canals. Hard enough in summer, much harder still in winter. You can carry snow inside, but what if your apartment is not warm enough to melt it? What if you have no wood to burn to heat it? Of course the authorities have granted everyone a steadily declining ration of wood. But declarations are easy, fulfilling them is not. Tell your cold, empty stove that legally it should be stuffed with wood.

Thank goodness for the Neva. Not very long, but long enough to save a city from dying of thirst.

Of course the Neva in winter is frozen over. One had to chop through feet of ice to get to water. And so they did, again mostly the women, some too old to carry the bucket of water once they extracted it, the frozen bodies of the unsuccessful scattered here and there. But even the old wanted to help, perhaps to assuage their guilt for consuming calories each day that could be going to their grandchildren.

The docent regularly saw the women gathered around holes in the ice off Nevsky Prospekt as he exited the Hermitage for the walk home. One day, after noticing an old woman struggling up the icy riverbank with a bucket of water, he made a quick calculation—

how dangerous would it be for him, in his weakened condition, to carry for a while this bucket of water for the old woman?

Before he could finish the calculation his shame at having even asked the question overwhelmed him and he called out to the woman with an offer to help. She was grateful.

"You are very kind, sir. May God and Mary bless you."

He carried the water for three blocks before her route took her in a different direction than his. She thanked him again, and he was secretly relieved. He stopped for a few minutes to regain his strength. He ate the small piece of bread he usually saved for the midpoint of his walks home.

As he returned to walking, he found his spirit growing lighter, but did not know why. It then occurred to him: It was a Friday, and he was nearing the block where the musicians play. The first time he heard them, he hoped they would be there again the next day. They weren't, but a week later they were, at the same time. And again the Friday after that. And now every week since, late Friday afternoons, they gather to make music in the storefront.

In the last few weeks there had been only four. The trumpet player had been missing. The docent didn't want to think about why.

But the four carried on, now alternating between the slow, melancholy chords of meandering tunes and others with a little more jump to them. The pieces seemed to wander, sometimes like a bird riding the wind, sometimes like a drunk, moving where they wished and inviting you along.

First one instrument led and then another, exploring the varying emotions of everyday life. This reminded him of certain painters, though he couldn't quite say which ones, maybe the Dutch Realists or that American he had recently discovered, Edward Hopper. He recalled that Stalin had banned the word *jazz* and had also forbidden the playing of the saxophone, such music deemed a purveyor of rebellious individualism and Western decadence.

So, stopping here to listen each Friday, as now six or eight folks usually do, is actually a crime. Or at least it is the witnessing of a crime. And to not have reported it is to have participated in it, reporting on others being a national pastime in the Soviet Union. Children were asked to report to their teachers any praying or icons they saw in their homes, workers were asked to report coworkers who seemed inadequately enthusiastic about their work, officials were expected to report other officials who failed to follow to the letter the latest program, or, for that matter, had allowed the ubiquitous photo of Stalin to hang askew. And so on in all areas of human activity at all times and in all places. Someone is always watching, someone is always listening, someone is always calculating the advantage for themselves of your fall.

CHAPTER 42

August 1937

No camp rule or ritual was more unwaveringly practiced than roll call. A prisoner missing from roll call was a cause for alarm, a prisoner missing from camp altogether was a cause for panic. A guard or camp commander who lost a prisoner was in genuine danger of becoming one himself.

Counts took place many times a day, but the most formal roll call was every night before lights out. Always outside, conditions be damned. It could be storming, freezing, hailing, or hot and mosquito infested—the roll call went on.

Everyone stood at attention in ranks as the count was conducted. On this night, the number came up one short. The official in charge demanded a recount. Still one short. Now everyone was nervous—an angry official was a threat to all.

Suddenly they heard a door slam. A man ran around the corner, buttoning his trousers, and tried to get to his place in line. A guard blocked him. The officer in charge approached him. The poor man tried to explain.

"I was in the latrine. I have the runs. There was nothing I could do. I apologize, sir."

An apology . . . in camp . . . to an officer. Almost funny.

The supervisor walked up and punched the man in the face, knocking him to the ground. He began kicking him with his heavy boot.

"You maggot. Do you think I care about the state of your bowels? Do you think you are on a cruise in the Black Sea?

He did not stop kicking. It looked as though he intended to kill him, an example for all to see and take to heart.

At this point Father Sergius left his place in line and walked up to the officer. He crossed himself and then spoke calmly but authoritatively.

"I command you, in the name of our Lord Jesus Christ, to stop."

The officer did stop. Father Sergius returned to his position and the man crawled toward his place in line. The recount continued.

When it finished, two of the zeks talked as they were hurrying back to the barrack.

"Can you believe what we just saw? How is Father Sergius still alive? I thought for sure the officer would shoot him on the spot. He did nothing. Acted like he didn't even hear him."

The other didn't look at him.

"What are you talking about? No one said anything. I was standing right next to Father Sergius. He never moved a muscle."

"But I saw him go up to the officer, cross himself, and heard him tell him to stop. Everyone saw it."

"No one saw or heard anything except you, my friend. Do you have a fever? Maybe you need to ask the Commandant for some vacation time—a trip to Odessa perhaps. Camp life is getting to you."

"I know what I saw. I know what I heard. It's a miracle."

"Miracles are for fools."

CHAPTER 43

February 1942

THE MOST WIDELY READ BOOK DURING THE SIEGE WAS, NOT surprisingly, *War and Peace*—in part because while no one was buying books, many people already had a copy (often unread), and not least because that historical situation so closely paralleled the present one. Then it was the French, this time the Germans. (Catherine the Great had made her court speak French; it seemed unlikely that Stalin would make the Politburo speak German.)

While many read Tolstoy, the docent read Dostoevsky, especially *Brothers*. Daniil thought Aleksandr a bit like Ivan—brash and skeptical. He thought of Lev as a kind of Alyosha, sweet-spirited and spiritual. He didn't find anyone that made him think of himself. But that changed when he re-read, for the first time since high school, *Crime and Punishment*. He was shaken by guilt-ridden Raskolnikov and by Sonia's love for him, and saw in her his own Sofia. At times he had to put the novel down, feeling it accused him, but he kept returning to it because it spoke of the possibility of redemption.

While many read, many others burned their books—not for the usual ideological reasons, but rather to keep themselves alive. Trees were light collectors, turning the warmth of the sun into cellulose. Paper was made from that cellulose, so burning a book was, in one sense, bringing the sun into one's home, a release of the sun's life-generating energy.

But with few exceptions, the docent could not bring himself to burn his books. It would be like burning children. A book was fuel for the mind—a bit of sun in another way, a sun that cast light on the human condition. A great book was a bright star. A private book collection a constellation. A great library a galaxy. The exception to his no-burn rule, consigned happily to the stove, were the pages of propaganda he had been assigned to read over the years. He was happy to find them at last useful.

One day, Pushkin's birthday in fact, Daniil was listening as an energetic voice on the hallway speaker read Pushkin's poetry aloud. Submerged in thought, he did not see Prodigal come padding up to him. But he felt something drop on the laces of his shoe. He looked down. It was a rat, a rather plump rat. How a rat managed to be plump in Leningrad in February of 1942 is no great mystery. Rats had thrived in desperate circumstance for many thousands of years, and with so many dead things in the streets of Leningrad, their food supply was everywhere.

The docent looked at Prodigal and Prodigal looked back. It seemed an offering, a "thank you" of sorts for its rescue, one poor creature doing what it could for another. It had to be accepted.

"Very kind of you, Prodigal. We shall have meat tonight."

Do not think this repulsive until you have been in their place. A drowning man does not criticize the quality of the rope thrown to him.

The docent picked up the rat by the tail. He stroked Prodigal and scratched behind his ears. He carried the gift to the kitchen. There was no longer water in the taps, but he had a bucket of water that he had brought home from the river. He poured some of in a bowl and washed the rat. Then he skinned it, hoping this would eliminate at least some of the potential contagion. He cut off the head and tossed it to the cat, an appetizer before dinner. Prodigal picked it up delicately in his mouth and carried it away.

Then the docent got out a frying pan. He lit the stove, using only one piece of wood and a pamphlet describing the current Five-Year Plan. He cut the rat in half and put it in the pan, adding a splash of paint thinner to create a nice crust. Having fried it the best he could, he put one half on a plate and set it on the floor. Prodigal came up to it and began to eat.

The docent took the other half to his table. He laid out a cloth napkin and a knife and fork. He always tried to make any meal besides bread a dignified affair. It helped with the illusion that he was not starving. He hoped he would not vomit it up. It would be a waste of needed calories—protein no less.

CHAPTER 44

March 1942

WHAT DOES IT DO TO A CHILD'S MIND TO BE GROWING UP surrounded by evil? Among other things, it normalizes what should never be thought normal. If there is never enough to eat, for instance, it weakens a child's needed sense that life is good and the future hopeful. The damage to the body is visible and measurable. The damage to the mind and spirit is profound but largely hidden—at least for a time. Sometimes the evidence comes out indirectly.

As in Luka's drawings.

"I have something to show you, Daniil."

"What would that bc?"

Aleksandr left the room and came back with a large scrapbook.

"It's Luka's drawings. I want you to see them."

"Of course. Be happy to. You have a talented son, Aleksandr."

"I have a disturbed son, Daniil. The blockade is changing him and how he understands the world."

Aleksandr opened the scrapbook to the first page. Written on it, in a child's hand, was the following: "'Things I've Seen or Want to See' by Luka."

"Just turn the pages, Daniil. They're in chronological order, starting six months before the invasion."

Daniil did as requested. The early pages were dominated by dinosaurs and horses, with an occasional drawing of a member of the family, sometimes a grouping, everyone always smiling. Titles indicated that a few of them were self-portraits, also smiling. They reminded Daniil of Rembrandt's fondness for capturing his own image.

Then a drawing of an airplane with a swastika on it.

"That one's from the end of July. Luka and I were out in the park and we saw a German reconnaissance plane fly low overhead. He asked what the 'thing' was on the wing of the plane. I told him, 'It's a swastika, Luka, something the Germans use to say who they are.'"

"'What does it mean?' he asked.

"I gave him a foolish answer.

"'It means that many people will now die.'

"I regretted it immediately, of course, but I couldn't take it back. He just nodded and said nothing. But look at the drawings after that."

The next few were battle scenes and explosions, the kind of things young boys like to imagine. Only at that time in Leningrad—as now—imagination is not required.

But these were not the disturbing ones. Boys will play war, cops and robbers, hunter and hunted even if raised in a bubble. Take away their toy six-shooters and they will use their index finger for a gun barrel and thumb for the hammer. As lion cubs will play in ways that train them for the kill, so the play of boys is filled with faux violence, preparing too many for the real thing. Lamentable, perhaps, but also normal.

Luka's drawings as the atrocities mounted were not normal.

The first one that raised concern was of an elephant. Not just any elephant. It was Betty the elephant, the one who had captured Yuri's attention as a boy many years before. It had become a zoo favorite, known by everyone in Leningrad, but especially adored by the children. In early September, the day before the Nazis and Finns officially closed the circle around the city, Betty's compound was bombed and she was crushed under the collapsed roof, crying out in pain and terror for hours in her death throes.

Unfortunately the authorities, to build up anger toward the enemy, spread the word widely, offering graphic descriptions of Betty's suffering both in the newspapers (including photographs) and on the radio. Luka absorbed it all and it came out in his drawings. They were primitive but conveyed clearly the agony of Betty's tortured end.

Later drawings were of apartment buildings on fire and people leaning out of smoke-filled windows. Then of stick figures standing in bread lines. Then of loaves of bread by themselves and of other food—drumsticks, apples, sausages, pies.

"Look at the changes on the faces of the people, Daniil. No more smiles. Only sad faces. And look at the details of the faces—no longer round, pinched instead. And the eyes—staring and empty. He's caught the eyes."

Daniil nodded.

"Yes, he has a gift for capturing the essence in a few pencil strokes."

"Yes, but the essence of what? Of loss? Of destruction? Of evil?"

"Of suffering."

"Right, and no child should have to see and draw such things. And these aren't the worst. Keep going."

The next drawing was a bank of snow with a hand sticking out, then a woman pulling a sled holding a small form wrapped in a white sheet. Then, surprisingly, a drawing of a cat. It seemed at first a break from the horror. But no. To the side of the cat was a disembodied hand—holding a fork.

The last drawing, unfinished, had nothing in the center of the page—a blank—but had an ornate and finely rendered border. At first Daniil thought it just a repeated element of design, but then he looked closer. Nooses, alternating with swastikas—a border of small nooses hanging from small swastikas, all around the page. Swastikas, nooses, and blankness. Maybe the drawing was finished after all.

CHAPTER 45

March 1942

THE DOCENT AND HIS FELLOW WORKERS AT THE HERMITAGE were not exceptions to the effects of "nutritional dystrophy." All were weaker, all were drained of energy and vitality, all looked to the others like phantoms, depleted parodies of their former selves. The docent knew, and sometimes told his tour audiences, that in Rembrandt's day the custom when a loved one died was to turn all mirrors in the home toward the wall—a sign of grieving. Now you did the same, or took them down altogether—a sign of grieving for yourself.

Yes, all were slowly—or not so slowly—dying, but all who could still came to work. It was not for the pay, because pay was largely irrelevant. It fulfilled a mutual need—of the Hermitage for sustaining its existence—symbolic and actual—and of the staff for sustaining their reason for living. And it was thought by all a defense of civilization itself.

The Hermitage needed a skeleton crew—ah, what an appropriate term—for tasks as mundane as sweeping up the snow that came in through holes in the roof from an overnight shelling or through gaping wounds in the walls where windows once separated inside from outside, an illusion shattered like the twinkling galaxies of glass sometimes covering acres of floors. Daniil had more than once helped to sweep up while others searched out materials to bandage the vast window openings. It felt, he thought, like sweeping the sky of stars.

The docent was there the morning after frozen pipes had burst in the night and flooded one of the basements where the floors were covered with stacks of delicate porcelain and china. A small army of cleaning ladies was sent to remove the water and rescue the precious objects. Because there was no electricity, they could use only buckets, not pumps, passing them in long lines up the stairs to the nearest window. For the same reason, the basement was filled with darkness as well as water. And as there was no heat, the water had to be eliminated before it froze, shattering the art it covered.

The docent was a candle-holder while the women worked. Much of the fragile art was under the opaque water, invisible to its rescuers. Working in the semi-dark and freezing air, wearing waders or tall rubber boots, the women shuffled rather than walked so as not to step on something precious. They worked all day, every bit as much serving the Motherland as any soldier on the front lines. And miraculously, if you believe in such things, nothing was lost or broken.

And people continued to come to experience the paintings that were no longer there to be seen. More soldiers at first, beginning the day after the first three, and then citizens of every kind, including, eventually, the blind.

And when they did, there were guides to show them the vacant frames. And to talk. Because talk was all they had to offer—a widow's mite. They did not have the paintings themselves, hidden far away as they were, but they had an accumulation of knowledge. And they had years of their own experience with the paintings. That would have to suffice. When a string breaks on the violin in mid-performance, a virtuoso finds a way to finish with the strings that remain.

All the docent had to offer his listeners was talk, but he found, as did the others, that he had more and more to say. He became dissatisfied with what he had said in the past before each painting. For years he had given only dates and technical details, and general observations about periods and styles and artists' careers. People didn't need much because the painting was there to speak for itself.

Now he had to *be* the painting. He was not simply a conduit of information; his words were the medium by which the painting existed, or failed to exist, for these particular people. He was a partner, a co-imaginer—with words rather than pigments—of Michelangelo, of Raphael, of his beloved Rembrandt. It made worthwhile the daily and increasingly dangerous walk from his apartment to the museum. Why squander precious and declining energy to complete a seemingly pointless task? Because, as Lev had said about his own potentially never-to-be-seen paintings, it kept him human.

Today, the docent had only one tour group—a dozen people. For some reason he noted that this was the number of Jesus's disciples in the Gospels. He found that random bits from his religious upbringing in his very distant past were resurfacing, perhaps a sign of the decline of his mind. It bothered him.

This group was a cross-section of Leningraders—from young to old, men and women and one child, some dressed like workers, others like store clerks, one man with an expensive-looking suit, and two soldiers. They all looked hungry, but maybe that was only because the docent felt unusually hungry himself. He had gotten up at 4:00 a.m. this morning in order to get in line for his bread ration. The ration had recently been increased slightly—the food czar, Dmitri Pavlov, was doing his best. The increase was not enough to keep you from starving, but enough to allow you to starve more slowly.

If the tour talks were getting more elaborate, the tours themselves were getting shorter. The Winter Palace itself was vast, and it was only one of multiple buildings of the Hermitage that housed the literally millions of works of art. For every room that one visited—for every painting frame or sculpture that one talked before—the body paid a price. And, as elsewhere, the price of stairs was especially high.

So what had been a multi-hour tour for those three soldiers who first arrived weeks ago asking to see the paintings, was now a smattering, a few rooms, a few frames in each room, longer talks before each one to store up energy for the walk to the next one. Even the speaking was punctuated, a few sentences between pauses, allowing moments for the docent to catch his diminishing breath.

Given the brevity of the tours, the docent always emphasized Rembrandt. And among the Rembrandts, he always spent his energy most profligately on *The Return of the Prodigal Son*. He didn't know why. And then again, he did.

Today, standing before the giant frame, he started as he had always started.

"Rembrandt van Rijn, as perhaps you well know, was a Dutch Baroque painter who was born in 1606 and died in 1669. He is widely considered one of the greatest painters of all time, and this painting, *The Return of the Prodigal Son,* is considered one of the world's greatest paintings. Rembrandt created this masterwork late in his life, right at the end in fact. Some have speculated that it may not even be finished."

He continued in his usual fashion, indicating the size of the painting, the biblical source, the use of chiaroscuro, impasto, and the like.

He planned to spend extended time on the rendering of each figure in the painting—the prodigal, the father, the older brother, the advisor, and the two women. But he found himself talking more and more about Rembrandt's life and how the painting was related to it. He didn't know why. And then again, he did.

"As I have said, the story depicted in this painting comes from the Bible. But the painting also comes from Rembrandt's own life. When we think of the great ones of the past, their greatness often falsifies for us their lives. Who wouldn't want the skill and fame and legacy of a Rembrandt? It must have been wonderful to be him, to accomplish all he accomplished."

A pause.

"No, it was not wonderful, especially not in the last decades of his life. And certainly not at the end."

The docent paused again to allow this bit of dramatic rhetoric to have its effect. Also to breathe for a moment. His legs were growing unsteady.

"Rembrandt was a heroic painter, but he was not a heroic human being, and he did not lead a heroic life. In his youth he was vain, self-indulgent, and ambitious. Not ambitious to serve his country or to help others, but only for himself, only to be admired and envied. Look at his early self-portraits; he is cocky and self-assured and excessively satisfied with himself.

"He later marries his beloved Saskia—he in his late twenties, she just entering her twenties. She is from a wealthy bourgeois family, he the son of a miller. Her family suspects, not unreasonably, that he is more interested in her money than in her person. He is clearly a social inferior. But there is no doubt that Rembrandt adores her. He puts her repeatedly in his paintings, once as a representation of Flora, the Roman goddess of plant life, of flowers and flowering, and a symbol of fertility, flourishing, and beauty.

"They spend their early years and her money together happily as his career ascends. But there is heartbreak too. Their first child—a son—dies soon after birth. And later a daughter does as well. And then another baby girl dies when just weeks old. Three painful deaths before finally a son, Titus, survives.

"But that blessing is soon marred. Just months after Titus's birth, Saskia dies, at the age of twenty-nine, perhaps from tuberculosis. Rembrandt is still in his thirties, but any steady happiness in his life has departed with her. The rest of it will be marked by scandal, chaos, economic disaster, failed relationships, ethical lapses, personal corruption, and eventually the collapse of his career."

The docent has surprised himself with the direction his talk has taken, but feels he cannot stop now. Because he has a point to make about the painting.

"Rembrandt hires a woman named Geertje to move into his house to take care of baby Titus. Not long after he starts an affair with her. It lasts for six years. He makes repeated promises to marry her. But he knows he will not, because Saskia, who always controlled the money she brought into the marriage, made it a stipulation of her will that all of it should go to Rembrandt, but only until he either remarried or died. A new marriage meant economic loss, and Rembrandt, always short of money throughout his life, and burdened with a huge debt from a house that he had foolishly purchased with Saskia, could not afford any loss of income."

The docent could see that his audience was taken with his gossipy tale, as good as a cheap novel. He felt ashamed for having reduced the great master so, but pushed on to the relevant end.

"Eventually Rembrandt hires a housemaid named Hendrickje. He soon makes her not just a maid but a mistress. Geertje is outraged. She leaves the house and sues him for breach of promise regarding his failure to marry her. She wins the suit but suffers a mental and emotional collapse. Rembrandt gets neighbors to testify that she is insane, and Geertje is committed to an asylum.

"The rest of his life is marked by repeated lawsuits, harassment by debtors, bankruptcy, and even his betrayal of his son, Titus, and his daughter by Hendrickje—Cornelia. He has the inheritance put in Titus's name to protect it from Rembrandt's creditors. When Titus is fourteen, Rembrandt has him legally agree to turn the rights to Saskia's property back to him should Titus die. He later redrafts his will multiple times, passing around money and property between himself, Titus, and his daughter, all with the shared purpose of having access to the money himself while shielding it from his creditors.

"It gets worse. After twelve years, Geertje seeks to get out of the insane asylum. Rembrandt tries to keep her there. She finally is allowed to leave but dies not long after. Meanwhile Rembrandt's career has cratered, as has his personal reputation. He takes money from clients for portraits he does not even work on. He borrows money that he does not repay. He has fewer and fewer commissions and then none. He's considered old-fashioned. He is a has-been."

The docent found himself getting emotional.

"Then the bottom, the nadir. Titus, a young man now, had married, and while awaiting the birth of his first child, Titus dies. Rembrandt's only son and his physical link to Saskia is gone. Soon after giving birth, Titus's wife dies too. Then only months later the plague visits Amsterdam in 1663—just as we, my friends, have been visited by a German plague—and it takes Hendrickje.

"Rembrandt van Rijn has outlived everyone he loved. His reputation—both personal and artistic—is shattered. He is considered by acquaintances a deceitful, devious, angry, manipulative old man. He has no reason to think anyone will remember him, certainly not with favor. He is destined for a pauper's grave, rented from the church, to be eventually emptied for someone else, his bones scattered only God knows where."

The docent, moved by his own words—and his own life—was silent, head bowed. The others are silent also. Their own troubles are briefly forgotten in contemplation of the sorrows of another. Sorrows transported from centuries ago by these chosen words about this particular painting—which they can only imagine. For guilt and sorrow are the docent's point.

"So where is Rembrandt in his own painting?"

One of the women answers.

"He's the prodigal."

The docent nods.

"Exactly. This painting, friends, which, God willing, you will someday see, is not just of a story from an old book; it is a story Rembrandt is telling about his own life. He is not painting someone else's story only. He is painting his own. *He* is the one who has wasted his inheritance. *He* is the one who has sinned against those who loved him. *He* is the one whose life is in shambles.

"Once, many years before he created this painting, Rembrandt painted the middle part of this story, putting both himself and Saskia in a painting traditionally titled *The Prodigal Son in the Brothel*. It must have shocked her family and confirmed their suspicions. It depicts Rembrandt as the prodigal of our story, leering out at the viewer, raising a glass of beer, seemingly drunk, a whore on his lap, modeled by his wife, no less.

"Although in our much later painting of the prodigal's return we do not clearly see the prodigal's face, can we doubt that Rembrandt saw the figure as himself—a man with a life more tattered than his rags, a man who has sinned against family and neighbor, a man deeply in need of a forgiveness that he doubts is possible?

"And if we had time, we could talk about the figure into whose robes the prodigal is burying his face. Who is he? Who is the father? Well, we do not have time for that question. But I thank you for coming today. This is the end of the tour."

With that he led them back to the entrance. They followed him without speaking.

CHAPTER 46

February 1920

DANIIL AND HIS GRANDFATHER BOTH THOUGHT ABOUT THE OTHER often. The grandfather wondered what Daniil might be doing in life. Daniil wondered whether his grandfather was still alive. By the time of the invasion there was little reason to think so. People *got* old in the camps, quite quickly actually, but they didn't usually *grow* old. At least not in years. Father Sergius lasted far longer than most, not least because he actually believed it was his calling to be there, quite literally the purpose of his life.

A guard once asked Father Sergius, with a tone of amazement and even respect, "How come an old guy like you is still alive?" Father Sergius had answered succinctly, "Because I still have assignments, I suppose."

When Daniil wondered if his grandfather was still alive, he also wondered whether it was something he should wish for. The camps were incubators of cruelty and pain. All were included—men, women, children, the rich and the poor, the high and the low, the religious and the secular, the Marxist and the capitalist, the loyal Party member and the activist dissident—from every race, creed, and color. Everyone in Russia—with few exceptions—knew personally of someone executed or in the camps, often quite a few. The terminally naive—and there were tens of millions—thought anyone arrested must have done something wrong. But many knew that the main reason the camps existed—by the tens of thousands throughout the vast country—was economic rather than for punishment or rehabilitation. They existed as fodder for progress, providing cheap labor for schemes of every kind, from gold mines to canals to scientific pursuits. And everyone knew that most who were arrested did not return; those who did were often mere shadows of their former selves.

No, it was not clear at all that Daniil should wish that his grandfather was still alive.

The grandfather, on the other hand, not only wished but prayed fervently that Daniil, and everyone in the family, was alive and doing well. He was not naive about conditions on the "mainland" (which is what both the camp and those trapped in Leningrad called the rest of the Soviet Union), but he believed in God's power to bless folks under the most difficult circumstances. Evil and suffering and injustice are real, he knew, but so are goodness and mercy and blessing. Even in the midst of the former, one could both receive and be a conduit of the latter.

The grandfather also remembered fondly the day that Daniil and Sofia were married. He had performed the ceremony himself, his last before his arrest. He often replayed the event in his mind, a memory of when he could openly and completely be a priest of God.

The ceremony took place at a small church in front of a small number of witnesses. The family wanted to faithfully honor God, the Church, and a thousand years of tradition, but without broadcasting one's suspect beliefs to a hostile world.

Everyone waited outside and then followed as Daniil and Sofia walked into the church together, with the grandfather waiting in front of the altar. Despite the solemnity of the ceremony about to take place, neither the grandfather nor Daniil and Sofia could suppress their smiles as they first made eye contact.

The wedding ceremony, like Yuri's later baptism, was saturated in symbolism, which is to say physical actions that point to spiritual realities. Most of the specific rituals, for instance, were performed three times, a reference to the Trinity.

Rings were blessed, lit candles were given to the couple to hold, hands were joined, and prayers were said, but the central event was the placing of crowns and a ritual dance around the altar.

In some Orthodox traditions the crowns are garlands of woven myrtle and flowers, but in Russia they are either silver or gold. The best man gave the crowns, tied together with a white ribbon, to the grandfather, who placed them on Daniil's and Sofia's heads. The best man then switched the crowns from one head to the other three times.

All of this had been rehearsed of course, but Daniil still felt like he was in the middle of an examination and needed to concentrate to get everything right. Sofia, on the other hand, felt completely happy and at ease. Both reactions were predictive of their futures.

The grandfather then read the story of Jesus's changing water into wine at Cana, after which Daniil and Sofia sipped three times from a shared cup of wine, symbolizing that from this point forward they would share everything in life—both joys and sorrows—which certainly proved to be the case.

At this point, the best man and maid of honor took the crowns from the couple's heads, and the grandfather wrapped their clasped hands in his stole. Then he led them around the altar three times in what is known as the Dance of Isaiah, while the choir sang three traditional hymns. It was a re-enacting of the Old Testament dance around the Ark of the Covenant and a symbol of the pilgrimage of wedded life on which Daniil and Sofia were embarking.

The grandfather closed the service with separate blessings for each of them. To Daniil he said, "Be thou magnified, O Bridegroom, as Abraham, and blessed as Isaac, and multiply as Jacob. Walk in peace and work in righteousness, as God commands."

And to Sofia, "And thou, O Bride, be thou magnified as Sarah, glad as Rebecca and multiply like unto Rachel, rejoicing in thine own husband, fulfilling the conditions of the law, for so it is well pleasing unto God."

At which point, all the witnesses together shouted, "May you live!"—a wish for prosperity, fertility, good health, and all-around well-being.

Whenever the grandfather worked his way through this memory he smiled, and he also remembered his own wedding to his beloved Inessa. And strangely enough, even after years in the camps, he felt that the "May you live!" blessing had been fulfilled in his own life.

CHAPTER 47

April 1942

EVER SINCE THE MASSACRE OF THE CHILDREN ON THE TRAIN AT Lychkova the previous summer, the families of Leningrad had been reluctant to evacuate their children. Eventually, however, the logic of evacuation became irrefutable. People continued to starve precipitously even with the arrival of spring. Food was still a wish more than a reality. The ice was going out on Lake Ladoga and the trucks had stopped running. No matter the size of the announced ration of adulterated bread, your body was not fooled.

Evacuation was risky, but at least it was a chance. Like all parents, Aleksandr and Yana did the calculation. Yana insisted that it be only one child. She couldn't imagine life with both of them gone away. So they calculated accordingly. Two adults and one child could get by on fewer calories than two adults and two children. They knew, thanks to the incompetence of the bureaucracy, that the food card of an evacuated child was unlikely to be suspended. That meant, if they were lucky, they could use four cards to feed three—at least until the end of the month and maybe longer.

The discussion then became "Which of our children?"

Again, Yana was adamant.

"It has to be Luka. Yulia is too young. She will not understand. Luka is almost eight. He is brave."

It was decided. Luka would go in the next evacuation. It would be by boat across Lake Ladoga. There had already been one recent evacuation by boat, and, despite islands of ice still floating on the lake, everything had gone well. Aleksandr would go with Luka as far as the departure point at Osinovets. The authorities allowed that much.

The children evacuating that day were mostly girls, and the accompanying adults were mostly mothers. Someone had decided to make the event festive—perhaps to raise everyone's sagging spirits. Maybe as a way to identify those departing—or simply out of idiocy—all the children were given white straw hats to wear.

So there they were, hundreds of children with little white hats, looking like a field of daffodils. A strong wind blew off the lake and every few minutes a gust lifted off the hats of a few dozen, like popcorn kernels exploding in a heated pan.

As they said goodbye there were, of course, many tears, festive hats or no. The youngest clung to their mothers and the mothers clung to them. They had to be pried away by those conducting the evacuation.

Aleksandr had a letter from Yana that he gave Luka. And a little speech.

"You must be courageous, Luka. Leaving us for a short time will help you and it will help your sister and your mother and me. We will pray for you. God will protect you. Please remember to pray for us as well." Even Aleksandr invoked God at such a time, for Luka's sake.

To show that he was, in fact, courageous, Luka stood at attention, as he had seen the soldiers do, and stuck out his hand.

"No, Luka. A man can be courageous and give hugs too."

With that Aleksandr hugged his son and kissed him on both cheeks.

"I love you, Luka."

"I love you, Papa."

He got on the boat and twenty minutes later it pulled away from the dock.

All the mothers and fathers and grandparents and friends stayed on the dock as the boat sailed out on the vast lake. No one was going to leave until the boat was out of sight. The crying had mostly stopped. Some were clearly praying. Finally, the boat disappeared over the horizon.

They heard them before they saw them—a distant hum from behind, growing louder, but still unidentifiable. At least to those who had never heard such a sound. Aleksandr had heard this sound before and he let out a wail. Those around looked first at him and then at the sky behind him.

"Fighter planes!"

It was as though the words called the raptors into being. They roared into sight overhead, coming from the southwest, heading for the horizon—a formation of six fighter planes emblazoned with swastikas, a pack of mechanical wolves hungry to feed.

The crowd on the dock screamed in unison. They flung their arms in the air, as though to grab the planes as they passed over. Some jumped up and down, others fell on their faces. Some shook their fists, others just shook. Some cursed, some prayed. Some lost consciousness, others wished they could.

All knew that it was the worst moment of their lives. And always would be.

The planes joined the boat over the horizon in mere seconds. No sound came back. Everything was left to the imagination, but nothing was imaginary.

They remained in place for an hour. No one left. No one could move. No one could face returning and giving report. They simply stood there, faced into the wind that continued to blow.

Eventually a woman screamed out and pointed at the water.

"What are those? My God, what are those?"

At first it looked like birds on the water. A great flock of birds. But no, it wasn't birds. The woman who screamed answered her own question.

"Hats! White hats! They are the hats of our dead children!"

And then she screamed what Marx and Lenin and Stalin and all the great Communists had always said.

"There is no God!"

CHAPTER 48

October 1940

If a man commits suicide in a Special labor camp, he is not necessarily suicidal. It is only reasonable, anywhere, to expect certain minimal conditions as necessary for one to wish to stay alive. Father Sergius understood this, but he never gave up his conviction that such conditions could be met even in a place that was a suburb of hell.

One zek, Dmitri, was a particularly hard sell on this conviction. He was what zeks called a "wick," someone whose life is as precarious as a candle flame, liable to be extinguished by any breeze. He had been coughing up blood for weeks. Most likely tuberculosis. The infirmary's wonder drug—aspirin—wasn't going to help. He was beaten regularly because he was thought to be a Baptist, much worse even than being an Orthodox believer. (At least the Orthodox were an ancient Slavic tradition.) Actually, he wasn't a Baptist, or even religious, but in Stalin's Soviet Union, what you were said to be was always more important than what you were. (Recall the joke about the sheep and the elephants.)

Finally, he had recently found out that his wife had died. He had no children. Even the Simonov poem requires someone on each end—one waiting and one awaited. With the only one waiting now gone, there was no point in being the one awaited.

Simply put, he had run out of reasons to subject himself to one more day of camp life. He saw it as an equation: His physical existence plus the conditions in camp plus any likely future equaled absurdity. What little energy he had left was directed toward eliminating himself from the equation. No life, no absurdity. The only questions now were how and when. He wanted to act before he lost his will to die.

Father Sergius understood what Dmitri was thinking without being told. He often knew the unspoken thoughts of others. He didn't conceive of it as reading their minds. Nor even that God was revealing to him their thoughts. Instead, he felt as though the other person was choosing to speak to him without words. They were usually asking for help.

The epistle says, "Bear one another's burdens." Father Sergius took that quite literally. He did not simply offer consolation to others. He took onto himself at least part of their suffering, making it a shared burden and therefore less. Prisoners simply felt better when around him, even when, as was often the case, he said nothing. His presence alone changed space and time.

Father Sergius tried to treat the receptive and the belligerent in the same way. As he once said to a fellow believer in regard to another prisoner who had cursed Father Sergius for his attempts to aid him, "It is our duty to find a pathway to each person's heart. God made each one, God values each one, God has sent us into the life of each one to bring out his image in that particular one, no matter how defaced it may be." He added, "There are no small encounters in this life. Each one is an opportunity—most often an opportunity to serve and to bless."

In this present instance, Father Sergius knew both Dmitri's despair and his plan. He noticed him eyeing the beam near the roll call site where hangings were conducted—both by the authorities and occasionally by an exhausted zek himself. When he saw Dmitri tucking a length of rope under his mattress, there was no longer any doubt. The man was a sinking ship. He did not want to be rescued. When Father Sergius spoke words of encouragement to him, Dmitri answered bitterly.

"Mind your own business, priest."

"You need something to believe in, Dmitri. Without that no one's soul survives, even if his body does."

"I believe in two things. First, the human need for justice. And second, the complete absence of justice in the world. My core belief is that this essential requirement for life does not exist. I draw from that certain logical conclusions."

"Good, believe in justice. Then believe in the God who created justice and makes it possible. If that is too much for you, believe that at least your own actions can be just—for the benefit of others. At the very least, believe in your own worth. Believe you are valuable."

"How can I believe I am valuable when everything and every moment says I am dung?"

"God says you are his much-loved child."

"You dare to speak of God? Here? That is obscene, even for a priest. Do you see God in this place?"

"I do."

"Where? Show me where."

"I see him in you."

Dmitri went away angry. Not long thereafter, he also threw the rope away.

When he did so, Father Sergius thanked God that he himself had been blessed with imprisonment.

CHAPTER 49

April 1942

The docent sometimes missed the Friday afternoon storefront music ensemble that was part of his regular walk home—last week in order to see a man about trading a piece of Sofia's jewelry for a half-kilo of horse meat. At the last minute he had backed out of the barter. He couldn't get out of his mind when he had last seen her wearing it, and it felt like he was trading Sofia for a mess of pottage. It was a sentimental decision that might prove decisive. His emaciated body had started to feed on itself and there was little left for the feast.

Every action had to be parsed. How much would it take out of him versus what would it contribute to living. The psychological and spiritual were considered as well as the physical. He had decided early on, for instance, that it was worth it—even beneficial—to continue playing chess with Aleksandr. But even last fall they agreed it no longer made sense to go to the basement when the shells or bombs started dropping. Better to die from a bomb than from the exhaustion of repeated trips to the basement and back.

So, more than once the docent and Aleksandr would be in the middle of a game when the sounds of not-so-distant explosions would rattle the windows. Yana and the children would head to the basement, while the docent and Aleksandr would not even pause from studying the board.

Once, when the bombardment drew unusually close, the docent asked Aleksandr if he thought they should leave. The reply reflected both their situation and Aleksandr's personality.

"What? Leave now? Just when I have taken your queen and am about to put you in check? You must be kidding! You are trying to break my concentration."

The docent laughed and they continued on.

Having missed the last two Fridays, Daniil approached the place of music with anticipation. But unlike in the past, there was no one else listening outside the window. And he could not hear any music as he approached. A look inside showed why.

There were only two musicians now left—the drummer and the saxophonist. The drummer sat behind his drums and the saxophonist held his saxophone, but both looked wilted. They weren't playing, nor even talking. Maybe they had just finished a piece. Maybe they were thinking about what to play next. Or maybe they were simply exhausted, showing up out of habit and stubbornness and love, but unable to actually do any longer what they had always existed to do.

The docent was about to leave when the saxophonist spotted him. He seemed to say something to the drummer, who also looked over to the window. The drummer tipped his hat with his drumstick and began to play—but so weakly that the docent couldn't actually hear anything.

The drums awakened the saxophonist, however, and the latter began to play as well. That seemed to encourage the drummer, who began playing loud enough that the docent could hear them both. He wasn't sure what, in fact, he was hearing. He wasn't even sure that the sounds could be classified as music. But purer musicians than these have perhaps never existed.

CHAPTER 50

April–May 1942

After the death of a child, nothing in a family remains the same. And no one. Food tastes different, the body feels changed, the mind is altered forever, even the air is revised. All relationships are amended—between people, among ideas and values, with God and with any speculations about a life hereafter. Even when the "I don't wish to live any longer" stage has dissipated, one's commerce with reality is more tentative. Confidence about "how things are" will never be completely restored.

Not that any of these things manifest themselves identically from person to person. Aleksandr went quiet. Yana went back to church.

She had been raised Orthodox, but after Metropolitan Sergius formally allied the church with the Communists, the family joined a Josephite parish in resistance. The parents were harassed into the grave and Yana fled religion altogether. Faith and practice simply became for her incompatible with a realistic life.

But Luka's death—so abrupt, so pointless, so horrific—dissolved all her previous thinking about what was real. Perhaps belief was foolish, perhaps it was unscientific, certainly it was counter-revolutionary, maybe even evil—but it offered the only thing Yana now cared about. It offered the hope that she would see Luka again.

Can one build a life—or even a life-shaping conviction—on mere hope? A slender hope? A retrograde hope? An unprovable hope?

Apparently one can, because Yana did. She wouldn't argue with Aleksandr about it. Not even discuss it. That one hope simply became the cornerstone of her life. Anything that contradicted it she simply ignored. And anyone. This hope, along with the face of Yulia, was the only thing that kept her from jumping out the window.

For Aleksandr, it was quite different. The change was as total as for Yana, but the manifestations were his own. Luka's death changed his personality. He lost his cynical edge. Not because he had any reason to be less cynical—he had more reason—but because he lacked the energy for it.

If belief became Yana's dominant characteristic, Aleksandr's was lethargy. Wit required paying attention. Snappy comebacks required caring. Satire about bureaucratic foolishness implied a standard against which foolishness is measured. Aleksandr no longer had such a standard—implied or otherwise. He simply didn't care enough to react to the world—or to his wife, or to his friend Daniil. He made Oblomov look hyperkinetic.

Daniil tried to set Aleksandr up for responses that would show he was still with us.

"Listen to this line from Stalin's latest speech," he would say.

Or, "Can you believe this photograph of Zhdanov in today's paper? His uniform is tighter than ever. No rationing in his house."

Nothing. No response. Not even an "I can believe anything."

The games of chess ended. Daniil felt another prop had been kicked away from his own life. He was a leaning tower himself and the tipping point was drawing closer. You could resist many things, but gravity, eventually, will have its way.

Yesterday he had seen Yulia on the stair, trailing her mother, a wisp. It was painful. Daniil had never seen a look that said so much: "I've lost my parents as well as my brother. It must be my fault. It should have been me instead of Luka. I must have sinned." All without words.

CHAPTER 51

May 1942

IT WAS POSSIBLE, IN FLEETING MOMENTS, TO HAVE GENUINE happiness in Leningrad even in siege time. When, for instance, the trams started running again in April of '42, people ran up to touch them, wept for joy, and conductors rang the bells continuously in celebration. As if to say, "Take that, you Nazi swine, our trams are running again!"

The Germans noticed.

Yes, they starve and bomb us, we ring tram bells. Not exactly quid pro quo, but it is something. Not all weapons are military.

Of much greater significance for the docent, Yuri came home on a short leave a few weeks after the trams started up.

He wasn't allowed to say exactly where he had been fighting, but the docent deduced that it was not far from Mga, southwest of the city. The fall of Mga last September, along with Tikhvin, had been disastrous, cutting off the last rail link to the outside world and any dependable inflow of food and other essentials. The supply lines across Lake Ladoga—whether ice or water—were heroic, but they didn't even begin to meet the city's most basic needs. So far, Mga was still in German hands.

While not a nationalist in the sense that Stalin would wish, the docent shared the national admiration for the armed forces, especially the vaunted Red Army. It did not matter that they melted before the Panzers in the early days of the war. Now they were fighting fiercely, even suicidally, to defend the homeland and eradicate the fascist infection. Having Yuri fighting on the front increased the docent's anxiety, but also his pride.

Daniil received notice that Yuri was coming home for a short leave—a letter from him vaguely indicating "sometime in the next few weeks." He found himself interpreting every sound on the staircase as Yuri's arrival. When it turned out not to be, he expressed his disappointment to the cat.

"Another false alarm, Prodigal. Like you listening hopefully for the scratches of a mouse behind the wall. Such is life."

Prodigal would sometimes look at him as though sharing the docent's disappointment, but more often would express the indifference for which cats are famous. But the simple presence of another animate being, indifferent or otherwise, was comforting.

Finally, after the docent had almost stopped thinking about the possibility, there was a knock on the door. Daniil almost fell in racing to it. There stood Yuri, Yelena, and little Anatoly, their three-year-old, named after his great-grandfather, all smiling broadly.

"Greetings, Father."

"Greetings, Son."

They hugged—a little longer than they intended perhaps. Then the docent hugged Yelena and Anatoly together.

"Welcome home, Yuri. You are looking well."

"I am looking alive, which is the best thing a Red Army soldier can say about himself these days."

"And doing his duty," Yelena added.

"Yes, of course, alive and doing my duty."

Yuri brought a box up out of the duffel bag he was carrying over his shoulder.

"I have something for you, father."

"What would that be?"

"Potatoes, carrots, and a tin of ham. Not as much as I had hoped, but more than you can get at the shops."

"No, Yuri. Keep it for yourselves. You have a family. I have plenty of food."

"You were never a good liar, Father. Of course I brought food for Yelena and Anatoly. This is for you. If you don't take it, I'll throw it away."

"Now *you* are the liar. But I will take it—with much thanks, Yuri. With much thanks. I will share it with Prodigal."

Anatoly had already spotted Prodigal and was trying to get out of his mother's arms. Many young children in Leningrad had never seen a dog or cat. They had disappeared altogether before they could be seen. The youngest children only knew of them in pictures, and the older ones were beginning to change how they thought of them.

The docent did not want to talk of war. Yuri had a few precious days to be a husband and a father and a son. Not that returning to Leningrad was an escape from war. It was only a withdrawal to a place where the enemy could kill you but you could not fight back. Unless one thought that dying with one's honor intact was a form of fighting back. Which the docent believed it was.

But Yuri was the one who brought up life at the front.

"It's a hard life, for sure, but I'm glad I'm there. I think of Yelena and Anatoly every moment, but I tell myself I am lucky to be able to defend them against those who wish them harm. Better me with a gun out there than sitting home waiting for them to knock on my door."

"Do you have friends out there, Son?"

"Well. I have comrades. We bond over a common enemy and a common cause and a common desire to protect our loved ones."

He paused for a moment.

"In some ways it's better not to let comrades become friends. They are too likely to be yanked away from you, or you from them. It's hard to bury a comrade, it breaks your heart to bury a friend."

The docent nodded. Yelena's eyes filled with tears.

Yuri went on, speaking more quietly.

"And it's harder yet when your comrades die because of the stupidity of leaders. Like when they removed our company commander. He was a good soldier, a good leader, and a good man. He told us we had two jobs—defeat the enemy and return home to our families. He said it was his job to accomplish the first and increase the odds of the second.

"One day last fall, the first days of October before he was called back to lead the defense of Moscow, the orders came down from General Zhukov to attack the German lines with no option for retreat. That's Zhukov's only strategy. Everyone knows it. Always attack. Never retreat. "Not one step backward" is how it's phrased in his orders. He once shelled his own soldiers when he could see that they were returning instead of advancing. It's officially a crime to be captured, you know. Retreat is always cowardice and treachery, never tactical, and punishable by execution on the spot. Of course he is the one back at his office giving orders, not the one facing the tanks with pea shooters."

Yuri was breathing more heavily. Daniil could tell that in his mind he was now back at the front.

"We had only rifles, and even some of those were hunting shotguns. We were weak from inadequate rations. We found ourselves attacking Panzers and machine guns. It was pure suicide. Our company was slaughtered. Every sane military strategy said we should retreat and report the situation, waiting for reinforcements.

"That's what our captain ordered. We fell back a couple of miles. Instead of reinforcements, we got a visit from the NKVD. Our captain was executed on the spot for cowardice and not following orders. Before they tied his hands behind his back, he turned and saluted us. Those few of us who remained saluted back. They could have executed us too for doing so. We didn't care."

I changed the subject.

"What are you going to do while you're home?"

Yelena answered.

"We're doing it now. Seeing you is our first stop."

Yuri added. "Then a walk to The Summer Garden."

"Ah, yes. Keep an eye out for Eugene Onegin or maybe even Pushkin's ghost."

Yuri laughed.

"Spare us the literary allusion, papa."

"I'm glad you recognize it as such."

"I recognize that it is time to go. I will see you again before I return to the front. Perhaps we can visit mother's grave together."

Daniil was glad that Yuri brought up Sofia. It kept her part of the family.

As he said goodbye, something came out of the docent's mouth without premeditation.

"God protect and bless you."

He knew immediately he was echoing his grandfather, who said those words at every parting. He could not explain to himself why he said it, but he was happy for Yuri's reply.

"And you, Papa. God protect and bless you too."

They all embraced. It was the happiest and saddest the docent had been in a long time.

CHAPTER 52

January 1921

When the secret police invite you for a conversation, it is not an invitation. You cannot decline it. And it is not a conversation. They already know what they wish you to say and they have ways of making you say it. Or at least sign it. And if you don't, they will simply find someone else who will—and make sure you regret not cooperating.

This was Daniil's second official interrogation, but his life was drastically changed since that first one a few years prior. Then he was a new high school student, barely aware of the wider world. Now he was a married man, with a wife and child, having just completed his first semester at university.

His family thought he was married and a father too soon. Daniil agreed but was fatalistic about it. Sofia was pregnant and he wanted to be an honorable man, as his parents had always taught. More importantly, he genuinely loved Sofia and was content with the idea of spending his life with her.

This time his interrogation took place not at school but, more ominously, at the local security headquarters, Bolshoy Dom, on Liteyny Prospekt, also known as "The Big House." Everyone knew of people who had entered there and never reappeared. No reason to think that would happen to him, but also no reason to think that it couldn't.

In the days before his appointment, Daniil rehearsed repeatedly in his head his prior interrogation. He wanted to be ready, but the Organs were expert in making sure you were never entirely ready for what they had in store. Surprises were part of their fun. He reminded himself not to be too clever. He had recently heard of a fellow student who when asked on a form who had conspired with him in his crime had written "Robespierre" and been taken directly to jail.

As it happened, Daniil's interrogator was neither warm nor hostile. He probably had half a dozen of these to get through today, and it helped to be calmly efficient. Emotions slowed things down and he avoided them unless they proved necessary.

Interrogations often started with some form of "Our investigation has concluded that you are engaged in anti-Soviet activities. Please give us your evidence." Self-incrimination was preferable to tiresome intimidation, unless the interrogator actually enjoyed intimidation, which many of them did.

But in this case, the agent started factually.

"You have just turned twenty, Mr. Aslanov. Is that correct?"

"Yes, sir."

"And you are married—to Sofia Pashanova, I see. And have a son, Yuri."

"Yes, sir."

Daniil understood the significance of the interrogator demonstrating that he knew their names.

"Starting life early, I see."

"Yes, sir."

"And you are midway through your first year at university. Is that correct?"

"I am, sir."

"I am happy to say that your record so far indicates you are doing well."

"I hope so, sir."

"That's an interesting word, Mr. Aslanov. Hope. What, exactly, are your hopes?"

Daniil knew this was where the real interrogation was beginning. He recalled the words of his mother to his sister at the time of his first interrogation: "The walls have ears, Polina. Whatever you say, say nothing."

"I hope for a good life with my wife and son and to serve my country."

"Very commendable. How, precisely, do you hope to serve your country, Mr. Aslanov?"

"I hope to study philosophy at university."

The interrogator barked out a laugh.

"Philosophy! Thinking big thoughts, eh, Mr. Aslanov? How is that going to be a service to our country?"

"Comrade Marx was a philosopher, sir."

The interrogator had been caught. He didn't like it. His face turned red.

"Of course he was."

It is not wise to trip up your interrogator and Daniil knew it. The man instantly turned Daniil's observation into something suspicious.

"Do you think it appropriate for a youth of twenty to refer to the great Karl Marx as 'comrade'?"

"Perhaps not, sir."

"And do you think you are as wise as the great Marx, Mr. Aslanov?"

"I do not, sir."

"That's good to hear."

The interrogator was back in charge.

"You have a grandfather, do you not? An Anatoly Aslanov."

"Yes, sir."

"What is his occupation?"

"He is trained as an historian, sir."

The interrogator slammed the table with his open hand, his voice now openly hostile. A change of tactics.

"I did not ask you about his training, boy! I asked you his occupation, his present occupation. Do not spar with me, boy. You will lose!"

Daniil recalled the well-known boast of the NKVD: "We know everything!" He weighed that against his mother's dictum and decided that evasion was futile—and dangerous.

"He is a priest, sir."

"Exactly. A priest."

Then in a calmer, even conciliatory voice, but with a hint of condescension:

"Is religion illegal in our country?"

Daniil didn't know. He thought it must be, but he didn't actually know. Fortunately, the man answered the question for him.

"No, Mr. Aslanov. It is not illegal. In fact it is explicitly protected by our new constitution. So there is no need to worry about your grandfather. It is fine that he is a priest if he wishes to be. We simply want to give him a choice."

Daniil had no idea what the choice could be. This was the surprise. The interrogator continued.

"Your grandfather was a fine historian for many years. He became a priest in the prime of life after the death of your grandmother, Inessa. We simply want to offer him the chance to be a historian again. Our new society needs intellectuals, perhaps especially historians, to guide the people into a new way of thinking, a new way of living. Your grandfather was a respected professor. There is a place for him in the new order if he wishes to accept it. But we cannot offer it to him if we do not know where he is. Do you see that, Mr. Aslanov?"

"Yes, sir."

"So where is he?"

Daniil should not have waited to answer, but he found himself mute. Finally he said what was actually true.

"I don't know, sir."

He did not know because the grandfather didn't want his family to know, for their own protection. He would simply show up from time to time to be with them briefly and then disappear. He liked to say, "I am like the wind in the Scriptures. You know not from whence I come and you know not to where I go."

So it was the truth, but it did not set Daniil free. The interrogator leaped to his feet and pounded the table again, this time with his fists.

"You do not know? You do not know? You expect me to believe that you do not know where your own grandfather lives? Do you think I am a fool?"

Words abandoned Daniil. He simply shook his head.

The interrogator sat down again. He sat for a long time. When he finally spoke, he returned to their earlier subject.

"We have established that you are in your first year at university. Is that correct?"

"Yes, sir."

"You filled out an application, did you not?"

"Yes, sir."

"The university accepted you based on the information you supplied in that application, did it not?"

"Yes, sir."

"If that information was misleading, or, let us say, insufficient, they might have good reason to reconsider their acceptance."

Daniil said nothing—which, despite his mother's advice, was not adequate. The interrogator shouted.

"You do not answer? Do you agree or disagree that the university might change its mind if they find they have been misled?"

"Yes, sir. They could change their minds."

The interrogator returned to speaking calmly.

"It would be a shame for a bright young man not to bc able to fulfill his . . . what shall I say . . . his hopes."

"Yes, sir."

"That could have lifelong consequences, could it not, Mr. Aslanov?"

"It could, sir."

"Yes, lifelong consequences. Instead of being . . . say, a philosopher . . . one might be instead a laborer—a digger of ditches, a cleaner of sewers, a stocker of shelves. Honorable proletarian work, no question, but not perhaps as satisfying for an intellectually gifted young man as working in a university as a philosopher."

Daniil remained silent.

"And it might have consequences for others as well. Who else might not find rewarding work? Who else, when he was grown, might not get to go to university?"

The interrogator straightened his papers and seemed ready to end the conversation.

"And all because one did not remember where someone else lived. Someone who was going to be given an attractive choice. What a shame, Mr. Aslanov. What a great shame. Perhaps your wife . . ."

He glanced at his notes.

"Perhaps Sofia will remember something."

The interrogator rose. Daniil raised his hand to stop him from leaving.

"I truly do not now where my grandfather lives. But he does visit us."

"Yes."

"And it is almost Christmas."

"Yes."

"And the family celebrates Christmas at my parents' home."

"I see."

And the interrogator did see. For the first time during their interview, he smiled.

"I wish you all the best at university, Mr. Aslanov. You may go."

CHAPTER 53

June 1942

Daniil had not seen Aleksandr for three weeks, not even on the stairs. He had spoken with Yana a few times, and even found an old wrapped candy in the corner of a kitchen drawer to give to Yulia as they passed one day. She had at first refused to reach for it, looking to her mother who nodded. Yulia took it with only the faintest of smiles, not sure she was as yet allowed to have a moment of pleasure.

Then one day there was a knock on the docent's door. It was Aleksandr. Daniil hardly knew how to greet him. The only thing that came out was insipid.

"It's you."

"Yes, it's me. I want to show you something."

He unrolled a poster.

"What is this, Aleksandr?"

"It's what it says. It's a call for musicians. They have reconstituted the Radio Symphony Orchestra. They started performing again weeks ago, but they are still short of musicians. The rumor is that they are going to play Shostakovich's newest symphony, the one he began here in Leningrad before he evacuated last fall. I hope I'm not too late."

Aleksandr had been critical of Shostakovich when he evacuated Leningrad last October.

"Gave that big speech in September. Said, 'We all are soldiers,' said, 'We are invincible and always at our post.' Then disappeared from his post when things got tough."

But he was now the composer's biggest fan.

"He's finished it. The Seventh has been played in Moscow and all over the world. Now they say it's going to be played here, where it most deserves to be played."

"That's great, Aleksandr. But . . . I don't know. . . ."

"But why do I care? Why am I telling you?"

"I guess so."

"Because, as you know, I am a musician, Daniil. An engineer, but also a musician—a good musician. You know I play the French horn. They are going to need horn players. The Leningrad Symphony was evacuated east last summer. They kept the Radio Committee Orchestra here to sustain the people's spirit, but most in the Radio orchestra have died or gone to fight or are too weak to even practice. There were only a handful left. They have the orchestra up and running again, but the word is that this new piece requires a huge orchestra, over a hundred players. They're going to need more than they have now. Conductor Eliasberg is desperate. They're even recruiting soldiers to play. I am a soldier. My horn is my weapon with which I will fight the enemy."

Daniil was speechless. He had not seen his friend this alive since the floating hats.

"So, you're going to volunteer. You're going to try out for playing Shostakovich?"

"Yes. Hell yes. They're desperate. I'm desperate. It's a perfect match. And to think, I almost traded my horn for a bunch of radishes."

"What if they don't choose you, Aleksandr?"

It was a serious question. Daniil was overjoyed that Aleksandr was animated again, but he was worried that his friend was setting himself up for a crushing disappointment. The odds seemed long at best.

"They have to choose me. It's fated. If they don't, I will complain directly to Comrade Stalin, Friend of the People. He will see to it. He needs my vote."

He said it with a straight face and struck his chest with a closed fist.

Then he laughed a profound laugh. Daniil joined him.

"You're back, Aleksandr. You're back."

"What does that mean?"

"Just that you're back."

And after a pause, Daniil risked an addition, putting his hand on his friend's shoulder.

"Luka would be happy."

Aleksandr nodded.

"Yana thinks Luka *is* happy."

They then embraced and cried together for a long time.

CHAPTER 54

February 1931

As much as prisoners loathed and feared them, the camp guards were not their main fear. That honor belonged to the criminals, the ones truly in charge in the barracks. In fact, in many cases they were officially in charge. The authorities often gave a criminal that role because they knew they were schooled in violence and intimidation and could keep order.

Even the guards feared the criminals, many of whom had murdered before and, having little hope of ever being released from a Special camp, had little reason not to kill again. In any dispute between the criminals and other prisoners, those who supposedly ran the camp, for their own safety, took the side of the thieves and murderers. Among themselves, the criminals, almost alone among those condemned to live and work there, operated on the honor system. And the way to gain honor was to be fearless and ferocious and abide by their own code.

A new prisoner, Pasha, a young university student, did not understand any of this. He had been shaved and fingerprinted (the latter a frequent act called "piano lessons"), but had not been given a tutorial on "life at camp."

He did not understand, for instance, that he was likely to be beaten—for pleasure—by both guards and other prisoners, that his food was likely to be stolen, that he would be given the job of emptying the shit from the latrines, that, young and healthy, he might well be raped. He also did not understand about his shoes.

Amazingly, he had been left with his civilian clothes, something much prized by zeks even when eventually reduced to tatters. Civvies were a link to a past to which many would never return.

But the thing that got Pasha in trouble were his shoes. They weren't especially nice shoes, but they were better than Viktor's and Viktor noticed. Like almost all the criminals, Viktor was covered in tattoos. Criminals used them to announce themselves and their exploits. The tattoos were a visual resume, declaring their criminal specialty, the times they had killed someone important or pulled off an impressive crime, and their hatred of authority, especially of the military. When they could, they took off their shirts during outside work to let everyone know their status. The most common symbol was a cat, but Viktor was especially proud of the wolf's head on his right hand. "Do not anger the wolf," he would say when threatening someone with a fist.

Viktor walked up to Pasha, standing by the stove, and placed his foot next to Pasha's.

"Yes, looks close enough. Give me your shoes, boy."

Pasha, as we've said, was not yet experienced.

"Why should I give you my shoes?"

Now Viktor was the one who did not understand. Is this boy stupid? Does he not know where he is? Does he think he can call the local policeman—or his mother—to protect him?

"You should give me your shoes so that I do not do this to you again."

With that he punched Pasha in the mouth, knocking him down, sending a white tooth bouncing across the floor. He began kicking him in the head, screaming.

"This is why you should give me your shoes, shithead!" Another kick.

"This is why!" Another kick.

"And this is why!"

The criminals called repeatedly kicking a down man "dancing," and some of them watched with a smile as the Pasha was welcomed to the barrack.

Suddenly the grandfather leapt between Viktor and the motionless boy.

"No, Viktor. You must not kill him."

Viktor's rage only grew. Father Sergius had broken an iron rule of the camps. Never, ever, interfere in a fight involving one of the criminals. This was not a fight, rather an execution-in-progress, but the rule applied. Viktor was even more amazed that the grandfather had stepped in than he was that Pasha had resisted giving up his shoes.

"Oh no, little priest. I must kill him. And now I must kill you. The only question is who goes first."

At that point, a voice rang out near the barrack door.

"Guards coming!"

Two prisoners grabbed the groaning Pasha off the floor and tossed him on a lower bunk. Everyone else either jumped into a nearby bunk or shuffled around. The grandfather remained standing in place.

Guards almost always entered in twos or more. The barracks could be as dangerous for them as for the prisoners. The first one in spoke.

"We heard yelling in here. What's going on? Discussing the merits of *Das Kapital* are we?"

Viktor answered.

"Football, kind sirs. Just football. Spartak fans versus Dynamo. You know how worked up football fans can get."

"Well, both those teams are crap. It's Moscow Stalinets for me. Now keep it quiet or you'll all end up in the cell."

"Yes, sir. Keeping it quiet here, sir."

The guards left and Viktor retired to his bunk. Everyone knew that nothing was settled. A great tree had begun to fall; it was only a matter of when and where it would land.

But everyone was shocked at where the tree landed.

The next night, five guards and the camp commander himself came into the barrack. No one had ever seen the commander in a barrack. Something ominous was in the works.

The commander spoke sharply.

"Prisoners Shch-232 and Shch-968, come forward. Father Sergius stepped out. Pasha, eyes and jaw bruised, looked at the number on his padded jacket and his face went white. A zek beside him nudged him forward.

"You two started a fight last night. This camp will maintain discipline at all times. You are assessed forty-eight hours in the punishment cell."

With that the commander and one guard left, and the remaining four led Pasha and the priest out.

Afterwards, the barrack was silent. This was a certain death sentence in winter. The punishment cell was essentially a hole in the ground, six feet by six feet at most, no furniture, no bedding, cement walls and floor, a flat wooden roof covered by dirt. And most important of all, no heat. With temperatures now well below zero, a prisoner might survive one night in the cell, but never two. It was a harsh sentence, even by camp standards.

Viktor had not moved. He was trembling. Everyone was looking at him. His voice shook.

"It wasn't me."

No one said a thing.

"It wasn't me, I tell you."

Silence. Everyone knew he was lying.

Viktor was now a taboo breaker, a heretic against camp gospel. In the camps, the lowest form of living thing was an informer. Informing happened all the time, but a known informer in a Special camp was as good as dead. In this case, his fellow criminals would kill him. If someone has informed once, they will inform again—on no one knows who. Killing him is the only safe thing for the criminals to do. The only honorable thing.

Pasha knew nothing of the punishment cell, but when he saw the opening with the ladder down into the dark, he began to cry.

"I am going to die. I am going to die. I am going to die."

Simple boy that he was, he spoke of justice. To the guards nonetheless.

"This isn't fair. I didn't start the fight. He wanted my shoes. I would have given him my shoes. I didn't even fight back. *He* punched *me*. Look, my tooth is missing. I didn't fight back. Did I, priest? You saw that I didn't fight back."

The guards couldn't even work up a laugh. They were too cold and wanted only to lock the trap door and get back to the warm guardhouse.

There was no bulb in the cell. Just enough light filtered in from the lamppost outside the door to allow them to make out each other's faces. The grandfather spoke quietly.

"Do not be afraid, Pasha. God has told me that we will not die here. We will die someday, and we must be ready for death, but it will not be now. It will not be here."

Pasha's terror made him resist hope.

"What do you mean, foolish priest? We are here two days in bitter cold. Without jackets even. This is the end. Oh mother! Oh father! Your Pasha is going to die in a hole a thousand miles from you! This is not possible! Not possible! Not possible!"

But of course it was not only possible, it was quite ordinary. Many thousands died unfairly every day in Russia, and not only in the camps. It was just a matter of how—a bullet, a noose, a beating? Of exhaustion? Of hunger? Of disease?

Of a broken heart?

Father Sergius tried again to calm him.

"I am here with you, Pasha. More important, God is here with us both. He does not always rescue. Sometimes, if we are blessed, He takes us to Himself. But God has told me that I must stay this time, that I must stay with you and that both of us have things yet to do for Him."

At that the priest began to pray.

"Oh Most Holy God. Be with us in this time of trial. Give us courage, give us strength, give us faith. Bless my brother Pasha, great God. Take away his fear. Draw near to him. Show Yourself to him. Give him peace."

The grandfather stopped praying out loud but continued praying silently. He did not know for how long—minutes? hours? He lost all sense of time. His body was still in the cell, but his spirit was somewhere else, lifted up, far beyond the camp, beyond the taiga, beyond this world.

At some point, even with his eyes closed, the grandfather noticed an increase in the light. He opened his eyes and began to smile. The cell was filled with a soft glow. Not bright, but palpable. And it was warm. The ice on the cement walls was melting. The boy was sitting on the floor, asleep but also smiling. The priest crossed himself and fell to his knees, giving thanks to God.

"Truly you are a mighty fortress. Truly you are both a strong rock and a guiding shepherd. Truly you love us and all your creation. We give thanks to you. We bless your Holy Name."

The light and the warmth stayed with them for two days. Pasha awoke halfway through. The grandfather asked him how he was feeling.

"I dreamed of my parents. My mother was praying for me to the Virgin of Vladimir icon. My father was telling me to be strong. It was more than a dream. I heard them. I spoke to them. I told them I was with you, that I would be okay. It made them happy. It made me happy."

The two said no more during the next day and night. Pasha was eager to sleep. He hoped to again speak with his parents. The grandfather spent almost the entire time in prayer. It made him happy.

When the guards came after two days to open the trap door, they were shocked to find the two zeks alive. They expected frozen bodies, they found smiling faces.

"How can this be? Why are you two still alive? Who has helped you?"

The priest could not resist an enigmatic reply.

"The One who helps all mankind. The One who can help you too."

Joy is a rare thing in the barracks of any labor camp, much less a Special camp. But there was joy and laughter when Pasha and the priest were ushered back. How was this possible? The other zeks took it as a personal triumph. Two people had beaten the system. No matter how. Once assumed to be dead, and now they lived. If they could survive, each one thought, perhaps I can too.

When asked about what happened, the grandfather only said, "God was with us."

Sasha tried to give more detail.

"I think it was angels. There was a light. And it warmed us. The priest prayed almost the whole time. Yes, I think it was angels."

Even the intellectuals did not protest. From that day on, most of the prisoners, and even some of the guards, began addressing the grandfather not as "priest," but as Father Sergius.

CHAPTER 55

June 1942

THE ONE-YEAR ANNIVERSARY OF THE INVASION PASSED WITHOUT much notice—public or private. Among the many things that disappeared during the blockade—people, buildings, hope—were calendars. Life was devoid of events to mark when there was really only one, seemingly timeless, event going on. Marking the invasion seemed masochistic.

But let us not be defeatist, a serious crime in these times. The trams were running again. The first winter had passed (though many loved ones with it). The bread ration was more than twice what it had been in December, providing almost a thousand calories if it had all been bread. Parks and other open land were being turned into gardens. A pipeline had just been laid across the bottom of Lake Ladoga, bringing fuel.

The slight ease in conditions didn't mean, of course, that people stopped dying. Months without enough to eat opened one up to the companions of starvation—disease, exhaustion, despair. Often the abused mind and body simply stopped working, case closed.

Which was increasingly the case with the docent—and maybe with the jazz ensemble.

Daniil could make it into the Hermitage only a couple of times a week these days. He had more to eat but less energy to show for it. Same for Prodigal, as Daniil observed.

"We are a matched pair, Prodigal. You are losing your fur and I have very little left to lose. But we have each other, which is something."

Today was one of the days the docent had made it to the museum. On his way home he stopped to rest after each block. At one point he found himself resting against a storefront window. His mind was not alert enough to tell him where he was.

Then he heard a familiar sound. It actually startled him at first, followed by a smile. It was the sound of a saxophone. He stood straight and turned around. It was the place of the Friday afternoon jazz fest. At first he couldn't see in because of the glare, but he cupped his hands around this eyes, his face pressed against the glass.

There, lying flat on his back on the floor, holding his instrument above him, was the saxophonist. He blew a few notes and then stopped, allowing the sax to rest on his stomach. Then he raised it again and played a few notes more. He did it repeatedly. Whether the notes linked together to form an actual composition the docent didn't know. What he did know was that he was witnessing a heroic expression of the human spirit. All his comrades gone, his own life seemingly going, and this man chooses to spend his last minutes playing music, staying, like Lev, a human being, staying himself—a maker of music—until the end.

The docent knocked on the window. He wanted to acknowledge what he was seeing. He wanted the man to know that what might be his last performance had an audience. But the man did not respond to the knock. His eyes were now closed, his saxophone lying on the floor beside him.

CHAPTER 56

August 1921

Sofia had never seen this look on Daniil's face. It was a combination of shock, anger, despair, and fear. The open letter shook in his hand like an autumn leaf in the wind. She assumed it announced someone's death, someone close. In a sense it did; it announced his own.

More precisely it announced the death of his hopes for the future—his, Sofia's, and Yuri's, their infant son.

"What is it, Daniil? What's in the letter?"

He didn't answer. He didn't hear the question. The external world had shut down.

She picked up Yuri, as though some danger were in the air, and asked again.

"Daniil, Daniil. Speak to me, my sweet. What has happened?"

He answered without looking at her, staring into space.

"I've been expelled from university."

"What? How? Why?"

He looked back at the letter and read from it.

"They say, 'for filing a false application.'"

"You're about to start your second year, Daniil. How could the application be relevant? That was almost two years ago."

"It's in the next paragraph: 'Applicant failed to disclose true social origins.'"

"That's all it says?"

"It's all they need to say. It's enough. It's more than enough."

"What does 'social origins' even mean?

"You know what it means, Sofia. It means whatever they need it to mean. In my case, it means bourgeois. Worse yet, much worse, it means from a religious family."

Yuri started to cry, and Sofia soothed him.

"What does this mean for us, Daniil?"

"It means everything, Sofia. It means we will live different lives . . . very different lives."

To himself he thought, *It means that no sin goes unpunished.* He believed he had protected his future (and his small family's future) when he was interrogated last Christmas, though the price was enormous. He was shocked and confused. He shouldn't have been. The explanation was simple—they are liars. He should have assumed it from the beginning.

Yuri continued to cry. Sofia did not.

"If that's all it means, then we are fine. We are together—you and Yuri and I. We will live this 'very different' life together."

With one arm she held Yuri, with the other she held Daniil.

"This is no tragedy, Daniil. This is just a turn in the road."

CHAPTER 57

July 1942

THE KNOCK WAS SO FAINT THAT THE DOCENT DISMISSED IT AS A random sound, perhaps imagined. When it recurred two minutes later, he went to the door and opened it. For the rest of his life, he wished he hadn't.

There stood Yuri's wife, Yelena, holding their three-year-old Anatoly. She said nothing, nor did she cross the threshold. She simply held up the telegram that so many wives and mothers had received in the last year.

"Your husband, Yuri Daniilovich Aslanov, died on July 1 in battle for the socialist motherland, true to his military duty, heroically and bravely."

When the docent saw the telegram—and without reading it—he dropped immediately to the floor—as though his legs had suddenly broken, which his heart surely had. The child looked down at him from his mother's arms.

"Grandpa fall down."

The docent rose, embarrassed at having prioritized his own grief. He put his arms around Yelena and the child and drew them in.

"How much more, Daniil Mikhailovich? How much more?"

She didn't identify how much more of what. She didn't need to.

He brought her in to the apartment. Yelena sat down and placed Anatoly on his feet on the floor. The child began to wander, spotted Prodigal and headed his way. The cat, wisely, fled into the bedroom and under the bed.

"It came last week. I am sorry for not telling you sooner. I couldn't get out the door. I couldn't get out of bed. Neighbors, God bless them, brought us food. They took care of Anatoly. I was paralyzed, Mr. Aslanov. Today is the first day I have left our building. I am sorry."

"Do not apologize, Yelena. You gave me one last week with hopeful thoughts about my son. One last week without despair."

The docent left unsaid a piercing irony. Having attended a church service for the first time in decades, he had found himself lately praying for Yuri and his safety. Asking God to protect him—even this morning, not knowing that he was praying for the life of a son already dead. But God knew. And let him keep praying. Yes, that's how it is with that God the priests go on and on about. It made him feel foolish as well as brokenhearted.

Yelena reached into her bag and pulled out a handful of letters.

"And there are these. I've been getting letters from a dead man. Yuri died ten days before the telegram arrived, more than two weeks now. Mail travels slowly and haphazardly from the front. Almost every day since he died, a letter from him has arrived, in no particular chronological order.

"They are both precious and repellant to me. I want to kiss every word and I want to burn them unopened. His cheerfulness oppresses me. He makes light of his danger. He speaks optimistically about our future. 'The three of us,' he writes. Then adds 'and more to come,' drawing a small smile. It's torture."

The docent simply nods and touches her shoulder.

"Every day I dread the letters coming. Every day I dread them no longer coming. I am a torn woman, split wide open, with nothing to hope for. Really, Papa, what is there to hope for?"

Anatoly has given up on the cat and wandered back within reach. The docent leans out and scoops him up into his lap.

"There is this one to hope for, Yelena. There is this one."

She begins to cry.

The docent knows his answer is a cliché, the same one he had used on himself regarding Yuri when Sofia died—another irony. Put our hopes in the next generation. Sacrifice for them. As the generation before sacrificed for us. Tomorrow will be better. Marx and Lenin both said so, the better future bringing us Stalin. Pain and suffering today, but oh, that golden future. It will be worth it all. It's the inevitable direction of history, an ascending vector. Even the capitalists believe it. Progress—nothing can stop it.

Nothing but a telegram.

CHAPTER 58

December 1935

Poetry in the camps was uncommon but not unheard of—recall the "Wait for Me" poem. Rarer still in the barracks during Father Sergius's many years in the zone was an instrumental musical performance. He arranged it himself, with the help of the criminals, in an effort to save a man's life.

The life that needed saving was that of Yevgeny Abramovich. He was a classical musician—a composer, a conductor, a master of multiple musical instruments. The mathematician claimed to have actually heard of him. He was newly arrived. No one, of course, knew why he had been sent to a Special camp, since no one asked such things, but someone speculated it may have had to do with his patronymic.

Yevgeny was in bad shape when he arrived and quickly got worse. Prisoners only got the full ration of food, slender though it was, if they fulfilled their work quotas, which were often unrealistic. It was, in the land of euphemism, called "nourishment scale," and it guaranteed deaths beyond counting. Not fulfilling your quota was considered breaking the law, and could lead to your sentence being extended. Yevgeny never came close to fulfilling his quota, which meant he got very little to eat. And didn't seem to care.

He was putting up no psychic resistance to his assigned fate. He never talked and would sit every evening on his bunk, staring into the distance. Sometimes you could see him moving his fingers in the air, as though playing a musical instrument of some kind.

One evening the intellectuals discussed among themselves a film that was popular in the late twenties. Some thought it magnificent, others sentimental trash. They defended their positions as though dueling with French troops during the Napoleonic wars. Thrusts of argument, parrying counter-arguments, high diction insults, libels against people's mothers.

When the topic changed, so did the alliances. Your friend on one subject became your enemy on another. What was clearly at stake was the need to win an argument even as one was losing one's life. It was the only evidence that something of value remained.

The film argument evolved into the question of the role of art in general to modern life. The still fully communized, of which there were a surprising number, said art was important only to the extent that it served the Revolution. This brought angry retorts from those who countered that art and artists provided a moral compass. Still others said art was little more than decoration. It made life prettier, but was a distraction from truly important things.

That's when they heard a new voice—Yevgeny's.

"I am sorry to interrupt, but I am forced to speak."

Things got quiet, because most of them had never heard his voice.

"There are things which have practical importance in life—such as how we organize ourselves politically and economically—and there are things which define us as human beings. Our art defines us. That is why bad art is dangerous as well as unpleasant. It defines us falsely, making it harder to live as we ought.

"I speak only of the highest art, the greatest expressions of the human imagination and spirit. I speak of Gogol and Dostoevsky and Tolstoy. Yes, and Shakespeare. I speak of da Vinci and Goya and Repin. I speak of Bach and Mussorgsky. These artists are of great value to the state because they enhance our humanity. How can a state be great if its citizens are spiritual pygmies? Men do not live by bread alone. No, nor by production quotas alone. We need scientists and technicians, but they deal only in complexity. Artists deal in profundity. We need knowledge of both to thrive."

At this, the musician began coughing. His speech had used up what little energy he had. He wavered unsteadily and then retreated to his bunk.

As did the others, allowing him the final word.

Father Sergius had listened intently to his speech and knew the man did not have long to live. He pondered how to help him.

He said to some others, "He is dying because he has been cut off from what sustains him. Not food, but music. How can we give it back to him?"

A criminal overheard this.

"I was in the red room a while back. There's a broken balalaika in a locker in there. I could . . . um . . . liberate it."

Many Soviet organizations had a red room, a place filled with pamphlets and books of propaganda, including those by Yaroslavsky and Stepanov proving that God did not exist. Even some camps had a red room, evidence for the laughable claim that the camps were fulfilling their stated political purpose of rehabilitation.

The red room in this Special camp was never used and was always locked, but a lock is just an encouragement to a professional thief, and so the criminal stole the balalaika and gave it to Father Sergius, who gave it one night to the dying musician.

The man came alive. First he hugged the instrument to his bosom. Then he labored over it for an hour. The wood was cracked, a string was missing (luckily it was a six rather than three-string balalaika), the others were frayed or unattached. He put it back in order the best he could, tuning each string expertly until it sounded as Euterpe intended. Everyone watched him from afar. A kind of anticipation filled the barrack. They went out to roll call with suppressed smiles. Perhaps they would all be punished when the instrument was discovered, as it surely would be. But perhaps not. What was there to lose?

After roll call and lights out, the musician started to play. He began with "Tachanka" and other folk ballads—"Kalitka" and "The Coach is Racing." Some of the zeks whispered along. When he played the famous dance song, "Kamarinskaya," a few quietly clapped in rhythm. He transposed classical pieces on the fly to make them work on a balalaika of five strings.

Everyone in the barrack heard something different. With each song the musician was telling the story of his life, but each person heard only his own story. The music took them back to places they would never visit again and to people they would never be with again. The sound created for a time a new heaven and a new earth. It remade reality. The camp no longer existed. For a time—a time outside time—they were profoundly happy, they were profoundly sad.

And then the guards came in. Four of them. Everyone saw them, but the musician kept on playing. Those nearest him motioned him to stop, but he knew he was playing for his own funeral. He would play until the end.

One of the guards started toward him, but another put out his arm and held him back. Miraculously, they listened for a few moments. Then the one who had held up his arm walked over to the musician. Father Sergius expected the man to grab the balalaika and break it over Yevgeny's head.

Instead the guard allowed the musician to finish and then complimented him.

"You are talented, sir. That piece is a favorite of mine. I played it myself as a student. But now you are finished. Come with us."

Yes, finished.

The guard took the instrument from him and the four led the musician away. As he passed the grandfather, he spoke.

"Thank you, Father. You gave me one last happy hour."

After they left, Father Sergius said to no one in particular, "He is a believer."

Which earned a quick retort.

"How do you know? His patronymic is Abramovich."

"I am not talking about religion. If you listened to his music, you know he is a believer."

The men in the barrack never saw him again. Word leaked back later that he had been transferred. Another euphemism? No one knew.

CHAPTER 59

July 1942

After the word of Yuri's death at the front, the interactions between Daniil and Aleksandr inverted. When Luka died, Daniil had tried in every way possible to comfort a devastated Aleksandr; now the roles were reversed. In truth, neither found comfort either desirable or possible. Finding comfort or consolation seemed a betrayal of the loved one lost. But each appreciated his friend's offer of solace.

What helped Aleksandr most was his successful application for the makeshift orchestra assembled to perform Shostakovich's Seventh Symphony. It didn't lessen the pain of losing Luka, but it increased his sense that he should continue to live. Daniil, now with neither wife nor child, had an even greater need for such a reason.

In search of topics for conversation with his wounded friend, Aleksandr gave the docent regular reports on the progress of the orchestra. His first practice, for instance, was grim indeed.

"We looked like coats hanging in the closet—with our bodies being the hangers. And it was worse when we took our coats off. The arms of the flutist were as thin as her instrument. But at least she made it to rehearsal. Eliasberg told us that the drum had died on the way to the hall, the first violin was dying at home, and the oboist was too weak to get out of bed."

Daniil was taken with his phrasing.

"Did he really speak of people as instruments? 'The drum died'? 'The first violin was dying'?"

"Oh yes. He is a musical taskmaster of the old school. He lives for the music. The players are equated with and less important than their instruments. When one fellow was late for practice because he was burying his wife, Eliasberg's only response was 'No excuses.'"

"Must be great for morale."

"Oh morale is not a problem. We're all grateful to be there. It's an honor. It gives our lives meaning, something more scarce these days than meat. Not the best collection of musicians ever, but perhaps the most courageous. We are an orchestra of the living and the willing. That will have to be enough."

That first rehearsal was scheduled for three hours but lasted only fifteen minutes. Some were unable to hold up their instruments for even that long. Eliasberg reported to the authorities that the score, which had been flown in on a small plane skimming over the waters of Lake Ladoga, was impossibly long and difficult and that the musicians were too weak to perform it. The authorities responded by increasing each musician's food ration—extra porridge—for the weeks of practice preceding the scheduled performance of the Seventh.

Meanwhile, the orchestra performed public concerts and radio broadcasts. It allowed the orchestra much needed practice. Eliasberg started with the standard repertoire—Beethoven, Tchaikovsky, Rimsky-Korsakov. They would have to work their way up to Shostakovich. And a potential audience had to get used to hearing and loving music again.

Aleksandr's mood had improved considerably over the weeks of rehearsal. He had grown less morose, less cynical. A report he gave Daniil of a musical revue he had attended proved he had regained his edge.

The event was a big performance at the House of the Red Army to lift the people's spirits. Almost entirely propaganda, it gave Aleksandr, who brought home a program, a cornucopia of material to riff on.

"You should have been there, Daniil. It was at the same time hilariously entertaining and a crime against art. Look at this list of songs performed by the Youth Ensemble: 'Anthem to the Bolshevik Party,' 'The Song of the Fighter Aircraft,' 'Songs of the Cooks'—now there's a salute to the proletariat for you—and 'The March of the Women's Brigade.' And later we got 'Everything for the

Motherland' and 'Cantata on Stalin' performed by the Red Army Song and Dance Ensemble.

"Can you believe that? Stalin gets a cantata. What's next, 'A Lullaby for Genghis Khan'?"

Aleksandr was, after a long time away, back on one of his rolls.

"But the piece de resistance for me was the NKVD Song and Dance Ensemble. Staggering incongruity! The most brutal organization in the entire Soviet Union, killers of millions, and they have the gall to form a song and dance ensemble? First they torture us with hot pokers; then they torture us with bad singing and dancing. Have they no conscience?"

Aleksandr was in such a good mood that Daniil got caught up in it a bit and started telling him of the time he had been to church with Lev. Aleksandr's response made him wish he hadn't.

"To church, huh. Never been myself. I've played so-called 'sacred music' here and there—they sometimes allow it as long as the texts are not included in the programs—but I haven't actually ever been in a church. What's it like?"

Daniil flinched. The question seemed like a trap, even from a friend. He hated his own suspicion, but suspicion was what kept people alive.

"Oh, I don't know. A lot of milling around, looking at paintings, listening to music and speeches. Not very interesting."

"Did your parents take you to church before the Revolution?"

"No."

That's twice, Daniil thought. *One more denial and I've caught up with Peter.*

He changed to their common subject.

"How's practice going for the symphony?"

"Well, the fellow doing the trumpet solo is a concern. He's a jazz trumpeter with no classical experience and is very anxious about it. And we still haven't played the symphony all the way through in one sitting, even though the performance is not far off.

"We better get to the performance fast. Seems like we are one or two fewer every rehearsal. The fellow next to me passed out and fell off his chair last week. A few people have grumbled about the difficulty and length of the score. Eliasburg wasn't happy. 'No complaining. Perform or I'll have your extra ration cut.' That put an end to it."

"Still not worried about popularity, eh?"

"Well, he's no easier on himself. He's come to some practices straight from the hospital. I saw him waver and clutch the podium three or four times today. Look, here's a drawing I made of him on the margin of my score. He's almost a shade."

CHAPTER 60

July 1942

MOST ZEKS MOURNED THEIR SEPARATION FROM WIVES AND CHILDREN and other loved ones. Others thought erasing all memories of their former life a key to survival. And one in the barrack had asked a fellow zek to write and tell his wife that he had died, so she could feel free to remarry and remake her life.

Father Sergius also mourned his separation from loved ones, but mourned most the loss of the Eucharist. Its regular performance is the soul of Orthodoxy and his own primary tether to transcendence. Having it forbidden was like forbidding him to breathe. Physically he could of course live without it, but, in a deeper sense, he could not live without it.

And so he didn't.

Father Sergius kept all the camp rules concerned with order. He kept most of the rules concerned with the distribution of goods, such as food and clothing. He tried to keep none of rules that were enemies of the spirit. The prohibitions against any form of religious practice were enemies of the spirit, designed ultimately by Satan, and therefore required to be resisted.

So Father Sergius often heard confession surreptitiously, and whenever he could, he held a Mass and performed the Eucharist. The latter was the most dangerous. He could hear confession while shoveling dirt next to the one confessing, both seemingly focused on their work. But passing out bread and wine and performing the necessary steps of the Eucharist was another thing entirely.

Which is why he tried to do it in the woods—when possible at a glade he had discovered with a tangle of vines that formed what looked like a natural cross. Father Sergius believed God had allowed him to discover that place and wished him to use it for this purpose.

Work details often waited near that edge of the forest and that glade—for work orders, for equipment, sometimes simply for a brief break from hard labor. Father Sergius frequently carried bread and wine in the lining of his jacket, and a small spoon in his sock, just in case an opportunity arose.

The elements were not hard to get. Bread was dispersed daily and one simply had to save a bit each day over time to accumulate enough. (And of course resist eating it when extremely hungry.)

And alcohol was available if one knew how to get it and could pay the price. The criminals seemed always to have a secret supply, and even a guard here and there would sell it to supplement his token income. Most people wanted vodka, but Father Sergius was only interested in obtaining wine—in fact, only a sweet red wine, as tradition stipulated.

One day a gang of twenty or so were told to wait beside the woods. It looked like they would be here for some time. Father Sergius had alerted the known believers to look for him in a situation like this. His taking off a shoe was the agreed upon sign that a Mass would be attempted. When he did so, five of the zeks wandered toward him.

But what about the guard? It was unusual but not unheard of that a guard was a believer. Father Sergius had identified three in this Special camp. He counted on the Holy Spirit revealing it to him, and then confirmed it by making a comment to the man using a term only an Orthodox believer would understand. Today there was only one guard and Father Sergius believed him to be one of the three. He walked over to him and spoke casually.

"I would like to spend a short time in the woods with some of the brothers if that would be acceptable."

The key words were "some of the brothers." Zeks did not call each other "brother." The guard would understand the meaning and the occasion. There was likely not a single person in this camp of many hundreds who the guard would allow to do this other than Father Sergius. It put him at risk, but perhaps he allowed it as an act of expiation for his own sins (which he knew to be many).

"Only for you, Father. Do not be long."

Yes, after years of seeing how Father Sergius lived for and served others, even some of the guards called him Father.

The six men slipped into the woods, found the glade, and prepared their hearts for the Mass. One of them acted as deacon, as he had done in his previous life. He stood beside Father Sergius, who stood facing the men with his back to the vine cross. With a nod from the grandfather, the deacon spoke first.

"Master, give the blessing."

Father Sergius did so.

"Blessed is the Kingdom of the Father and of the Son and of the Holy Spirit, now and forever and to the ages of ages."

The men responded.

"Amen."

Father Sergius then began a long series of petitions, some from the Divine Liturgy and some from his heart in response to local camp conditions.

"For everyone confined to this camp—prisoners and others alike—may they feel your presence, your peace, and your forgiveness even in this place. And may they live."

After each petition the men repeated, "Lord, have mercy."

There was of course not time to perform the entire liturgy. This pained the priest because he loved every part of it. He longed to do it slowly and completely, to savor it as one would a great meal, because it was great and it was a meal unlike any other.

With the required prompts from the deacon, Father Sergius included fragments of other parts of the service: "Commemorating our most holy, pure, blessed, and glorious Lady, the Theotokos and ever-virgin Mary, with all the saints, let us commend ourselves and one another and our whole life to Christ our God."

He even offered as the sermon a few words of encouragement to the men.

"Men, do not despair. The God who made you loves you and is with you—even here. He calls you to live as his child—even here. Seek the good—even here. Seek it in each one you meet—even here. Seek it in yourself. Amen."

He then moved to that for which the entire Mass exists: the Eucharist. He removed the bread and small vial of wine from his jacket and the spoon from his sock.

He told the story of Jesus with his disciples at the Last Supper breaking the bread and pouring the wine.

At the prompting of the deacon, he said, "And make this bread the precious Body of Your Christ."

Then, "And that which is in this Cup, the precious Blood of Your Christ."

Adding, "Changing them by Your Holy Spirit."

The deacon said, "Amen. Amen. Amen," and Father Sergius went on.

"So that they may be for those who partake of them for vigilance of soul, remission of sins, communion of Your Holy Spirit, fullness of the Kingdom of Heaven, boldness before You, not for judgment or condemnation."

Then he invoked Christ's mother again, "Especially for our most holy, pure, blessed, and glorious Lady, the Theotokos and ever-virgin Mary."

There was much else he wished to do and say, but time was short. Already some of the men were looking back toward the camp in fear.

Father Sergius broke the bread into pieces and slowly ate one. He touched the vial of wine to his lips, taking a few drops.

He then offered the bread and wine to the deacon on the spoon, afterwards looking to the men and saying, "With the fear of God, faith, and love, draw near."

The men did, some with tears in their eyes. Just as the last one wet his lips with the wine, there was the sound of breaking branches and the guard pushed into the glade. He looked frightened.

He rushed up to Father Sergius, who looked at him calmly.

"Me too. Please, Father, me too."

The priest administered to him the elements, and the guard kissed his hand. Father Sergius looked at them all and said, "Save, O God, Your people, and bless Your inheritance."

The guard responded, "We must get back immediately." He walked behind everyone as they left the woods, pointing his rifle toward Father Sergius and the other prisoners in case someone official happened to see them coming out.

CHAPTER 61

August 1942

August 9, 1942, the 335th day of the siege, was one of the few days in the last thirteen months in which people woke with expectation of something good in their lives. Everyone knew it would start in the late afternoon. The lucky ones would pack the huge Bolshoi Philharmonic Hall, only seven miles from the front lines. The rest would hear it, standing in the gathered crowd outside (with the hall doors left open) or on one of the hundreds of thousands of speakers spread permanently throughout the city.

And the Germans would hear it. Especially the Germans. They would hear it, like it or not. Additional large speakers were placed near the front, pointing in the direction of the enemy. The message was clear—"You can kill us, but you cannot defeat us. Our spirit is stronger than your evil. We defy you."

The army helped out in another way. During the day, right up to the time of the concert, General Govorov reigned down 3,000 artillery shells on the Nazi heads, keeping them hunkered down and away from their own guns. Some called it "symphonic artillery."

A thousand citizens showed up in clothes they hadn't worn for over a year, though it seemed like a hundred years. Only their best, another way of defying the barbarians outside their gates. Many women wore make-up for the first time since the blockade began. And a few hundred soldiers were present, picked for their exceptional service and showered with honor by all. (Mayor Zhdanov, afraid the Germans would shell the hall, was absent.)

Daniil was there too. Each musician had been given a small number of tickets for family or acquaintances. Aleksandr presented one to him with the formality of a religious ceremony.

"I give you this, Daniil, because you are my friend. And you know the saying; 'An old friend is better than two new ones.' You have shared both your life and your resources with my family. You shared our happiness when Yulia recovered from sickness. You comforted us when Luka was taken from us. You have been a great friend when I was desperate, and I owe you more than I can ever repay."

And then, afraid perhaps of appearing sentimental, he added with a small smile, "And this is also a thank you for letting me trounce you so often in chess."

Daniil did not have formal clothes to wear, but he went in the right spirit, knowing it was one of the most significant nights of his life.

The stage was full with eighty musicians. Empty chairs with instruments on them were intermingled among the performers, representing those who had begun practicing for the event but had died before it could take place, including two soldier-musicians who were killed at the front.

Conductor Eliasberg, looking like a stick inside his too-large tailed jacket, started with a short speech.

"A great occurrence in the cultural history of our city is about to take place. In a few minutes, you will hear for the first time the Seventh Symphony of Dmitri Shostakovich, our outstanding fellow citizen. He wrote this great composition in the city during the days when the enemy was, insanely, trying to enter Leningrad . . . and Europe believed the days of Leningrad were over. But this performance is witness to our spirit, courage, and readiness to fight."

And so they began.

The first movement is a battle of instruments that represent the battle going on in and around Leningrad—and in each human heart. The massed strings, supported by the winds, open the symphony and represent the people, symbolizing the peace of the city before the attack. Then the forces of destruction enter, slowly at first, barely detectable, in the form of the snare drum. Initially the flutes and piccolos are louder than the snare. Evil often arises subtly, unnoticed, sometimes with a smiling face.

While the woodwinds dominate initially, and the violins reenter, the snare continues to build, undaunted, growing louder minute by minute. The timpani, cymbals, xylophone, and trumpets come in on the side of the snare. The sense of sharp conflict increases. Dissonance increasingly dominates. The collision of sounds grows unpleasant and goes on and on. The listener wants it to end. It does not end. It builds. The forces of destruction are winning.

The authoritarian snare drum is increasingly sinister, repeating its martial, machine gun-like rat-a-tat-tat over and over and over, suggesting the relentlessness both of this battle and all war, and even the inexhaustibility of evil generally in the human experience. The two sides—strings versus percussion and horns—push back and forth, each trying to establish dominance.

Shostakovich wanted this episode within the first movement to be repetitive and painful—and it is. Just as are the unrelieved days of the blockade.

Daniil watched Aleksandr playing his French horn, unsure which side his instrument is on. Unlike the formal, stiff posture typical of Russian performers, Aleksandr bobbed and swayed as he played, like a boxer engaging his opponent—in this case death, the void—totally absorbed, because he was playing for his lost son.

A wistful flute solo arises, reminding us again of the possibilities of peace, but perhaps also suggesting that this serenity may be the stuff of dreams, not of reality. How can such dreams survive in a world dominated by power and violence?

Then the violins and companion strings reassert themselves, supported by the flutes and reed instruments, not overcoming the dissonant forces, but at least showing they are still present.

A melancholy bassoon solo follows. Lives have been lost, more will be lost, a great city is being destroyed. It is only right to grieve.

As the orchestra and the audience do grieve, there comes a quiet recapitulation of the movement's opening. The strings and the clarinets play quietly, but the snare of evil is simply biding its time. Eventually, at the end of the movement, the snare returns, supported by a single trumpet. The movement ends quietly, but with anxiety about the future.

The struggle goes on, in varying moods and with varying outcomes, in the second and third movements. The second is a momentary reprieve from the ominous first, a recalling of past joys, with a mood of sad reverie. This continues into the third with allusions to the country's huge natural expanse. But there is also melancholy and anguish. A recurring theme seems to be that only by sticking together will people survive, as heard when the entire string section later returns with the passage from the movement's opening. If evil is persistent, so must be the united resistance to it.

And yes, there is a kind of victory in the last movement. But it is not a swaggering, military-parade victory. It is a tragic victory, won only after much loss. Evil will be defeated, but the price of victory is great sacrifice. It will only be achieved through suffering. And no victory is permanent. Even as the symphony ends with a triumphant swell, repeating one last time the opening theme, one can hear the threatening drums lurking behind it, suggesting, "We are still around; we will be back."

Optimism, hope, courage, endurance—tempered by realism, readiness, and wisdom. A work of art saying "No" to oppression, to evil—and saying it not just to Nazi oppression, but to all oppression everywhere, including that grown at home.

The tragedy of this work is that there will always be tyrants, there will always be suffering. What the piece offers is the hope that despite that there will always be people—whole communities—who will stand against the one and offer comfort for the other. Evil will always be present, but so, perhaps, will be humanity's willingness to resist it.

Even in the first few minutes of the concert, people wept, thinking no doubt of those they had lost. They savored every note, every bow movement, every flash of drumsticks on the snare. The long symphony was not too long for them—they would be happy for it to go on all night—but as it approached the hour mark, it began to get too long for some of the players.

As feared, the winds began to falter first. Even the musically illiterate could hear it. The conductor stared at them, as though trying to give them energy through his eyes. The audience grew anxious. Would they be able to finish? How discouraging if not.

Then a man stood up in the front row of the audience. He stood at attention, back straight, arms to the side, head elevated. He said nothing. Then another a few rows away did the same. Then another and another. All at attention. All silent, willing their strength to the musicians.

Soon the whole auditorium was standing, a spiritual counterattack against all that opposed life and goodness and how things ought to be. An army of lovers of music, willing their compatriots to finish their sacred task. They were soldiers of art resisting the destroyers of civilization.

It was effective. The wavering musicians rallied and the performance finished strongly. For a moment—after the last instrument ceased vibrating—there was complete silence in the hall. Then a roar of emotion that defies metaphors. It was aesthetic appreciation of course, but it was the heart cry of a people oppressed—beaten down, starved, murdered—and at the same time a cry of triumph and hope: We have overcome, we will endure, we will flourish, there is hope.

The applause and stamping of feet went on, it seemed to Daniil, for as long as the symphony itself. A young girl brought flowers to the conductor. Those in the orchestra who could stand did so, with serious faces but joy in their hearts. Those who could not stand waved.

Daniil looked to Aleksandr, who he had watched closely throughout. Aleksandr was neither standing nor waving. He sat in his chair, his horn on the floor, his elbows on his knees, his head in his heads—sobbing.

Thinking no doubt of that armada of floating white hats.

CHAPTER 62

August 1942

Father Sergius believed in miracles; he just didn't think of them the way most people did. He did not, for instance, think them unusual. It wasn't simply the commonplace idea that life itself is a miracle, it was that he thought of the transcendent as so frequently revealing itself within the immanent world as to not be surprising. In fact he resisted the word *supernatural.* He once explained it this way to Daniil.

"If by 'natural' you mean 'that which is composed solely of matter,' then yes there is another level—the supernatural or transcendent.

"But if by 'natural' one means 'that which is the true quality of reality,' in which God and spirit infuse the merely physical, then there is no need to think of something 'above' nature, a supernatural realm. Nature—the nature of things—is made up of both the spiritual and the physical, not separate but interwoven, because God made things that way. The spiritual is embedded in the material. There's no need for a separate, second level. In heaven, we're told we will have bodies—new ones, but bodies. Read the letter to the Colossians."

As a young man, Daniil enjoyed it when his grandfather got worked up theologically.

"So you disapprove of people speaking of transcendence or the supernatural?"

The grandfather smiled.

"It is not my place to disapprove. Perhaps it helps some people. It's just not how I think of it. For me, the nature of reality is supernatural or transcendent only in that it transcends our finite expectations. The natural is itself supernatural. We think too small."

Father Sergius also thought the miraculous often hid itself, especially from those suspicious of it. An angry camp official who disliked him once ordered a guard to search the priest for anything forbidden. The guard, who Father Sergius did not know, patted him down. He discovered a small copy of the Gospels, but did not reveal it to the official standing across the room.

"I found nothing, sir."

A pure miracle? God erasing from the guard's mind what he had discovered? A coincidence? The guard happening to be a believer (or simple admirer) and not wanting to get the priest in trouble? Or a middle ground—explainable as a coincidence but one divinely ordained. Or something else? Father Sergius didn't feel it necessary to choose.

How Father Sergius survived to such an advanced age in the camps was a mystery even to him. It was quite rare. A man was old at fifty if he had lived even a year or two in the camps—and Father Sergius, who was middle-aged when he arrived, had been in detention for two decades. He recalled the time previous when he thought he had died, only to be sent back again. He hoped the next time he would be allowed to complete the journey.

Eventually that day came.

When it became clear one night that Father Sergius was at the point of his liberation from the camp, which is to say, when the barrack recognized that he was dying, he was urged to go to the infirmary. One of the fellow believers in the barrack offered to call for a stretcher.

But Father Sergius only smiled.

"No, no, my brother. Only God can restore me to health, and this time I think he is choosing not to. I am satisfied—in more ways than one."

"Then what can we do for you?"

"You can fetch Father Seraphim from barrack twenty-seven. Just tell him what is going on with me. He will know what to bring."

With that he closed his eyes.

Another prisoner heard the request and volunteered to go. It was not a safe thing to do. He could be shot for being outside his barrack at this time of night, but Father Sergius had recently helped him write a letter to his family, and he wanted to repay him. Besides, he knew the guard on duty and suspected he would be willing to help.

Eventually the prisoner returned with the priest. He was much younger than Father Sergius. Most in the barrack didn't know he was a priest at all.

Father Sergius opened his eyes when the priest came up to his bunk.

"Ah, Father Seraphim, thank you for coming."

"Thank you for calling for me, Father Sergius. It is an honor. If you think your time is short, Father, perhaps you would start with the general confession."

"Yes, I do believe my time is short indeed, too short certainly for me to identify all my sins."

With that Father Sergius repeated words of confession he had spoken often himself and, as part of his dutics, often heard from others.

"I confess to the Lord my God before you, reverend father, all my sins which I have committed up to the present day and hour, in deed, word, and thought."

Father Sergius smiled. He had done what was needful. But he wanted to do more and so continued.

"I confess to you God, in the presence of Father Seraphim, my sin of anger and judgment against the new guard when he struck me. I confess saying my prayers by rote, without thought or conviction. I confess to thinking too often of my pain and not enough of your suffering—for me, so long ago, and yet also at this very moment. I confess envying believers who have been martyred for their faith, something I have selfishly desired. I confess taking pride in not being an oppressor of others. . . ."

He continued for a long time. Father Sergius did not run out of sins to confess, but eventually he was clearly out of energy. Father Seraphim stepped in.

"God knows your sins, Father. He also knows your heart. He has forgiven all the sins you would confess and also those you might have forgotten. I think God would like you, one last time, to partake of his body and blood."

The grandfather nodded his agreement.

"Yes, yes. Please."

He felt deeply weary, but also deeply blessed. And full of anticipation.

Father Seraphim reached into his sleeve and pulled out a small wad of paper and a thin vial.

He repeated the words of the Eucharist as Father Sergius partook of the bread and the wine.

He then reached into the pocket of his padded jacket and withdrew another small vial. Anointing the grandfather with oil, he prayed for his healing, even if healing seemed unlikely and even undesired.

"O Holy Father, physician of our souls and bodies, heal Thy servant Sergius from every physical and emotional affliction."

With that the grandfather's head rolled to the side and he withdrew into unconsciousness. Or perhaps into a kind of superconsciousness. Who knows what goes on in the mind of the dying when they are past reporting?

He lay in that state for the rest of the evening. The barrack rarely paid close attention to a prisoner dying. It was simply too common to be noteworthy. But in this case, there was an unusual stillness. No card playing. No joking. No bullying. No talk even except for whispers. Whether they liked him or not, everyone sensed that their lives would be worse for his passing.

Some stood a kind of vigil, next to his bunk or further away. Just before lights out, a guard came into the barrack. It was the guard who had allowed them communion in the woods and participated himself. He pretended to be checking on the barrack but everyone knew why he was there. He went over to the grandfather, unconscious on his bunk, took off his cap and discretely crossed himself. After a few moments in silence, he left.

Exactly when Father Sergius's spirit left his body, no one knew. He did not rise in the morning and it was soon confirmed that he was dead. Everyone filed out silently to begin a day of hard labor from which the grandfather had been freed. One prisoner—Dmitri, the man he had persuaded not to kill himself—called back toward his bunk.

"May your memory be eternal, Father Sergius."

Others nodded in agreement.

CHAPTER 63

August 1942

Not long after learning of Yuri's death, the docent descended into a mental and spiritual coma. It could not have been more than a few days because when he resurfaced he found himself still alive. Apparently his mind had shut down to protect itself from the unprocessable. A limb can become paralyzed from a blow; so can a mind.

He reawakened to discover Prodigal licking his face. They stared into each other's eyes for a time, and then the docent stroked the cat's head before touching his own face.

"I am still here, Prodigal. That's disappointing. How long have I been away?"

Prodigal answered with a meow. Daniil interpreted it as, "Who cares? Feed me."

After another couple of days, the docent decided, despite a persistently high fever, to make his way to the Hermitage. It marked his surrender to the responsibilities of still being alive.

No one at the museum gave any indication that he had been away. As a volunteer rather than an employee, he was simply given things to do whenever he appeared. Now that he was back, he was asked if he wished to lead a tour later in the week. He agreed. He did not offer any information about Yuri, and no one asked.

On the morning he was to give the tour, the docent was weaker than usual, and the fever had not abated. He shared with the cat his uncertainty about whether he should go in.

"What do you think, Prodigal? Should I risk it? I'm not well. As nice as it would be to ride the tram again, I don't have the fare. That means walking. Walking is free, but it has a high cost of its own."

The cat seemed to be paying attention, but for its own reasons. Daniil smiled.

"You're right, Prodigal. What does it matter that I'm not well. I haven't been well for a long time. Few have. I will likely never be well again. But I must still live life as best I can. I must still do what work I can. And most of all, your look tells me, I must feed my cat."

And so he did, meagerly. And then walked unsteadily to the museum.

The docent had been giving tours of the painting frames quite regularly since tours had begun last December. The number of visitors had grown over the months, especially now in summer. Today, for the first time in one of his tours, there was a blind woman in his group, with a companion. A blind person in an art museum—no touching allowed—was now, he thought, entirely reasonable.

"When there were paintings on the walls, it would have seemed to make no sense. But now there are only frames. Everyone is blind. Perhaps everyone has always been blind in one way or another, including me. Why did I not always conduct my tours in a way that even a blind person could profit from what I said?"

Lately, the docent had often skipped a stop at the frame of *The Prodigal* in his tours. He didn't know why exactly. He found himself increasingly uncomfortable talking about this painting that meant more to him than anyone still left in his life—even Anatoly, though he would not admit it. But today he decided to end the tour today at Rembrandt's masterpiece.

He began as usual.

"Rembrandt van Rijn, as perhaps you well know, was a Dutch Baroque painter who was born in 1606 and died in 1669. He is widely considered one of the greatest painters of all time, and this painting, whose frame you see, *The Return of the Prodigal Son*, is the world's greatest painting."

A small change.

The docent then moved on to descriptive and stylistic comments. He mentioned each of the figures in the painting. When he spoke of the barely discernible figure in the shadows as perhaps the prodigal's mother, the blind woman asked a question.

"You say the mother is faint in the dark corner of the painting, if that's her at all. Why is the mother not more prominent? Is she not important?"

Daniil wondered why he had never asked himself that question. He wasn't satisfied with his answer.

"Well, the mother is not even mentioned in the parable. So let's give Rembrandt at least a bit of credit for including her, even if only in the shadows."

The blind woman didn't seem satisfied either, but said no more. Daniil moved on to what the critics say about the painting.

"Commentators often point out the lack of movement in this painting, notable in contrast to the action depicted in so much of Rembrandt's art. None of the characters is moving. Each seems confined to their own world, their own thoughts.

"Some call the composition 'static.' I prefer to call it 'quiet.' Better yet, 'still.' That nothing is moving is fitting. The painting captures an eternal reality more than a temporal moment. It depicts the stillness at the center of all things, at the center of creation if you will. What is happening here is not a detail of everyday life; it is foundational to all of life. The philosophers would say that, metaphysically, it deals with essence, not accident."

Daniil did not care that he was losing his audience. He was now talking to someone other than those in front of him. He moved, as he had done in recent talks, from aesthetics to biography, only this time he went much further than he had ever gone before.

"This is perhaps the last painting in Rembrandt's life—a life that has long been collapsing around him. He has struggled against financial ruin for years, and has mistreated and betrayed many people in that struggle. His reputation—both personal and artistic—is as tattered as the clothes of the prodigal in this painting. Worst of all, his son, Titus, the only surviving link to Rembrandt's beloved but long deceased wife, Saskia, has recently died."

Daniil then crossed boundaries he likely would never have crossed if he were not weak and feverish, passing from biography to autobiography. He turned away from his audience and stared at the large, blank space within the giant frame.

"I too once had a wife, like Rembrandt's Saskia. Together, like the Rembrandts, we had a son. His name was Yuri. He was the only child of mine and my sweet Sofia. He was both wise and strong, like his mother. Our only child, but he was enough. Sofia died before the war. Yuri died a few weeks ago. Killed defending Leningrad. Killed defending his country. Killed defending his wife and child.

"Van Gogh said of this painting, 'You can only paint a painting like this when you have died so many deaths.' Like Rembrandt, I too have died many deaths. Too many deaths. Too many."

The people in the tour began exchanging glances. Daniil didn't notice. He was staring at the wall. In fact, he was now seeing the painting, back in its frame, a frame no longer outlining a blank space, but enclosing once again a sacred space.

He went on, unaware that he was saying aloud what was in his heart.

"Brothers and sisters, this is the greatest painting of all time, itself depicting the greatest truth of all time—that reality has at its center love—and, because of that, forgiveness."

His face darkened and his voice caught.

"But why is such forgiveness necessary? Why was such sacrifice necessary? It is a repeated theme in Rembrandt's work—suffering and sacrifice, often involving father and son. Across this very room you would once have seen Rembrandt's depiction of Abraham about to sacrifice Isaac—father and son—the father's knife to his son's throat, but the sheep in the background to be sacrificed instead. And, were it still here, you would see Rembrandt's *The Raising of the Cross*—God the Father accepting the sacrifice of God the Son as the grounds for forgiveness. And who else is in that painting, helping to crucify the Christ? Why, Rembrandt himself, in his artist's beret, looking out at us as he helps to lift the cross into place.

"Yes, Rembrandt says in that painting, 'I put Jesus on the cross. My sins put him there, not anyone else's. I, Rembrandt, put him there. And so, bystanding viewer of this painting, did you.'"

A few in the tour walked away with a wave of the hand. They did not come to hear a sermon. The docent was too lost in his own reverie to notice.

"Yes, father and son. Sin and sacrifice. Betrayal and forgiveness. It's everywhere in Rembrandt. It's everywhere in life."

The docent, head burning, felt himself growing weaker. But he knew he must say more. The painting, which he now saw clearly on the wall, was starting to come alive. The face of the older brother was no longer the one Rembrandt painted. It was his own older brother, Maxim, from whom he had long been alienated. The face of the seated counselor becomes the face of his father.

"Yes, the prodigal in our painting has betrayed his father. By wanting his inheritance while his father is still alive, he has wished his father dead. And then he has taken his father's gift to him—his precious inheritance—and dishonored it. What the father created through his dedication and labor, the son has uncreated, despising it by wasting it on foolish things."

Daniil saw the face of the servant girl change to the face of his sister, Polina—witness. And there in the dark shadows is not the prodigal's mother, but his own. He turned back to his hearers. His voice was low.

"I am also a betrayer."

He let the words sink into his own ears.

"I betrayed not a father but a grandfather. Like the prodigal says of himself, I say of myself—I am unworthy."

He touched his forehead with his right hand, as though in wonderment at his own words. Or at his own past actions.

"My grandfather—his name is Anatoly Ivanovich Aslanov—was a history professor. He was married to Inessa Artemovna. When she died too soon my grandfather became a priest. This was after the Revolution."

A few more people left. This kind of talk was dangerous to listen to as well as to speak.

"My grandfather loved me. I was his favorite grandchild, just as my brother, Maxim, always claimed. He taught me how to ride a bike. He taught me about art, including about this painting we are speaking of. He taught me about God."

Daniil put out his hands and shrugged his shoulders in a gesture of incomprehension.

"And I betrayed him. The authorities asked me where he was. I said I didn't know—and I didn't. They said they merely wanted to offer him his old job back—as an historian. I knew this was a lie. Or should have known."

He paused.

"No, why do I continue to deceive—deceive even myself? Of course I knew it was a lie."

He turned back to look at the painting that was still there in his visionary eye.

"But they threatened us. They threatened me, my wife, and child. And our future. And I knew they were not bluffing. I knew you could trust them to keep their promises."

As he looked at the painting, the face of the father changed to that of his grandfather, taking Daniil's breath away. He finished with a shaking voice.

"And so I betrayed my grandfather. I told them we would be celebrating Christmas at my parents' house. (Isn't that a nice irony? Christmas and betrayal wedded together.) And I told them my grandfather would be there."

Daniil went down to one knee.

"Which he was. And they arrested him. And no one who loves him has ever seen him since."

As he looked to the painting he visualized in the frame, he saw the back of the head of the prodigal, his face buried in the father's robes. The prodigal then turned his head and stared out at the docent. Daniil saw that the face was his own.

The docent collapsed. The people fled. The blind woman said to her companion, "We must get help."

CHAPTER 64

August 1942

At one time Leningrad officialdom demanded with each fatality the "cause of death." That was before the causes were so multiple and plentiful as to render any one of them moot. And before the deaths themselves were too numerous to calculate. It was like counting the grains of sand on the beach.

Death from starvation for sure—but often only indirectly. Who can discriminate death's cause between starvation and the diseases it propagates—dysentery, typhus, scurvy, chronic diarrhea, heart failure . . . despair? They are symbiotic, each feeding on the other—coconspirators. It would be comical for the docent to go to a doctor now. "Of course you are dying," they might say. "Who isn't?"

Actually the docent was proud of his body, wasted though it was. It had fought hard. It had done everything a body can do to preserve itself. But now all its savings had been spent. You could say he was dying of bankruptcy. Bankruptcy of the body, bankruptcy of the social system, bankruptcy of goodness, bankruptcy of the human condition. His life tried writing one last check, and it had come back marked "insufficient funds."

He thought of reaching out to Aleksandr, but he was two flights of stairs away—an impossible gulf. Besides, his friend and family faced their own abyss. No one could help him now—and he did not wish for it.

The only one left to share his passing was Prodigal. The docent had already set out on the floor all his remaining food, pitiful though that was. Without the docent, the cat's only future lay in the slender hope of finding rats—or, as Daniil hoped, of being taken in by Aleksandr, Yana, and Yulia.

Prodigal seemed to know its master was in his last moments. It came to the side of Daniil's bed. It lacked the strength to jump up, but the docent reached down and picked it up and placed the cat on his chest. Prodigal turned a couple of circles and rested itself in a tight ball.

Daniil smiled a last smile and stroked it. Prodigal's fur was almost gone. Its ribcage was the size of an apple, but to the docent the cat felt luxurious. It licked his hand as he stroked and even started to purr.

Daniil felt completely satisfied as his life drained away. He welcomed Death as a friend, a rescuer. He drifted into a beautiful hallucination.

His grandfather stood at his bedside. Not as Father Sergius, but as Grandfather Anatoly Aslanov, the man he had known as a boy, only now much older. He wore a muted gold shirt and had a reddish blanket over his shoulders. His silver beard lay on his golden chest—two precious metals.

They spoke.

"Hello, Daniil. I am so glad I have been allowed to come be with you."

"Yes, Grandfather. I am glad too. When did you die? I have often wondered if you were still alive."

"Oh, not long ago. Not long ago at all."

"And where? Where did you die?"

"In the place I was supposed to be, Daniil."

The docent's face lost its peace.

"I put you there, didn't I, Grandfather. I put you there. Please, Grandfather. I beg you to forgive me. I am so sorry. I didn't know what I was doing."

The grandfather placed his hands on Daniil's shoulders. He looked him in the face and then glanced to the side.

"Oh Daniil. You have been carrying this burden for so long. It is a burden of your own making. You didn't put me there. God put me there. God knew it was where I was supposed to be, where I was created to be. There was no chance of me not being there."

"You are saying this to comfort me. Even the meaning of my name convicts me, Grandfather."

"I am saying this because it is true."

"True, Grandfather? Is there even such a thing as true?"

"There is, Daniil. And the truth will set you free."

"Free from what, Grandfather?"

"Not free from. Free to. Freedom to be the wondrous creature you were created to be. Free to know intimately the One who made you."

"But what about, I don't know, my failures? My sins, I suppose. My betrayal?"

"The world is filled with many words, but the last word, the very last word, is love. And love forgives all things. Do you believe that, Daniil?"

"If you say so, Grandfather. If you say it is so, I will believe it."

"Not because I say so. Believe it because it is how the world was made—an expression of the defining quality of the Maker. A truth that will always be true."

"That's hard to see, Grandfather."

"Yes, as in the question you asked me as a boy. The answer is still the same, Daniil. Love is always there for us—since Creation—but it has to be accepted."

"Like the child who accepts a sweet?"

"Yes, like a child who accepts a sweet."

"It's a good story, isn't it, Grandfather?"

"Yes, the best and truest of all stories. And there are people waiting to celebrate the story with us. Let's go together."

The docent nodded. His grandfather smiled and faded away. Then Daniil faded away too, also smiling.

EPILOGUE

Aleksandr found Daniil's body the same day of his passing. By this time in Leningrad, with the trams and buses again running, and vegetable gardens in the Field of Mars, it was even possible to get an individual grave. And Aleksandr saw to it that his friend did.

Not that the siege and suffering were over. It would run another sixteen months, almost 900 days in all, through a second winter and part of a third—more bombings, more shellings, more death in its many costumes. The blockade would kill more people in total than the bombings of Hamburg, Dresden, Hiroshima, and Nagasaki combined, likely the most deadly siege in human history.

But it was not, as Hitler predicted, the end of Leningrad.

Aleksandr and his family, for instance, survived. Yulia, in time, grew beautiful and married well. But neither she, nor Aleksandr, nor Yana ever filled the hole left in their hearts from the death of Luka on the big lake, nor wished to.

Yuri's wife and child, Yelena and Anatoly, also survived. She eventually remarried and Anatoly became, serendipitously or providentially (make your choice), an art historian, combining the passions of his grandfather Daniil and great-grandfather Anatoly, after whom he was named.

And let us not forget Prodigal. He was, indeed, taken in by Aleksandr's family. His fur grew back and he lived to a ripe old age.

Rembrandt's masterpiece returned to the Hermitage, along with all the other art. Orbeli's children, who he wept to see departing from that train station, returned home. The Hermitage reopened its doors, the paintings returned to their frames, and *The Return of the Prodigal Son* became and remains its most visited work of art.

And the city eventually got its name back—the apostle's name.

Daniil Mikhailovich Aslanov, docent of Leningrad, one person, one sufferer, of a number so big that we cannot conceive it. One person, with one choice, who accepted, at the very end, that love surpasses all things—even when everything around him argued otherwise.

THE END

Also by Daniel Taylor

FICTION

The Mystery of Iniquity. Slant Books, 2022.

Woe to the Scribes and Pharisees. Slant Books (at the time an imprint of Wipf & Stock), 2020.

Do We Not Bleed? Slant Books (at the time an imprint of Wipf & Stock), 2017.

Death Comes for the Deconstructionist. Slant Books (at the time an imprint of Wipf & Stock), 2014.

NONFICTION

Believing Again: Stories of Leaving and Returning to Faith. Cascade, 2025.

The Skeptical Believer: Telling Stories to Your Inner Atheist. Bog Walk Press, 2013.

Creating a Spiritual Legacy: Sharing Your Stories, Values, and Wisdom. Brazos, 2011.

The Expanded Bible. Thomas Nelson, 2009, 2011. A reference work created with Tremper Longman and Mark Strauss.

In Search of Sacred Places: Looking for Wisdom on Celtic Holy Islands. Bog Walk Press, 2005.

The New Living Translation. Tyndale House Publishers, 1996, 2004. Senior Stylist.

Is God Intolerant?: A Christian Response to the Call for Tolerance. Tyndale House Publishers, 2003.

Before Their Time: Lessons in Living from Those Born Too Soon. Co-authored, Dr. Ronald Hoekstra, M.D. InterVarsity Press, 2000.

Tell Me a Story: The Life-Shaping Power of Our Stories. Bog Walk Press, 2001. (Previously published as *The Healing Power of Stories*. Doubleday, 1996.)

Letters to My Children: A Father Passes on His Values. InterVarsity Press, 1989. Reprinted by Bog Walk Press, 2005.

The Myth of Certainty: The Reflective Christian and the Risk of Commitment. Word, 1986. Re-issued by InterVarsity Press, 1999.

The Treasury of Christian Poetry. Revell, 1982. Coeditor.

ABOUT PARACLETE PRESS

Paraclete Press is the publishing arm of the Cape Cod Benedictine community, the Community of Jesus. Presenting a full expression of Christian belief and practice, we reflect the ecumenical charism of the Community and its dedication to sacred music, the fine arts, and the written word.

SCAN
TO
READ
MORE

Learn more about us at our website:
www.paracletepress.com
or phone us toll-free at 1.800.451.5006

Raven

The Raven, to ancient peoples, represented light, wisdom, and sustenance, as well as darkness and mystery. In the same spirit, Raven Fiction reflects the whole of human experience, from the darkness of injustice, oppression, doubt, and pain to experiences of awe and wonder, hope, goodness, and beauty.

YOU MAY ALSO BE INTERESTED IN